DEAD QUIET

JOHN MAHAFFEY

NEMESIS SERIES BOOK 3

Dead Quiet
Published by Crosswind Press
The Woodlands, TX

ISBN: 978-1-7375093-2-5
FICTION / Thrillers / Suspense

Cover by Donna Cunningham
Interior design by Wolf Design & Marketing,
wolfdesignandmarketing.com. Copyright owned by John Mahaffey.

CROSSWIND PRESS

FROM THE AUTHOR JOHN MAHAFFEY

Special thanks to these wonderful folks at My Word Publishing who bring their book magic to make it all happen: Polly Letofsky for her book business smarts, Donna Cunningham for her amazing cover design skills, Jennifer Bisbing, for her dedication to making this book series flow, Carly Catt for her keen eye for editing, Victoria Wolf for making the typeface jump off the page, Mary Walewsky for reaching readers, and Ralph Scott and Kendra Murray at Squeaky Cheese Productions for giving voices to my characters.

PROLOGUE

CAREFUL NOT TO WAKE HER, he slipped out of bed, crept across the carpet in his socks out of the room, and tiptoed down the stairs to his office. When Trey McCall's mind raced, he often retreated into his sanctuary to pace and think.

A year and a half had passed since Bobby McCall, Trey's eldest son, and Desiree Richards, Lucky Richards's widow, referred to by the McCalls as fugitive disciples of Lucky Richards, had disappeared from Vancouver. No sightings, no rumors. He was not so much bothered by how they vanished but more so about where they had gone and what they were up to. Were they together or going it alone?

On the home front, Nemesis and The Circle M flourished. Trey's son Jefferson, a four-time All-American selection in golf and a graduate of North Texas University, turned twenty-one and was well on his way to following in his father's footsteps as a premier player on the PGA Tour. The future appeared bright for the McCall clan, except for one lingering complication. As long as Bobby McCall and Desiree Richards remained on the run, they posed a constant threat to the safety and security of the McCalls.

CHAPTER 1

WHAT WERE THE ODDS, Trey McCall wondered. Maybe a hundred million to one, or higher, that both Robert McCall and Desiree Richards would both miraculously still be fugitives at large with almost every investigative agency in the world hunting for them, for years. Even the Nemesis supercomputer, Warlock, couldn't pin them down. The only hope was that one, or both, broke from cover. Judging by their history, Trey bet the impatient Robert McCall would be the first to make a foolish move—he wasn't wrong.

BORED TO TEARS, Robert McCall stuck close to his beach cottage in Biloxi, Mississippi, for what seemed an eternity. Going by the alias Ray Cunningham, he lived a secluded lifestyle on the water. Money was not the issue. He'd raided every hiding place where he and his late partner Arte Mercer stashed the loot they'd stolen years ago. Loneliness was the issue. It ruled his life.

As he stared at the battered *Biloxi Belle* fishing charter coming in to dock after a full day at sea, Rob thought, *Everyone on the Gulf Coast accepts me as Ray Cunningham—no questions asked.* On a recent jaunt on the *Biloxi Belle*, Ray thought he caught the boat owner's wife, Bev Williamson, staring at him from her seat across the galley. He stared back, then realized hers was an unfocused gaze of someone just killing time, mindlessly fixated on nothing out of the ordinary. That was it! *Nothing out of the ordinary* was driving him bonkers.

Perhaps a catnap on the couch would give his mind a chance to reset. Voilà! Ray awoke with a fresh take on an old idea. Excited, he hurried into his cramped office to rummage through a pile of contacts. At the bottom of his desk drawer, he found the address book with the number for Boris and Natasha, a pair of whiz kid computer geeks. A couple he had history with on projects that should have been wildly successful—but weren't. Unable to reach them on his first three attempts, Ray hesitatingly left them a message to give him a call ASAP.

At two a.m., Ray's cell phone buzzed, waking him from a sound sleep. "Are you serious?" Checking his watch, he answered groggily, "What kind of idiot calls at two in the morning? Better make it good, whoever you are … I'm losing sleep over here."

"Nice to hear your voice again; glad to see that temper hasn't changed. You called me, my friend, just returning your summons," a familiar male voice chided.

Proof positive of what Ray always believed, computer geeks slept during the day and foraged at night. During their middle-of-the-night conversation, Ray hemmed and hawed around about the three of them getting back together. And how nice it would be to take revenge on Nemesis for ruining their lives. As soon as the dialogue became superfluous, Ray instructed him to think about it and call him when they made up their minds.

One week later, the trio met in the Breeze Bar at the Beau Rivage Hotel and Casino in Biloxi.

Ray ordered beverages and coyly asked the wonder team a simple question. "Do you two think you could break into Warlock's cyber-crime program and listen in on the Nemesis super snooper?"

"Well, ah … Ray, is it now? What the hell do you think we've been working on ever since we got blindsided by that freak-ass computer?" Boris spit out his rebuke and rolled his eyes. Then he calmed down to explain. "In response to your question—of course. I discovered a backdoor into the mainframe, as well as the password to get in. You see, Noah Bouchard, the man who built and programmed Warlock, is fascinated with one particular eighties action movie. And he uses its title as his password—Top Gun. Once I get inside and covertly insert my program, we'll be able to monitor progress on all their cases, raid their archives, and stay ahead of any investigations coming our way. Did that sufficiently answer your question?"

Staring Boris straight in the eye, Ray asked, "Yes, it did." No thanks or praise, he followed with, "By the way, could you and Natasha retool the old Affluente plant to manufacture sun protection products? The reason I ask is that a month ago, on a lark, I drove by the old Affluente factory in Biloxi to check it out. It was for sale. Out of curiosity, I picked up a flier. The investment company that owned it was willing to unload the old place for pennies on the dollar. The old factory is now mine."

Smiling ear to ear, Boris and Natasha glanced at each other and nodded. "But, of course, we could make the adjustments. No problem. It's the perfect time to jump back in, while Nemesis's guard is down," Boris added.

Ray smirked and greedily rubbed his hands together.

WHILE RAY CUNNINGHAM jawed with Boris and Natasha in Biloxi, Noah Bouchard was in Trey McCall's office at The Circle M attempting to explain his newest computer brainchild, Loki, to Trey. Concerned about possible vulnerabilities to Warlock, Noah purposely left a back-door entryway accessible to only the brightest hacker, one who could figure out his password. Noah changed his mainframe password to "Top Gun" so all communications conducted were rerouted to Warlock's little brother, Loki, in Texas. A clever ruse to lead the hacker down the wrong rabbit hole. Even the most skilled cyber nerd would have no way of knowing the switch had taken place and would think they were communicating with Warlock. Programmed to deceive, Loki was equipped with three tiers of files, accurate but outdated ones to add credibility, semi-accurate ones designed to misconstrue, and fabricated ones to misguide. Nemesis flagged unsuspecting visitors and ranked them according to their threat level, one to five—five being the most severe. Loki collected, sorted, categorized, and filed data for the Nemesis agents to investigate. It all sounded good to Trey, but tech lingo stood beyond his grasp.

Overdosed on scientific terms spouting out from the brilliant Noah Bouchard, Trey left it to the group of cyber gurus, opting for a more genteel calling to work with his son on his golf game at the practice range. Trey was forced by injury to give up his dream of a second golf career on the Senior Tour to assume the role of coach. And, alongside Tara, co-manage their son Jefferson, who was preparing to launch his own professional golf career.

What a welcome reprieve it was from external threats and concerns to challenge the elements outside in the fresh air, perfecting the talents necessary to master a game that required one's full attention. Determined that his son avoid the pitfalls that derailed Trey's shortened career, he insisted everything be done by the book as far as the Tour was concerned. With grandiose aspirations for his son's success, Trey rattled off a litany of different shots for Jefferson to execute. Each one came off as if it were second nature. The last was Trey's favorite.

"Now let's see that controlled baby fade you've been working on," Trey remarked nonchalantly. With a slightly open stance, promoting an outside-in swing, Jefferson created the most beautiful high left-to-right shot that dropped out of the sky so gently that it barely made a mark on the green. Pleased with the result, the two smiled at each other.

"Yeah, just like *that*! You know where that shot always works? Major championships like the Masters, that's where," Trey remarked and gave his son a high five.

Among the most advantageous accomplishments in his son's stellar amateur golf career was Jefferson's fifth-place finish in the US Open the previous year. As a low amateur in the championship, he qualified for a spot in the upcoming Masters. A true competitor, Jefferson loved center stage and performed best under pressure. Father and son worked in tandem, tailoring Jefferson's game to fit the Augusta National Golf Club's unique, challenging layout. On a majority of the holes, high draws off the tee and high soft fades into the firm greens were called for, but when the Southern winds kicked up, swirling through the massive pines, innovation and imagination were essential. Working toward a common goal, Trey and Jefferson looked forward to April, where throngs of patrons would gather at the first "major championship" of the year in Augusta, Georgia. Ordinarily, such a massive collection of humanity would be cause for alarm for the McCall family. However, at the Masters, security was taken to its highest level including a no-fly zone over the property during tournament week. The McCalls learned over the years not to allow threats by others to interfere with the way of life they made for themselves. Awareness of their surroundings was key.

CHAPTER 2

MEANWHILE IN BILOXI, thanks to the expertise of Boris and Natasha, Ray Cunningham gloated over the retooled plant. Each product contained a sun protection factor (SPF) exclusively formulated for the Gulf Coast, which was just a bunch of BS cooked up by Ray, Boris, and Natasha, to attract the attention of the Mississippi tourist crowd. Production costs were a fraction of previous projects thanks to Boris's robotic innovations that substantially streamlined the manufacturing process—fewer hours and fewer workers. For now, the three entrepreneurs financed the whole show out of pocket, using the monies they'd made from the defunct Affluente scam and expecting to attract investors after their new product was established.

As a token of appreciation for including them in another opportunity at the brass ring, Boris and Natasha presented Ray with a one-of-a-kind gold Rolex Submariner wristwatch with a blue sapphire face sporting small diamonds for eight of the hours of the day on the dial. Blood red sapphires at twelve o'clock, three o'clock, six o'clock, and nine o'clock indicated directions on an internal compass. Ray was both delighted and surprised by the gesture and promised never to take it off.

Perfect, the vain little twerp fell for it. Just as Desiree predicted, Boris thought as he picked up the phone to call Montreal.

Now forever on Ray's left wrist was a customized chronometer with multifaceted capabilities, including a state-of-the-art miniature spycam with audio and video tracking and ingenious functions to measure blood pressure, stress level, heart rate, and the like. The timepiece was financed and requisitioned by a long-lost friend and investor in Montreal—engineered and assembled by Boris—monitored primarily by the party residing in Quebec.

CHILLING ON THE VERANDA of her posh condo near Montreal, Desiree Richards sipped a cocktail and smoked a cigarette while enjoying the cool, sunny afternoon. Her phone vibrated by her side, a call she expected from Boris with a heads-up about Ray and the spycam–watch Desiree asked Boris to give him. Smiling as she hung up, Desiree moved inside to her bedroom for an hour nap. She shed her clothes and glanced in the mirror. Following months of rehabilitation and healing from reconstructive surgery to her whole body, Desiree was thirty pounds lighter, no longer a bottle blond, and looked twenty years younger. A stranger even to herself, a giggle escaped her mouth, as she stared at her reflection. *My, oh, my*, she thought. *What a babe!* After one more glance in the mirror, Desiree yawned and climbed between the Egyptian cotton sheets of her king-sized bed.

As she tossed and turned, her suddenly kindled PTSD mind wandered about, then settled in a cave at the rear of an abandoned mine in Alberta to relive a haunting nightmare. *Desiree paused to catch her breath and relight her flickering torch. As soon as she struck a match all hell broke loose. In a flash, she had to scramble for her life to escape the claws of an angry grizzly. A glancing blow from a giant paw sent her skidding across the damp floor, crashing into the far wall.*

Petrified and defenseless, she prepared herself for the worst. By sheer luck, she discovered a cramped escape tunnel, shimmied her way out into the sunlight, and hustled downhill to an abandoned shack. Desiree tended to her wound as best she could and waited for dusk. Then snuck to the highway where she thumbed down a sympathetic motorist who took her to an emergency care clinic. Treated and bandaged, she cabbed it to a motel to recuperate. Two days later, free and clear, Desiree drove to Montreal stopping along the way to retrieve bags full of cash she'd hidden from past swindles.

Desiree smiled as she dreamed. A gust of wind blew the sheer curtains in her bedroom and ruffled her long chestnut-colored hair, waking her from her snooze. Giddy from the tickling hair, she gazed around to ensure she wasn't still dreaming. She yawned and stretched, put on a top and some shorts, and went outside to her veranda.

It was shaping up to be a lovely sunset with all the pastel colors building layers in the sky. She poured another cocktail, lit a cigarette, and contemplated her future as the sun sank below the horizon. The smartest thing for her to do would be to hunker down in her condo and enjoy the rest of her life doing whoever and whatever she wished, with more money than she could ever spend. But that went against her nature, seeing that there were individuals who seriously wronged her—folks who needed to be dealt justice—her kind of justice. Desiree had a plan she knew would work given the skills of her confederates Boris and Natasha.

Her target was Bobby, or Robert, or Rob McBride, or Ray Cunningham—whichever name he was currently using. Shortly after Boris and Natasha left college, Desiree employed them when no one else would. Because of Desiree, Boris and Natasha walked away with millions in cash and a solid reputation as IT geniuses, for which they were eternally grateful. Because of those close ties with them, she knew Ray was working the old "Lucky Richards's scam" in Biloxi.

Thanks to the Rolex watch on his wrist, Desiree monitored the little traitor's movements twenty-four hours a day. If Ray adhered to the Richards model, he'd abscond with all the proceeds as soon as profits began to wane and leave the others in the lurch holding the bag. Up-to-the-second data provided by the spycam on Ray's watch gave Desiree a window of opportunity to move in ahead of Ray and sweep the coffers clean. The icing on the cake would be to secretly betray Ray to Nemesis before she vanished into the sunset. Trey McCall would have no recourse but to turn his son over to the authorities, bringing dishonor to Nemesis and the McCall legacy.

A delightful scenario, indeed! Furthermore, what a marvelous way to distract Nemesis. For decades, Desiree baffled the best at the cybercrime giant. They thought she was dead. Best to leave it that way for now. She enjoyed the anonymity as she carried out her duties as Supreme Leader of a regenerating noble family consortium. Patience was her ally; it would take time to assemble bona fide champions to her cause.

ALL THE WHILE, PLAYING HIS PSEUDO ROLE as a dedicated IT entrepreneur working in conjunction with Ray Cunningham, Boris came up with several more innovative ideas using AI (artificial intelligence) components to further reduce the number of employees needed on the line at the Biloxi factory.

Natasha developed the addictive formula they'd use in the products—christened Amor del Sol. In her new lab, she blended common ingredients found in most suntan products with simple appealing fragrances, laced with enough narcotics to addict the user. It was made available in three alluring scents—vanilla, eucalyptus, and jasmine—and attractively packaged in a handy decorative four-ounce plastic spray bottle, for easy application of the non-greasy formula dry to the touch after absorbed into the skin.

What amazed the Amor del Sol information techs was how the public continued to fall for the same scam over and over. More baffling was how past hustles (Eclipse and Affluente) ended the very same way, for the very same reason. Simply put, the public bought the promise of the fountain of youth. And management, wanting to squeeze out every last penny, waited too long to sell out. Boris and Natasha were getting rich off it so they figured, what the hell, why not?

No one outside of Boris, Natasha, and a few mindless employees ever saw Ray Cunningham at the refurbished plant. For as long as possible, Ray wanted to remain a silent partner, to give himself mobility. It mattered not to Boris and Natasha as long as they received their just rewards. Given the potential riches ahead and Ray's history of disloyalty, the geeks had taken precautions. Their ace in the hole was Desiree, who recorded every move the little weasel made day and night.

Spring break in Biloxi was only a month away, a venue that provided an excellent business barometer for them in the past. Why not give it another go? By then, there would be more than enough Amor del Sol in storage to last through the beach blowout. As a final touch, Natasha introduced pheromones into the formula to enhance physical attraction and amplify the feeling of well-being produced by the narcotics.

NO LONGER IDLY BOUNCING off the walls, Ray now had a project to keep him busy. He cleared his mind of useless thoughts to focus on preparations for the upcoming influx of wild teens and young adults, who would soon bring chaos to the now peaceful, white sand beaches in Biloxi. Brimming with confidence, Ray was positive the third running of his idol's master scheme would be the charm. Previous failures were due to flawed last-minute deviations from the plan by inept personnel at the helm. Like its creator, Lucky Richards, his disciple saw only the purity of the mastermind's design. If allowed to run its intended course, it could not fail.

FARTHER WEST ON THE VERANDA outside of the chairman's office at The Circle M, Trey and Tara admired the mirror reflection of blue sky off the lake as their conversation drifted to the elusive fugitives. Noah Bouchard joined them to inquire if they had any questions about Loki, their newest asset.

"Only one." Trey looked up and smiled at his friend. "Did you fill Tara in on all the particulars and nuances of our newest cyber spy? If so, I'm good on that front. Although, there is something else that I would like to ask your opinion about. It's going on two years since my son Robert fled Canada and Desiree Richards disappeared for the umpteenth time to who-knows-where. Things don't add up, something's cooking, but I don't know what, where, or who is involved. Trying to figure it out keeps me up at night."

"Yes, I explained Loki to Tara, who is now familiar with all its functions." Noah shifted in his chair, a confused expression on his face. "About the other, those are an awful lot of unknowns, my friend. Seems like you should be overjoyed that your delinquent son has gone to ground for this long, maybe the boy has seen the errors of his ways and somehow repented. On the other hand, he could be afraid to call attention to himself with so many people searching for him. Whichever, one would think you'd be pleased not to have him in your hair." Noah grimaced. "Desiree's another animal altogether, calculating and elusive. Smart enough to lie low for as long as it takes to regroup and literally lick her wounds." Noah stopped as he turned to leave. "Tell me this: what more can you do that you're not doing now?"

Trey shrugged. "Nothing that I can think of. Still, I can't help wondering—where's Murphy? You know that guy who always shows up in the end to screw everything up?"

"Son, that's the nature of our business—any business for that matter. If those two are out there planning something individually or collectively, with our new resources, we'll know soon enough," Noah said on his way out the door to go pack for his return home.

Tara excused herself to visit the lab and familiarize herself more with Loki. Trey settled into his comfortable leather chair at his desk to contemplate. Waiting was the hardest thing in crime investigation. It promoted boredom and frequent naps. Just as Trey tilted his head back and yawned, his cell phone buzzed. On the other end, cockier than usual, his son Jefferson challenged him to a nine-hole golf match. Unable to resist, Trey went into the office bathroom to change into golf attire, trying to recall how long had it been since he'd bested his boy in a match. *Too long,* he thought and smiled.

WITH THE MASTERS COMING UP, it was time to give Jefferson some real competition. As Trey approached the golf facility, he saw his former caddie, Dance Johnson, now a fixture on his son's bag, hard at work with his new boss, talking strategy about the Augusta National Golf Club. Dance referenced the swirling wind that played havoc on the par three twelfth, sandwiched in between the difficult par four eleventh and par five thirteenth, known as "Amen Corner." Year in and year out, players in contention fell victim to the thirteenth by challenging the right front hole location on Sunday. Rather than playing to the center of the green, leaving a relatively easy two-putt par, many a bold player found Rae's Creek running in front and right of the green—dampening their chances to win the championship. There were plenty of holes to be aggressive on at Augusta National, Dance stressed to Jefferson—the twelfth was not one of them.

Due to the huge number of patrons who showed up for the practice rounds on tournament week, savvy Masters participants often came to Augusta early to take advantage of a few days of uninterrupted focus on the course. Something Trey did in his previous Masters appearances and found it helped immensely. Dance was already at the course checking things out when Trey, Jefferson, and Tara arrived in Augusta on Thursday prior to Masters week. The McCalls found the house they rented, unpacked, and settled in. As they drove down Magnolia Lane on Friday morning, Trey observed the expression on Tara's and his son's faces. It was like Trey's first reaction when he took in Augusta National for the first time—the look of awe, reverence, and respect. Jefferson was still in a daze as he registered for his first Masters, surrounded by all the history and tradition.

Friday morning, the atmosphere was abuzz with major championship electricity as the McCall trio made their way through the clubhouse. Confronted by old contemporaries, the elder McCall had battled on courses all over the world, and old memories flooded the former player's mind. When he introduced these legends to Tara and Jefferson, their eyes lit up, visibly impressed that these icons of the golf world knew Trey and played against him—many lost to him. Damn, Trey missed these guys and the competitions they'd shared over the years. An impromptu reunion was something Trey had not anticipated, yet greatly appreciated.

Practice rounds went well; Jefferson worked on his shot making and Trey gave him invaluable course management suggestions on optimum positions in the fairway and, most importantly, on the greens with their swells, ridges, and diabolical slopes. Dance listened and added suggestions of his own. As they played, it amazed Trey that so many players came up to say hello—more so that patrons outside the ropes remembered him and requested his autograph. Even with the airtight security measures at the Masters, Nemesis training kept him ever vigilant of his surroundings.

For the first few days at Augusta National Golf Club, Jefferson settled into his rhythm to embrace the true essence of the Masters. There was much more to it than the explosion of springtime in Georgia, resplendent in all its colorful regalia. There was the reverence and respect the patrons displayed for the contestants and the venue as well as the parade of overzealous scoop-crazed media who invaded the event. The history and the tradition memorialized in the clubhouse, around the grounds, and on the golf course were a steady reminder of how truly exceptional the championship was in the world of golf. Trey saw in in his son's eyes and reverent manor, Jefferson wanted to make his first Masters a memorable one—the first of many more to come.

Wednesday morning, during their last practice round, Trey

thought he heard a familiar voice shout at him from the other side of the fairway on the seventh hole. Making sure he wasn't imagining things, Trey squinted in the direction of the sound. He grinned ear to ear when he recognized Ace Hershfield, one of the veteran cameramen from Trey's days working in television. A legendary character, Ace got his nickname from filming the first live hole-in-one on television back in the day. As old friends do, they chatted about the glory days and fresh developments in broadcasting. With a sly smirk on his face, Ace clued him in about some of the execs Trey had worked under back when. It seems they were unceremoniously let go last Friday after a merger, and the new management brought in their own people. *What sweet karma,* thought Trey. They parted the company with the promise to keep in touch. When he caught up to his son at the seventh green, Jefferson asked who he was visiting with back in the fairway.

"An old and trusted friend, a straight-up guy who always had my back. A cameraman I hope you see around a bunch during your career. Remind me one day to talk to you about karma. Seems the older I get, the more real it becomes. Now let's see what we can do to get you in that last pairing on Sunday afternoon."

WHILE TREY AND JEFFERSON mapped out their strategy to conquer Augusta National, Trey's eldest son, alias Ray Cunningham, launched his spring break test run for his outdoor sun products under the Amor del Sol label in hopes once the party freaks latched on to it and spread the good word, the feedback would be positive. For maximum exposure, Ray purchased booth space at all the popular beaches for the week. Monday through Wednesday, they distributed free samples and brochures to the beach crowd, with instructions on how and where they could purchase additional merchandise. After Wednesday, the product was available for cash or debit card only.

For the first three days, Amor del Sol goods flew off the shelves in the booths. Thursday would be the true test—would the party freaks pay money for the stuff? A few hired alpha studs and babes praised the effects of the products to the crowds and directed their followers to the booths to stack the deck. By Saturday afternoon, Ray had to hire more staff to keep the booths stocked. Sunday morning, they had to limit the amount of product sold per customer to one, which made the merchandise more desirable, and by week's end, they were down to only a few cases of products left at the plant. By all indications, Amor del Sol was a rousing success.

NEMESIS AGENTS AT THE CYBER LAB headquarters in Texas picked up a load of gibberish from a familiar region during spring break—the Mississippi Gulf Coast. Most of the banter had to do with a revolutionary array of sun products called Amor del Sol. More than likely it was just another fad sweeping the mob at spring break. Miranda, who did not believe in coincidences, thought Amor del Sol had "Lucky Richards scam" written all over it. Rather than bother Trey, Tara, and Jefferson at the Masters, she shared her findings with Slim McCall, a brilliant logistician for Nemesis, currently manning the helm in Trey's absence. Following Miranda's explanation, Slim agreed there were similarities. He concurred it was best to spare the McCall clan any added angst on the eve of young Jefferson's first Masters.

Instead, Slim sent Rich Martel and Samantha Smithwick, over to Biloxi to check things out. The youngest-looking agents in the Nemesis organization easily fit in with the beach crowd demographic. At Slim's suggestion, they were to touch base with Bud and Bev Williamson to make sure they were all right, then monitor the beach activity.

Rich was a veteran of numerous missions and trained under Tina Tremblay, one of Nemesis's most experienced agents. Conversely, Samantha (Sam) was on her first field assignment, gung-ho to impress the front office. Sam and Rich were dating, which would ordinarily prevent them from working as partners. In that this was more of a fact-finding exercise than a dangerous mission, an exception was made. Besides, Sam trained with the elite forces at the ranch and was capable of taking care of herself.

The sun broke over the horizon on Wednesday with the promise for another day of scorching temperatures along the coast. Rich and Sam slipped into their swimsuits, donned casual attire over them, and were off to meet with the Williamsons at their charter boat office. The owners of Buddy's charters were glad Nemesis sent them over. There was a matter Bev needed to talk over with Rich and Sam.

Troubled, and to ensure complete secrecy, Bev persuaded them to cruise the bay in the *Biloxi Belle* before the Nemesis duo joined the spring break rabble-rousers. As soon as the charter boat cleared the bay, Buddy set the controls in a slow, wide trolling circle so he could join in the conversation pertaining to one person in particular, who she and Bud had been associated with for some time.

Uncertain where to begin, Bev cut to the chase. "Now, I can't say for sure that this fella is who I think he is, but I have this gut feeling. It's the shape of his eyes and face that remind me of a young man from one of my and Lucky's adventures. Just a mixed-up kid back then, caught in the middle of a big mess the way I saw it. Anyway, this guy has gone to a great deal of trouble to disguise himself. Still, I've got a strong feeling."

Rich glanced over at Sam and then back at Bev. "So, who do you think this fella really is?"

"Goes by Ray Cunningham now, but I think he's really Bobby McCall."

"By chance, could this be the guy?" Rich showed Bev a photo of Robert McCall he pulled up on his cellphone.

Bev nodded. "Might be … he's older, hair's longer, a different color, and he's got a beard, but the eyes and shape of the head are right. Could be him."

Rich handed Bud the phone. "Captain, check out this photo. What do you think … Could our suspect be Robert McCall?"

"Yeah, that's him, absolutely."

"*Hmm,* that definitely puts a new slant on things. If Bobby McCall, alias Ray Cunningham, is going to be around during spring break, it's best I remain in the shadows. We met briefly during his last visit to The Circle M, though long enough that he would remember me. Which leaves Sam to do all the snooping among the beach crowd." He flashed a sly grin. "By the way, she fills a bikini that shouldn't pose any problem."

In reaction to the compliment, Sam paraded around the galley like a swimsuit model. Beautiful in every sense.

As for Rich, he planned to stay on the periphery in disguise in case she needed assistance and scoped out the crowd for Ray. On the way back to the dock, Rich called Slim with the bombshell Bev dropped on them. Surprised but not shocked at the news about his nephew being behind a new scam, Slim concluded it all fit in with the Richards's modus operandi. There was no use in getting the McCall trio worked up at the Masters; they would be back home from Augusta in four days, anyway. By then Slim hoped they'd have a positive ID on Ray Cunningham; meanwhile, he instructed Rich and Sam to keep an eye out.

DURING THEIR FIFTEEN-MINUTE DRIVE from the house to the opening round of the Masters, Trey and Tara did their very best to keep their emotions hidden from Jefferson. Inside, the anxious parents' bellies churned. In contrast, their boy seemed quietly confident on the ride down Magnolia Lane, seemingly oblivious to the electric atmosphere surrounding the opening round. Patrons roamed the grounds in record numbers on a glorious spring day, already standing three deep at the first tee waiting for Jefferson's group. As was the custom at the Masters, after their warm-up and final putting session, Masters security escorted Jefferson McCall and his two playing competitors through the crowd to the first tee, some thirty yards from the putting green.

From outside the ropes on the right, Trey and Tara watched Jefferson drill his first tee shot of the day right up the center of the fairway, a considerable distance past his playing partners, which drew an interesting reaction from one of them, who silently mouthed, *Wow*. As they walked past the throngs of people lining the fairways, one of the players in the group peered over at Jefferson about to strike up a conversation—but backed off. Jeffersontook no notice; his eyes were glued straight ahead, focused on nothing but the job in front of him. He exhibited a cool, confident air, common to the likes of a Jack Nicklaus or Tiger Woods. The other two in the group glanced at each other, likely wondering if this kid was going to be the next great player.

After a perfect drive at the first, Jefferson hit his second over the green in an almost impossible place from which to save par. Although he pitched the ball to eight feet, a remarkable feat indeed, he failed to make the putt. A bogey five for Jefferson at the first hole of his first Masters. Fearing the worst, Tara hung her head. Beside her, Trey grinned.

In a hushed voice, she muttered to him, "What in the world is wrong with you, Trey? Jefferson just screwed up his first hole! It could completely destroy his confidence for the rest of the week."

Trey shook his head no. "I don't think so. Be patient. You'll see. It was something I'd hoped would happen early in the round to get Jefferson's attention. All morning he's walked around in kind of a dazed craze, a frozen funk. He needed something to shock him back to reality, to set his mind right and get his game face on."

At the second, Tara watched her son reach the par five in two shots. From across the green, his first putt just grazed the top edge of the cup and stopped three and a half feet past the hole, leaving him one of the fastest, trickiest putts at Augusta National. Thinking about his miss at the previous hole, Tara covered her eyes with her hands. Calmly, the Masters rookie rolled the ball right in the middle to get back to even par. After a bogey at the fifth, a birdie at the seventh, and pars at eight and nine, Jefferson stood at even par going to the tenth. On the second nine, eight solid pars and a single birdie on the par five fifteenth got him to one under. A decent start for the first timer. And at the end of the round, Tara took in a deep sigh of relief when she realized it was the first full day in weeks that she hadn't thought about Jefferson's older stepbrother Bobby.

In round two, Jefferson shot even par, giving him a two-day total of one-forty-three, well within the cut line to play the weekend. Saturday, he was paired with a four-time Masters champion, and wall-to-wall patrons followed them from start to finish. Ignoring the distractions associated with being paired with a legend, Jefferson shot a two under par seventy. On the final day, Jefferson shot an incredible sixty-four, an eight under par round that included eagles at the par five thirteenth and fifteenth holes, capped by an incredible up and down from the right bunker on eighteen to save par. A tie for third earned him a Masters invite for the coming year, plus exposure and experience on one of the biggest stages in all of golf.

Unlike many talented golfers who couldn't bring it to the arena, Jefferson McCall not only brought it, but he thrived on being in the spotlight with a fearlessness yet sensible attitude—a credit to his father who helped instill those traits in his son. The comradery Jefferson and his caddie, Dance, developed was similar to that of Dance and Trey back in the day—an almost unbeatable combination. Dance's easy-going yet dedicated personality lent itself to the way the McCalls approached life and the game. With his top three finish at Augusta, Jefferson qualified for four invitational tour events as well as two major championships he was not exempt from already—the Open Championship and the PGA Championship.

Counting on her son's ability and Trey's advice as Jefferson's manager of record, Tara graciously declined a multitude of sponsor exemptions on her son's behalf. As good as Jefferson was, she and Trey saw no reason for the boy to be beholden to any tournament. Deep down, both knew seven tournaments were more than enough for their son to secure his players' card.

Immediately after they arrived back at The Circle M midday Monday, Jefferson joined in the festivities as he greeted congratulatory shouts with high fives and slaps on the back to the overjoyed Nemesis extended family. After the celebration, Slim asked to see Trey and Tara in his office.

SEATED BEHIND HIS DESK as his nephew and niece-in-law entered his office, Slim handed them a folder—an up-to-the-minute account of activity on the surveillance in the Gulf Coast. As Trey read through the dossier, the smile on his face turned to a frown. "Is this for real?"

Nodding, Slim explained. "I'm afraid it is. Seems that your prodigal son is at it again. On my orders, Rich Martel and Sam Smithwick went to Biloxi to check things out. During an interesting boat trip with the Williamsons, they picked up some good intel from Bev—who swears the guy behind this Amor del Sol ploy is definitely Robert, using the alias, Ray Cunningham. At the moment, Rich is parked on the periphery, invisible to prying eyes, while Sam is working the crowd to see what she can dig up there. If Bev is correct, Ray's arrival in Mississippi directly coincides with Robert's departure from Canada."

Pausing to catch his breath, Slim continued. "Coincidently, Mac is on board. I filled him in once he got back with a couple of those Quarter horses he bought from Reanna's old man in Bandera. It will probably come as no surprise to you that Mac has had it with that little son of a bitch—his words—and is ready to be rid of that useless mongrel for good. Can't say I blame him. The boy never had a mind of his own, that's for sure. But I understand if you feel differently since he's your flesh and blood. Anything we need to add to our plan?"

"No, Uncle Slim, given the same circumstances, you've done exactly what I would have done. Let's see what comes from being patient. Although, I think I'll send Ty Dossier and Miranda Stevens to Biloxi, giving us two more bodies on the ground. Thanks for handling this while we were away, the Masters would not have been the same for Tara, and with this on our minds as well. By the way, you do know you're my favorite uncle, right?" Trey chuckled.

Slim nodded again, smiled, then frowned—*Hell*, he thought, *I'm his only uncle.*

WHILE THE FOLKS AT NEMESIS discussed strategy, Ray and Boris assessed the encouraging results pouring in on their trial run of

Amor del Sol. During the mass invasion of youthful bodies on the Gulf beaches, Boris flew high-altitude drones over the melee below to capture the festivities on video. Initially, Boris adopted drones as a security measure for the factory and storage areas at the Amor del Sol property. Why not use spring break to sharpen his navigating skills with his new toys? With the range and stealth of drones, nothing escaped the lenses of his cameras.

One evening while they viewed an accumulation of drone videos, a familiar face popped up on the screen. Enraged, Ray had Boris reverse the video back to the face in the crowd and freeze the frame.

"No way, it can't be. It's impossible," Ray said, shaking his head. "How could they be onto us already? Do you two have any idea who that asshole on the screen happens to be? Well, do you?"

Before Boris could respond, Ray blurted out, "That son of a bitch's name is Rich Martel, one of the top agents working for my father at Nemesis. Sic your drones on the crowd and find him. I want to know his every move. Who he's with and who he talks to. You got that?"

Boris nodded as Ray stormed away to walk off his anger, absently wandering along the beach under a full moon until the waves lapping on shore calmed him down. *Could be just a coincidence.* Maybe Rich and some friends came to spring break to check out the babes, have some beers, and relax for a while. Yeah, that was probably it.

Search as he might for the next few days, with his drones prowling the skies, Boris did not locate Rich anywhere in the vicinity. What Boris didn't know was that as soon as Rich suspected Trey's missing son was in Biloxi, he dressed up as an ice cream vendor to move around unnoticed in the crowd. The disguise worked perfectly.

After a few days of holding his breath, Ray exhaled with a humongous sigh, satisfied that Rich had gone back to Texas.

CHAPTER 3

AS SOON AS THE MADNESS of spring break, coupled with the fear of discovery by Nemesis wore off, Ray again found life in Biloxi monotonous and searched for an interesting hobby to calm his restless mind. Times he spent on the water with the Williamsons on the *Biloxi Belle* mellowed him out and cleared his mind. Perhaps he should get a boat of his own. Although he knew so little about them, he now had time to learn. Why not? So he scoured marinas in the area for a boat of his own, testing various types and sizes to get a feel for the differences in maneuverability. Finally, Ray decided on a mid-sized vessel, versatile enough to navigate coastal areas as well as the deep water where he'd once hooked a marlin. A month after Amor del Sol went into full production, he found the boat he was searching for in an ad posted at a nearby marina. Slightly larger than he'd figured on, it was a beauty in pristine condition and the price was right. Although he was super rich, Ray was still very much a cheapskate.

"A deal of a lifetime" is how Wilmer Braun the builder and owner of the boat phrased it. Everyone knew him as Old Man Braun, a German nautical engineer who immigrated to Mississippi toward the end of WWII. Drawn to the sea, the man loved boats and was enthralled with submarines. For an extra two grand, Braun threw in a submersible he'd disguised to resemble a large dolphin or Mako shark, fin and all. It was engineered to attach to the underbelly of Ray's new boat by powerful electro-magnets controlled by switches on the sub and in the lower cabin of the host craft. Access to the sub was through a watertight trapdoor in the floor of the mothership. Ray patted himself on the back for thinking ahead to the end game and a viable escape plan—just like Lucky Richards would have done.

Now that he had a project and a hobby, Ray's disposition changed; he actually smiled on occasion. Only one thing would make it better: female companionship. Happy hour at the Half Shell Oyster House was an excellent spot to pursue his mission. As soon as he cleared the door, Ray spotted the dynamite waitress, no bigger than a minute, with jet-black hair, big dazzling eyes that drew you in, and a remarkable figure he remembered from previous visits. As he settled at a high-top table in the bar, she scurried over to take his order.

Before he spoke, she stopped him. "Dos Equis, salt, no lime, and a Jack back, am I right?"

"Yeah, how'd you know?" He smiled.

"Good memory, I guess. The name's Willa Rae, and you would be Ray Cunningham. I check out all the cute guys, just a habit of mine. Just in case, you know." She smiled back and winked.

Seizing the moment, Ray was careful to play the gentleman, to not overindulge in the alcohol department, and to tip her generously. She wrote down her phone number on his receipt with a little heart drawn at the end. Then said, "FYI, in case you were wondering, everything about me is natural."

Wow, Ray thought as he drove home, she's very much the spitfire he'd witnessed lay out patrons that took liberties like copping a feel or pinching her ass. Once inside, Ray popped a beer, sat on his couch, and stared at his phone, building up the courage to call. Two beers later, he invited Willa Rae over for a drink and a midnight stroll on the beach. Eagerly, she agreed.

An hour later she showed up. Dressed casually in shorts and a tank top, her hair down on her shoulders released from the ponytail she wore at work, Willa Rae depicted the ultimate temptress. Moonlight surrounded her, giving off a wicked aura of temptation. Ray invited her in and offered her a drink. She brushed against him on her way to the couch.

"I'll have whatever you're having," Willa uttered in a low, sultry voice and curled up on the end of the leather couch, pulled a cigarette out of her purse, and lit it without asking if Ray minded. Ray went to the bar for a couple of Dos Equis and an ashtray. He returned with their drinks and his only ashtray. Sporting a sly grin, she patted the leather cushion for him to nestle in beside her. After a few swigs of her beer, Willa Rae finished her smoke, moved even closer to Ray, and whispered seductively in his ear. Following a vigorous erotic session on the couch, they slid into the spa attached to the pool out back. In no time, steam was rising off their naked bodies as the jacuzzi jets poured over them.

In the tranquil setting, with gentle waves slapping against the dock and lightning bugs dotting the night, they chatted about themselves, their jobs, family histories, plans for the future. When she mentioned her last name was Braun, Ray gulped and pointed to his new purchase tethered to the dock. "Unbelievable, did you know I just bought a boat and a mini sub from your father? Who, in his words, gave me a deal of a lifetime."

She laughed. "Yeah, I know, he asked me to check you out, a bit after the fact I'd say, but my father is eccentric. He wanted to make sure you were worthy of owning one of his masterpieces before he cashed the check. My dad is the suspicious type. If you consider all that was going on at the time he left Germany, who could blame him. And being the obedient daughter that I am, I felt a *thorough* investigation was in order. By the way, you passed."

Befuddled, Ray smiled but remained speechless.

"Don't let that go to your head. Now that you've measured up, we can take your new acquisition back over to my dad's in the morning; he'd like to talk to you about a couple of things."

"Sounds good to me, I think. Should I be worried? About your dad, that is."

"Naw, he's a really cool dude, smart as hell too. Do us both good to listen to what he says. Word of caution, his first name is Wilmer, whatever you do, do *not* call him that. My suggestion is that you refer to him as Professor or better yet Doctor. Titles he earned in the academic world." With that, the devilish seductress took him by the hand and led him back into the bungalow.

AT NINE A.M., Ray and Willa shoved off in the *Kismet*, the name he'd given his new boat, for a twenty-minute ride up the coast to the Braun estate. They skipped over the calm water admiring the bald cypress and Southern magnolia trees that dotted the shoreline. Folks wetting a fishing line off an old jetty waved a good morning hello. While a couple of playful dolphins swam alongside *Kismet*, darting here and there. Dr. Braun was waiting at the dock when they pulled in; instead of tying up the boat, he climbed aboard and directed Ray to continue farther up the coastline. At the third bend, Dr. Braun instructed Ray to bear hard right into a narrow waterway leading into a cove surrounded by huge, ancient spreading willow trees that formed a natural canopy. At the end of the cove, larger than a barn, sat a tall wooden boathouse with a cavernous entrance the good doctor opened by remote control. Slowly Ray pulled in and tied up to a wooden piling.

They exited the *Kismet* onto the steel-reinforced dock. The inside of the building was monstrous, with room enough for two or more boats the size of Ray's. On their left, further down the dock, was the mini sub he'd purchased from the good doctor in their recent transaction. Deeper back in the structure was a workbench and tool station loaded with parts and utensils necessary in construction and repair of marine vessels. Everything ran off propane generators sitting on the concrete floor across the back wall. Over to the side sat the drafting room and office, where Dr. Braun drew up his bold creations.

Ray nodded his approval at all he had taken in so far. Old Man Braun smiled broadly and motioned for Willa and Ray to follow him to the two-passenger sub. An impressive feat of ingenuity, it had taken the old fella years to build the fuselage of the sub from scratch. He'd methodically assembled each component from capsule, to cockpit, to dashboard, to battery housings and switches, to fuses and backup safeguards. Quite possibly the most over-engineered submersible ever created, it could run whisper-quiet on battery power for up to three hours fully submerged at a speed of twenty knots, equipped with an oxygen supply that would last three-plus hours, for two adult passengers. With amazing maneuverability, its motion on top or under the surface mirrored those of a large dolphin or short-fin Mako shark.

Fascinated by what he heard, Ray listened to the old man explain how simple it was to guide the machine, in his words, "even a young child could manage it." Paramount of all, the fuses and batteries had to be properly maintained and monitored constantly, and an abundant supply of backup batteries were mandatory on board in case of malfunctions. Life or death depended on battery function. Different shades of blacks, blues, and greys colored the outer shell of the sub, from the tail to the dorsal fin, down to the snout of a dolphin or shark. From the cockpit, the operator had a three-hundred-sixty-degree view through reinforced plexiglass. Truly a work of submersible art.

After the tutorial, Dr. Braun took a small sailboat back to his estate, leaving Ray and Willa alone in the mini sub to put it through the motions. Most of the rest of the day, the couple dived deep into the offshore gulf waters, surfaced, bobbed, and weaved in the waves in the two-passenger sub they dubbed *Mako*. Willa threw her head back in sheer delight having the time of her life. Ray was ecstatic. Believing he'd won her over, he anticipated a rowdy replay of the previous night when they got back to his bungalow.

They maneuvered *Mako* into the boathouse as the sun dipped toward the horizon. Hastily, Ray secured the mini sub to a piling and put its batteries on chargers. Anxious to get Willa to his place before dark, he slammed the throttles all the way forward on *Kismet*. Less than thirty minutes later, they walked hand in hand from his dock toward his cottage. Before they reached the door, Willa turned to give him an indifferent kiss, thanked him for humoring her father, and headed for her car she'd parked there the night before.

Crestfallen, Ray shouted after her. "Willa, wait. Where are you going? I, ah . . . well . . . thought maybe you'd want to stay over, you know, after last night, today, and all."

She pretended not to hear him and kept moving toward her car, waved ta-ta over her shoulder, and was off.

For a while, Ray sat on the front steps of his bungalow hosting a one-man pity party with his head buried in his hands, wondering what in the hell he'd done wrong.

WHEN WILLA GOT HOME, Wilmer Braun was waiting, anxious to hear about the previous day and night she spent with Ray. Although his concerns were genuine, they were not necessarily for fatherly reasons. He was adamant about the trip to Isla Segura off the coast of Peru to meet with an old college chum who managed the island for an international pharma syndicate. It must be a matter of great importance to Fritz Gruber and the mob for him to fly over three thousand miles to meet in person.

After an uneventful flight of six hours on a privately chartered jet, Dr. Braun and Fritz reminisced about their college days while they sipped Mai Tai's beachside. Fritz was quite the *player* back then; it was good to find out he hadn't changed much from the old days. They chatted about the nightspots and the ladies.

"Oh, the memories, but I wonder, my friend." Wilmer Braun cocked his head. "Why did you summon me all this way to meet face to face? It intrigues me. Must be hush-hush, top secret, and all that."

Still smiling, their history fresh in his mind, Fritz sighed. "Very well, to the point as always. Wilmer, have you ever heard of something called Affluente?"

"Indeed, I have. It was a cosmetic concern near the shipyard in Biloxi that went belly up," Braun replied.

"Okay then, have you heard about anything similar being manufactured in that area recently? Reason being I got word from a reliable female source in Montreal about a popular new product being turned out down there on your coast," Fritz confided to his countryman.

"Not to my knowledge. However, my daughter Willa is a waitress in one of the most popular bars in town—she hears gossip all the time. I'll ask her and get back to you," promised Dr. Braun, who was now mildly curious.

Fritz raised his eyebrows. "If you two come up with solid information, we will make it worth your while."

Instead of his usual afternoon nap, Dr. Braun walked the beach to mull over their conversation. What if he and Willa Mae circumvented Fritz and the cartel to pull off a scam of their own. Whereby, Ray Cunningham disappeared permanently. Earlier when Fritz mentioned a reliable female source in Canada. Dr. Braun knew precisely who he meant: Desiree Richards. Braun and Desiree did *business* in the past. They weren't exactly allies or adversaries—they were opportunists. Desiree, a master at playing all sides against the middle, was the one who prompted Dr. Braun to sell his boat to Ray Cunningham.

While her father enjoyed the amenities of Isla Segura, Willa Rae kept an ear out for any new activity at the docks in Biloxi. She picked up a rumor at the Half Shell one night that some dude purchased the old Affluente factory and retooled the place to produce sun care products known as Amor del Sol. Evidently, the new goods were the most popular sun products along the Gulf Coast.

Fritz slowly nodded when Wilmer gave him Willa Rae's news. "Good to hear. That confirms our information. You see, decades ago, there was a guy at Isla Segura by the name of Lucky Richards, a real con man ahead of his time, with a solid plan for scamming millions of people by means of social interaction. On its face, the scheme is genius, if not tampered with, probably fool proof. *Fool* being the operative word since its failures have all been due to faulty leadership. We're watching to see if it's worth offering them a partnership, which will only occur if we're convinced Amor del Sol will have greater longevity than its predecessors. If you and your daughter keep us up to date on the operation there in Biloxi, we'll cut you in for a nice piece of the action."

Dr. Braun grinned and thought, *Then again, that may not be necessary.*

AFTER WILLA MAE LEFT so abruptly, Ray remained on his back steps with his head buried in his hands until the lights of her car disappeared into the night. Still in a daze, he wandered over to the pool bar to grab a beer, then strolled the beach to sort his thoughts. One thing was for sure: Willa had his number. Was she worth it? Smitten as he was, the answer was yes, just thinking about her changed his gloomy mood. Memories of last night rushed in. He cracked a huge smile and thought, *Yessir, that one is sure worth it. I'd bet my life on it.*

A few days later, after an apology for her rudeness and a romantic afternoon together with a spa and romp, Willa casually mentioned Amor del Sol. Apparently one of her customers at the Half Shell overheard a rumor that the mob had taken an interest in the product.

Ray about jumped out of his skin and leaped up to phone Boris and Natasha. Willa eavesdropped on the conversation, catching only Ray's side of the conversation. In no uncertain terms, Ray ordered Boris to shut down the plant until further notice. Then for Boris and Natasha to leave the state pronto to a faraway location like Hawaii. Once it was safe to resume production, Cunningham would let them know.

"BORIS AND NATASHA—REALLY? If Rocky and Bullwinkle show up, I'm out of here. Money or no money."

DR. BRAUN EMBRACED the tropical ambiance, laid back and island casual. Just as he ordered a second umbrella cocktail from one of the enchanting wait staff, an unexpected phone call from his daughter interrupted his blissful state. He listened to Willa recant what she'd overheard from a conversation Ray had with a dude named Boris. Her father burst out laughing so hard he almost had a heart attack. "No wonder Lucky Richards's scheme hadn't worked with imbeciles like Ray at the helm. Too bad Lucky himself didn't get the opportunity to fully implement his plan. The ruthless bastard should have owned the world." Dr. Braun instructed Willa to hang tight and stay close to Ray.

CHAPTER 4

MINDFUL TO HEED THE ADVICE he gave Boris, Ray scrambled to make arrangements for Willa and him to hide out in Key West until things cooled down. In no real hurry to get there, Willa and Ray followed the western coastline of Florida until they reached Surreal, their accommodations near Key West. Ray tied the *Kismet* up in the slip they were assigned as part of the deluxe resort package. If they were to stay for an extended time, Ray would make sure they basked in the lap of luxury. Their rental residence featured an ocean-view three-bedroom, three-bath layout with a private pool and jacuzzi shielded on three sides from the public. Actually, Willa Rae dreaded going down to the Keys with a guy as moody and unpredictable as Ray. However, given the lavish surroundings, she decided to put up with his issues.

SIX THOUSAND MILES WEST of South Florida, Boris and Natasha arrived at their condo at Kaanapali Beach on the island of Maui. In exchange for ownership in a Maui condo, Boris paid off a large gambling debt to a mob bookie for a college buddy who got in over his head with no way out. On the outside, by modern standards, it was quite ordinary. To Boris, it oozed old-time Hawaii featuring a thatched roof and a bamboo-accented entrance. As they moved around inside, Boris and Natasha marveled at the polished dark hardwood floors. Walls covered in murals depicting Hawaiian folklore and pastel blue ceilings gave it a tranquil air, and sturdy wooden furniture topped with cushions and pillows highlighted by likenesses of island flowers and plants and ocean scenes gave the interior a tropical flare. A granite-topped island with a chef's prep sink was center stage in the kitchen. The window side offered diners an unobstructed view of waves crashing on the beach. The refrigerator, oven, stove, a pantry, custom cabinets, and granite countertops took up the wall side. Two identical bedrooms featured king-sized beds and walk-in closets. Each had a marble tub and shower in the bathroom. A sliding door led out back to the pool and pathway to the ocean.

"Check this out!" Boris said as he slid open the door. The scent of gardenia and plumeria wafting in on the breeze, combined with the sound of waves crashing ashore only a hundred yards away, made him giddy. He glanced over at the hammock strung between two large palms swinging to and fro in the wind. In the distance alongside the beach walk leading to civilization, he glimpsed restaurants, convenience stores, and tourist hotels. Activities huts dotted both sides of the path advertising deep-sea fishing, whale watching, and island tours. Tomorrow morning they'd go exploring—but for now, the beach was calling.

Boris turned around to ask Natasha a question, but it was too late. Bikini-clad, she beelined for the sand. On her heels out the door, Boris spotted a man across the way staring at him, which was probably not that unusual, being that he was white as a sheet, having not been in the sun since he began working for Ray. Yet, there was something about the man that bothered Boris, something eerie and threatening.

By the time Boris reached the beach, Natasha had dived into the water and now challenged the incoming waves head on. Laughing and giggling like a schoolgirl, she splashed water on Boris as he waded into the tepid ocean surf. Glancing back at the shore, Boris noticed the man from the condo complex sitting on a wooden bench, watching them, jotting down notes, and talking on a cell phone.

WHEN AN ADDICTED GAMBLER, deeply in debt to the mob, suddenly paid off his entire tab, it raised a huge red flag for the syndicate. Especially if the angel who gave the dude the money was named Boris. Then it became Fritz Gruber's role to delve into the computer nerd's history. A cursory glance at Boris's background showed the cyber genius was involved in a few computer scam operations that made him some decent coin. He disappeared briefly, then almost overnight, Boris and his partner Natasha moved up in the world to Affluente. Speculation had them currently involved with Amor del Sol, a deal the mobster was keeping an eye on for a possible hostile takeover in the future. Straight away, Fritz put a man on Boris and Natasha—a ruthless trained assassin just waiting for the okay to take them out.

FROM THE BEGINNING, Boris was the front man for the couple; he was fearless and spoke his mind. In reality, the true brains of the duo was Natasha. Even though Boris took credit for what they developed in the lab, she was the one who actually conceived it—Boris built it. Without the goth guise she preferred, Natasha was breathtakingly gorgeous. With her auburn-streaked dark brown hair draped down on her shoulders, glistening emerald eyes, and enticing figure, Natasha was hard for any man to ignore—which freaked her out.

With the pick of the litter, she chose Boris. When they were young and naïve, he had been there to rescue her from a brutally abusive relationship. From that day forward, they shared an unbroken bond of loyalty. What she didn't know was Boris needed her far more than she needed him, to maintain his macho image in the real world.

An honor student her whole life, Natasha, christened Millicent (Millie) Snowden, chose computer science as her major at Northwestern University and stayed for her master's. Then to MIT in Cambridge, Massachusetts, on a doctorate scholarship. She was top of her class, working on her thesis, when a tenured professor Dr. Lawrence Habersham convinced her to let him tutor her through the process.

Small in stature and grossly unattractive, sporting a bulbous nose, scraggly tufts of greasy mousy brown hair, with tobacco-stained teeth, Dr. Habersham was a despicable excuse for a human being, who possessed no loyalty to anyone save for himself. Professor in name only, he did not have the credentials to qualify as a janitor much less a teacher.

By virtue of a glowing fake resume, he was hired on the spot and entrenched at the school for two decades. The libelous prof published studies in several computer science journals adopting plagiarized materials he stole from grad students under his tutelage. School magistrates blocked blowback from victims to prevent any hint of impropriety involving the institution. Hearsay around campus had it that the lecherous old coot used his tenured position to bed some of his loveliest female grad students.

One day Boris spotted Millie in tears during one of their classes. After class he asked her if everything was all right; she broke down and opened up to him about Dr. Haversham. How he physically and mentally abused her to the point she couldn't stand it anymore. Livid, Boris went directly to the tutor's office to confront him. Pinned to the wall, the tenured freak protested, then cried like a baby, and begged for his life. Boris let him go and watched as the defeated little worm slid down the wall, and he left him weeping in a heap on the floor. Instead of slamming the door, Boris left it open so students who passed in the hall could view the despicable coward in all his glory.

Hand in hand, Millie and Boris left school for good that afternoon. Off together, to face what the world had to offer. Millie assumed the new nickname Boris gave her. *Boris and Natasha, very Goth noir,* they thought. They'd been together ever since.

FRITZ'S MOB ASSASSIN in Maui took as many photos on his phone as he could and sent them to his boss, who circulated them worldwide to his operatives. An IT man working for the syndicate in Seattle recognized Natasha as a girl he was in graduate school with at MIT. Without a doubt, she was the smartest one in the whole damn school. Oddly, she and a boy left school together under suspicious circumstances, all swept under the carpet by the administration. What an asset she would be if the syndicate could ever get their hands on her; it would make dealing with the new-age crime-fighting macro-computers a whole lot easier. Could be even Nemesis wasn't aware of her capabilities.

BACK AT THE CIRCLE M driving range, Chairman Trey McCall and Jefferson worked on the never-ending process of perfecting the fundamentals. Even the best that ever played often ran afoul to some fundamental issue they'd taken for granted—usually poor alignment. For Jefferson, it was aiming too far right, which caused him to work across his body, losing power and accuracy. Even after a top three finish at the Masters, Trey felt his son needed to make a minor adjustment for the following two weeks.

Harbour Town Golf Links on Hilton Head Island, South Carolina, and Colonial Country Club in Ft. Worth, Texas, had narrow fairways and tiny greens, complete opposites to those of Augusta National. Thanks to the minor alignment correction, Jefferson played consistently better through the week in South Carolina. Then shot a bogie-free sixty-three on Sunday afternoon to jump into the top five at Harbour Town.

Colonial in Ft. Worth was next on the circuit, a course where Trey McCall had a couple of runners-up finishes in his heyday. Jefferson and Trey were there on Monday morning to play a practice round. Colonial Country Club was a shot maker's paradise that required pinpoint accuracy. Trey walked every hole to lend his course knowledge to his son. Their dream was to add Jefferson's name to the Wall of Champions alongside the likes of Ben Hogan who won at Colonial five times. Past champions were the who's who in professional golf.

On day one, Trey sweated bullets, stayed in the shadows of the spreading oaks as much as he could, and hoped his son did not detect his anxiety. Ever vigilant, Jefferson picked up on Trey's angst instantly and asked his mom what was up. In her straightforward manner, Tara explained to her son how much this tournament meant to his father during *his* career. Not quite the Holy Grail to Trey, but it was close.

With a nod of understanding and determination etched on his face, Jefferson walked past his father, going to the first tee. Before he reached the tee box, he turned and gave his dad a wink.

As they walked down the rope line left of the fairway, Tara asked Trey if their son was all right.

"No, babe, he's not all right—he's perfect" was her husband's reply.

Paired with two past champions, Jefferson was last to tee off in the group. After the two veterans hit their drives, McCall stepped up to his tee shot.

Gently nudging his wife, Trey whispered, "Listen."

When Jefferson made contact, it sounded like a cannon shot; the ball exploded off the clubface and landed in the right side of the fairway, miles past his playing partners. Oohs and aahs followed from the gallery—along with a huge grin from his caddy Moondance—who sensed greatness when he saw it.

"Watch and remember this day ... it's just the beginning," Trey whispered to Tara.

Brimming with confidence, Jefferson blistered a high fading five iron to a back-right hole location to within six feet of the hole, then calmly rolled the eagle putt in the middle of the hole. On the second hole, Jefferson wedged his second shot a foot from the hole and tapped it in for a birdie. As the round progressed, Trey kept making bizarre statements: "Oh my God, he's there. I can't believe it. Watch out, world, here he comes."

Although Tara did not exactly know where her husband was coming from or what all of that meant, she knew it must be good. As if anticipating her question, he continued, "The zone, the frigging zone, our boy has discovered it. With his talent, no telling how many records he's going to set."

At the end of the first day, Jefferson led Colonial by two shots. For the rest of the week, Jefferson kept the pedal to the metal to capture the title with a birdie putt at the last hole to win by one. His father beamed with pride at what Jefferson accomplished, then shed a tear when his son dedicated the win to Trey at the trophy presentation.

It was dark when the McCall trio trudged toward their SUV for the drive back to the ranch. Only the cleanup crews remained at the course. Jefferson took one last gander at the eighteenth green to lock in the memory of this day forever.

IN THE FLORIDA KEYS, Ray caught a snippet on the news about Jefferson McCall, a newcomer to the pro Tour, capturing the Colonial Invitational in Ft. Worth. Seething, Ray shrieked, "Well, doesn't that beat all? You lucky little shit!"

In the adjacent room, Willa overheard him and asked, "Who won the lottery?"

"Nobody. But my piece of crap stepbrother just won about a million bucks hitting a little white ball around a pasture. Screw him and screw golf." Cunningham rambled on as he walked toward her voice.

Willa Rae stared deliciously into his eyes. "Tell you what, why don't you come over here and let me take your mind off your troubles."

Later, after they tidied up the cushions on the couch and neatly arranged pillows, Ray made reservations at a highly acclaimed Italian restaurant only a few minutes' drive away.

BEFORE LEAVING BILOXI, Ray shed his shaggy appearance for a more casually sophisticated one, hair still long but layered and tapered, his beard neatly trimmed and tidy. He sported the dapper, mega-buck-inheriting, private-jet-traveling, yacht-sailing, limo-riding, trust-fund-baby demeanor.

Because of the new look, an observant maître d', Lorenzo, recognized Ray when he came through the front door of Russo's. Strategically placed by the mob, Lorenzo was a sophisticated type of mercenary, who operated away from the fray. With access to the skinny on just about anything or anybody you wanted to find, Lorenzo was very much the *man.*

Exhibiting a debonair European man-of-the-world aura, he seated the couple on the veranda with a breathtaking view of the ocean. Willa Rae took in the gentle breezes that filled the air and watched the waves lap up on the shore. A crescent moon in a cloudless sky freckled with sparkling stars lightyears away made for quite a romantic setting. Her expression mellowed as if she was beginning to forgive Ray's annoying habits. After Lorenzo introduced the waitstaff for their personal dining experience, he quietly slipped away to make a phone call.

Concealed in a grove of palms out of earshot from any guests or staff, Lorenzo sent photos he just took of the couple to a mob colleague on the left coast in California. Not five minutes later, his friend Carmine texted back. Best he could tell, the male favored a kid who'd been part of the Affluente fiasco, Rob McBride. As far as the hottie, Carmine had no idea.

Later that evening, as Ray and Willa Rae were leaving, Lorenzo said, "Thank you, young lady, and you as well, Mr. McBride. Hope you had a marvelous evening." Absent-mindedly, Ray nodded his head and strolled to their car in the lot.

After they were both seat-belted in, Ray turned to Willa and asked, "Did that guy in the monkey suit just call me Mr. McBride?"

"Yeah, so what? He must have mistaken you for someone else. No big deal, right?"

He glared at her and roared, "No big deal, she says, no big deal to you—to me, it's a very big deal."

She leaned forward and said in a raised voice, "So what! Haven't you ever called somebody another person's name, are you some kind of Mr. Perfect or something?"

Just as he was about to explode, Ray caught himself, exhaled loudly, and uttered quietly, "I guess you're right. Sorry, I'm just a little on edge tonight. Yeah, he must have mistaken me for someone else, happens all the time. You're right."

Seconds after Ray burned rubber leaving Russo's parking lot, Lorenzo called his current employer to tell him about the identity of a gentleman he believed he'd uncovered at the restaurant. Mob-run pharmaceutical companies were concerned about small fringe-pharma operations eating into their profits. What started out as small potatoes had grown to an uncomfortable sum. Ray Cunningham's outfit fit that profile. Confirmation from Lorenzo that Ray Cunningham was actually Robert McCall caught the attention of Fritz Gruber and the syndicate elite.

Not only was the mob onto Ray, so was Willa Rae. Back when she asked him about Amor del Sol, Ray flipped out and called his partners to shut down the plant. Then the maître d' at Russo's called him Mr. McBride, and Ray blew his fuse again. A notion popped into her mind. Perhaps she and her father could use Ray's paranoia to their advantage. As difficult as it was for Willa to stomach, she needed Ray to think she had his back. Later on down the road, it might come in handy. When she proposed her idea to her father, Wilmer smiled. It fit in nicely with his scheme to misdirect the mob and the mystery woman in Canada.

SEEMED EVERYWHERE THEY WENT on Maui, the big man they saw shortly after they arrived on the island was there. Boris mentioned it to Natasha, who said it was a small island and was probably a coincidence. No way. He was sure the man was tailing them, and it freaked him out. To be safe rather than sorry, Boris booked a redeye flight for the two of them back to the mainland for the next day.

They played tourists all day, then Boris and Natasha took a limo from Kaanapali to the airport at 11:30 p.m., barely in time for their United flight. Last they saw of their shadow, he was waving his arms and screaming at the United agents that it was imperative he get on the 12:30 a.m. LAX flight. As he and Natasha boarded, Boris turned toward the ticket counter and gave the fat man the middle finger. At that, the man went berserk and plowed through the crowd and security personnel to get at Boris. He didn't get far. Armed police showed up and zip-tied his massive wrists behind his back. Then jammed him into the rear seat of a squad car and drove him to jail. Through it all, the giant relentlessly cursed his prey.

Safely aboard their plane for the five-hour flight to California, Boris and Natasha weighed their options. It was best they split up for now; whoever was watching would be on the lookout for a couple. Natasha had a close friend who lived in a remote part of northern California, a running mate she had not seen since college. New Orleans piqued Boris's interest. He'd always like the food, and you could easily get lost in the crowd there. When they got to the gate, Natasha exited first, Boris followed a few minutes later so as not to appear as a couple.

Natasha waited until she got outside the terminal to call Talley Marsh on the burner phone she bought in an LAX gift shop. At the other end of the line, the reaction was a shriek so loud it almost burst her eardrum, and in Talley-talk, it meant Natasha was welcome to stay as long as she wanted.

CHAPTER 5

AFTER PARTING WAYS WITH BORIS, Natasha assumed her given name, Millie Snowden, to simplify things. As she got her bearings, her phone signaled the text Talley promised with her current address. She leaned against the wall and contacted an offsite rental agency to bring her car to the terminal. When it arrived, she gave the driver a nice tip, put her friend's address in her GPS, and drove out of the airport in the direction of San Francisco.

When she got to San Francisco, she took Highway 101 North across the Golden Gate Bridge on a scenic drive through the Carneros wine region on the way to Talley's horse farm in Napa. Instantly Millie was attracted to the woodsy, homey, eclectic feel, and her justifiable fatigue from her eight-hour drive from LAX vanished. Talley bounded out of her farmhouse, down the wooden steps, with a glass of Napa Valley cabernet for each of them. After customary hugs and kisses, they settled on the porch that worked its way 360 degrees around the house.

Out of habit, Talley offered Millie a joint, which she politely refused, then a cigarette, which she also rejected.

Shocked, Talley said, "Well, I never thought I would see the day, my little 'Sissy' turning down her two favorite things. Hope you didn't give up sex and drinking as well. If so, you can just set your boney ass back in that gas-guzzling tank you drove up here and vete de aqui. In case you've forgotten your Spanish, loosely, that's 'get your ass outta here.'"

Unable to hold back, they both burst out laughing. Millie took a cigarette to appease her former college roomie. Nicotine-free for over a decade, she enjoyed the little buzz she got from the Marlboro Red, and the Napa cabernet went down smoothly. Having forgotten her sorority nickname Sissy that Talley laid on her was of little concern since it brought back fond memories. Before too long, the two room-mates weaved about in their attempt to replicate some of their old dance moves to vinyl's Talley dug out of rock-and-roll songs from the Beatles, Stones, and Boz Skaggs. Talley slipped off the porch into a patch of ferns that softened her fall. She bounced up like it was an everyday occurrence, then poured more wine into her glass. Out of nowhere, a truck rolled up, and two hunks slid out. Undeterred, Talley fired up a joint ready to take flight.

Noting the confused expression on Millie's face, Talley slurred, "Not to worry there, little Sis, those two just come up here from time to time to service me. Silly me, I forgot today was Wednesday, or is it Thursday. Fuck it, let's get naked. How 'bout it, y'all?"

What a quandary. Millie was far from being a prude, yet this was so bizarre. Should she or shouldn't she? She glanced at the guys who had already shed their clothes awaiting orders. Millie lit a joint, turned up a bottle of wine, drained half, and took a big hit off the joint, then stripped and gave it the best she had for the team. *Sissy* woke up with a splitting headache, thirsty and hungry as hell. The foursome was still naked, bodies tangled in awkward positions, and most of them still California dreaming.

Painfully, Talley raised her head and grinned at Millie, then said, "Well, how's that for a welcoming committee? Watching you with those two last night, I'd say you had the time of your life, never seen bigger grins on those fellas' faces since we began having these little square dances. Hey, I hope you don't mind if I call you Sissy from time to time … old habits die hard, kiddo."

Old habits die hard, no shit! Millie thought. She was lost as to all that went on in the trenches the night before. However, Millie remembered she did her best to mimic her hostess. There was suddenly a flurry of activity all around her when the boys realized they were already late for work down the mountain. The two young men scrambled around, picked up various articles of clothing, distributed them to the appropriate party, dressed, gave the girls goodbye kisses, and abruptly left. Talley and Millie did not bother to get fully dressed. In bras and panties, they stumbled to the kitchen to make coffee and find something to satisfy their incredible hunger.

Instinctively, Millie lit a cigarette and took several drags before she remembered she no longer smoked. She finished it and lit another, put a shot of Jack Daniels in her coffee, and tried to make sense of last night. After half a pack of smokes and three Jack and coffees, Millie was toasted again and semi-passed out on the couch. Before she went completely out, she wondered if her new life's slogan was destined to be, *Fuck it*. She'd forgotten how it felt to freewheel it like she and Talley had done so many times back at Chico State. Did life with Boris stifle her adventurous side? Had he held her back rather than let her fly? Like she was right now higher and higher, spinning out of control until . . .

Millie crashed hard and didn't wake up until mid-afternoon; she felt alive and excited. Talley strolled in, cigarette in one hand, beer in the other, sat down on the couch with Millie, and offered her a smoke—this time Sissy accepted. Being back with Talley made her feel liberated. To make up for lost time, they talked for hours about everything under the sun, filling each other in on gossip and about their future. The notion that Boris held her back from her full potential gnawed at Millie. *Best not to dwell on the negative,* she reminded herself.

If memory served her right, Talley graduated with a science degree and went on to get her master's in chemistry from USC in Los Angeles. Millie wondered … With her computer talents and Talley's skills as a chemist, an idea surfaced—a scheme she tossed around in her subconscious in her drug-induced state. Hesitant to approach Talley, now emboldened with a false sense of courage, Millie thought, *What the hell,* and went for it.

Millie disclosed her hypothesis to her college chum, "With my experience operating in the world of social media and your talent as a mixologist of delectable narcotic chemicals, we could pull off a masterful scam. Being a veteran of Lucky Richards's schemes that failed, I understand the flaw."

Here's my take. "The original Richards's scheme shied away from social media because it was not yet as powerful as it is now. I say, we incorporate a more malleable social media early in the process as a tool to swarm our products, much like a rave. Organized on the spur of the moment, we disperse stockpiles of finished product warehoused in Biloxi. Create enough swarms on the dark web, in different locales, at different times, on the same day—we make millions."

Shaking her head, Talley brought her back to Earth. "That's all bullshit. What kind of heavy shit have you gotten yourself into, kid? Talking drugs, web, mob, swarms. And who in the hell is Lucky Richards? Wow, that's some mighty heady garbage you're hauling around in your head, girl."

Totally exhausted, Millie took a minute to collect herself, then related her story to Talley including Lucky Richards and his infamous scam.

Talley, her face screwed up in an ominous scowl, set Millie straight. "Well, that explains a lot. Still, your *fantasy* plan is mostly crap, too contrived, and would meet the same fate as your previous attempts. Although, parts of it have merit. Give this a listen, hear me out before you shoot holes in it. You mentioned there are warehouses full of products over in Biloxi. Those two gents who kept us company yesterday are in the transportation and logistics business, with access to planes, long-haul semi-trucks, and cargo ships. If you can get them into those warehouses one night, their crew can load the contents in the cargo holds of a ship and be at a private dock in Texas before anyone in Biloxi knows the stuff is gone. In Texas, they load it on our big-rig semis and drive it here. I have more than enough storage at the farm to hide it all until we decide how we want to proceed."

Dumbfounded, Millie would have never thought good-time Talley would come up with such a plan.

When she found her voice, Millie asked, "Woah, who knew? Okay, I spilled my story about life after school … how about you filling me in on yours? Somehow, I think it's going to be a whole lot different than I would have guessed."

After they cleaned up and dressed warmly for the chilly air up in the hills, they strolled the grounds while Talley played guide.

Talley picked up where the conversation left off, "While I was still in college at Chico, I subsidized my income by working as a part-time lady of the evening for the old lady (a.k.a. Ma) who owned this place. Learned a lot of tricks of the trade but mostly how to read people. For some reason, the matriarch took a liking to me, and when she was diagnosed with stage-four liver cancer, the elderly lady revised her will. Ma left me the Slice of Heaven, all her money, plus the records of what the house of ill repute brought in every month. She included a ledger with the names of repeat customers, their occupations, phone numbers, and addresses. I was surprised to find out how many were leading citizens, politicians, lawyers, even members of law enforcement. It was ammunition Ma used to remain autonomous. It's mine now, to use now if necessary. Let's just say, sons tend to follow in their dad's footsteps."

As they made their way around back, Talley pointed out the enormous barn, stables, and the corral that backed up to the face of the mountainside. Further down to the right was a series of six one-bedroom, one-bath cabins where the girls entertained clients. Judging by how clean they all were inside, Millie guessed they were still in use.

Inside the stables were eight large horse stalls, four on each side, with hay bales stacked at either end. A trap door camouflaged by a bale of hay led down to a basement area roughly the same square footage as the floor above, used for storing sensitive items and doubling as a safe room with all the comforts of a small apartment. Industrial generators filtered water from a mountain stream and provided power to run the appliances down below. Millie's eyes lit up as she took it all in—the best was yet to come.

The back end of the corral butted flush against the mountain; a remote-controlled keypad, hidden inside a hollowed-out rock, regulated an oversized garage door Talley faux-painted to match the mountain. The door fit so snug, its outline was impossible to detect unless someone knew it was there. Talley pressed the button on a key fob, and the door glided up into the face of the mountain to reveal a cavern so vast it appeared the excavation took out a majority of the lower part of the mountain. To ensure it was more than adequately supported, the walls and ceiling were reinforced with solid steel beams. Millie denoted there was plenty of room for all the Amor del Sol products and more. As Millie surveyed the rest of the space, she focused on what resembled small bales of hay stacked along a side wall and asked Talley what they were.

Laughing out loud, Talley informed her guest, "Oh, you silly girl, that's some of the shit that got you so messed up last night. We grow our own weed up here, and it's got quite a hit, as I'm sure you can attest."

After she swore Millie to secrecy, Talley clued her college BFF in on a few of the shady deals she was working on the ranch—other than growing marijuana. Like keeping horses around to bolster the pretense that Talley was running a legit horse farm. And opening the bordello on weekends for the locals to enjoy the company of the college girls who still came down from Chico.

After enough for one day, they went inside to warm up. Sure her friend was serious about going into business together, Millie lit a cigarette and got them both a beer from the fridge. Comfortable with a fire in the hearth, they weighed their options. Finally, after polishing off half a case of beer and a pack of cigarettes, they came to a conclusion. It was only right for them to combine their skills. Together they could weave a wicked web of misconception to amass a fortune at the expense of an unsuspecting public.

A WEEK LATER, under the cover of darkness, a cargo ship coasted to the dock closest to the back of the warehouses in Biloxi and tied up. After carefully scanning the dock with night-vision goggles for security, the crew exited the boat and quietly approached the packed warehouses. An hour before dawn, their ship was loaded and on its way to Texas. Oblivious to it all was the lone guard at the front gate listening to classic rock in his earbuds, who never saw or heard a thing. As soon as the folks at Nemesis found out about the theft, they were understandably upset with the shoddy job done by the security company at the warehouses. All that product gone without a trace.

IN KEY WEST, Willa was sick and tired of Ray's repulsive demands. One morning he walked into the bedroom after his shower to find her packing a suitcase. Fed up with the Keys, Willa wanted to go back to her father's house to get her fingernails dirty again, working in the boathouse. And most likely no one would be searching for Ray at the Braun estate.

He asked calmly, "How about some company?"

She said maybe, if he stopped ordering her around like a slave and expecting her to drop everything to cater to his every whim.

What with the maître d' at Russo's calling him the wrong name and all the lies the kid tried to keep straight in his head, timing for her scheme was perfect, and he fell for it. If he thought she was leaving, it would give him the excuse he needed to exit the Keys. All she had to do was make it seem like it was his idea. What a predictable dumbass. Truth was, they would both be safer at the Braun home rather than out here in the open. Only a few folks knew where they had been. No one knew where they were going, just the way Willa wanted it.

CHAPTER 6

BACK AT THE BRAUN ESTATE after an uneventful boat trip from the Keys, Ray and Willa woke up after a restless night of overactive minds. First coffee, then they'd deal with the mess. Out of habit, Ray tuned the TV to a local news station to get caught up on the lies of the day. Glad to be home, Willa actually smiled at him and handed him his cup. He'd just taken a sip of the steaming hot brew before he spit it out all over the marble countertop on the island.

Willa shrieked, "What the hell, Ray, my coffee can't be that bad. Who's going to clean up that mess? Not me, not this time."

Ignoring her rage, Ray held up his hand for quiet, and said, "Clam up, princess, did you hear what the reporter just said? Somebody stole all my shit out of the warehouses down here last night. Can you frigging believe it? All that money out the window. It's not like I had it insured or anything. All that money—just gone."

Just what she needed; the kid was throwing another tantrum. Then again, maybe it really was exactly what she needed. Settling him as best she could, Willa cradled his head to her bosom and talked to him in a low, calming voice. "Just think about all the opportunities we can tackle without having to deal with that stupid sunscreen shit to peddle. Good riddance, I say, then we start afresh." It was all bullshit, but he took the bait again.

Ray scratched his head. "Yeah, that's what we'll do, start all over, without those losers hanging on. To tell you the truth, I've been thinking the same thing. Yeah, we'll hang around here and busy ourselves with the boat and the sub. We'll just put this minor setback behind us. Move on down the road like Lucky Richards would do."

Willa snickered at his reference to his mentor. The very thought of Lucky settled Ray down, leaving him open to suggestion.

For weeks, she farmed him out to the workshop in the boathouse to work on some new innovations her father dreamed up for *Kismet* and *Mako*. Engrossed in his work, Ray lost track of time, and Willa did too, concentrating on a strategy with her dad to eliminate the childlike idiot.

During one of Ray's juvenile fits, he'd accused his ex-partners Boris and Natasha of robbing the warehouses. Which played right into the Braun's scheme. Willa's job was to convince Ray that whoever stole his merchandise intended to do away with him. Then persuade him that they must work out escape routes, by land and sea if trouble comes knocking. If for any reason they got separated, they'd rendezvous at a prearranged location. Fear was a powerful motivator; Ray bought in. At Willa's suggestion, he agreed to random escape drills to keep them sharp.

For a month, they practiced. By land, Plan A was simple, they drove the Range Rover they'd hidden behind the house to the rear entrance to the estate and escaped on the back roads. Plan B, by sea, was more complicated. In practice, they hastily maneuvered *Kismet* with *Mako* secured to its bottom out of the boathouse to the open water of the bay. If it was for real, once they reached the deep water, they'd open the seacocks to scuttle the *Kismet*, board the sub through the trap door in the floor of the mothercraft, and flee underwater. *Mako* had enough oxygen and power for three hours, max; more than enough to get to the east coast of Florida.

For as long as a threat remained, the couple shared responsibilities. Ray made sure *Kismet* was lined up in the boathouse for a hasty exit, fueled and ready to go at a moment's notice. Willa kept the Land Rover full of petrol and maintained the life support systems aboard *Mako*.

ON A CLOUDLESS SUMMER MORNING, the sun beat down on the Mississippi Gulf Coast, temperatures threatened to reach the high nineties. Even with the giant fans at full speed, it was stifling inside the boat house. Ray was dripping sweat as he checked out the GPS, radar, VHF, alarm panel, SART, and other equipment on the bridge of *Kismet*. Whistling along to a song on the radio, Ray barely heard the chime of his cell phone—it was Willa.

"Listen carefully. There's no time to argue. They are on their way here right now. Put plan B in play *immediately*, where you scuttle the boat and escape in the sub. Never mind about me, I'll take the Land Rover and meet you later at our prearranged rendezvous."

Ray instantly dropped what he was doing to cast off the lines, jump to the controls, and fire up *Kismet*'s engines. With *Mako* affixed to the belly of the boat, he gunned the engines as soon as he cleared the doors of the boat house and flew down the short channel out to the bay toward the deep water.

As soon as he reached the predesignated coordinates, Ray cut the engines, went below, and opened the seacocks. Then he entered the mini sub through the trap door, sealed its hatch, and released the magnets that secured it to the hull. As designed, *Mako* dropped away from the mothership. Ray engaged its engines and set course for the deep water.

When he reached his second set of coordinates at the deepest part of his journey, Ray made his course correction for the west coast of Florida and settled in for what should take only another twenty-five to thirty minutes. He was relieved he wouldn't be underwater much longer; he suddenly felt a bit claustrophobic and anxious. As if on cue, every warning light and blaring alarm went off at once. His entire instrument panel blinked red, and a voice screamed at him. Engines shut down, lights went out and back on as soon as the backup batteries kicked in. Another voice blared out that the backup battery power was low: *Replace, Replace.* To his surprise, Ray discovered the usually overstocked battery bin was empty.

Odd, he thought, but at least this time it wasn't his mistake; *Mako* was Willa's responsibility. Slowly his tiny ship descended, the controls no longer responding to his commands. At this point, Ray should be panicking. Instead, he was amazingly calm, actually finding his situation humorous. He giggled, then busted out laughing.

Robert McCall, alias Ray Cunningham, stared out his porthole and saw a magnificent marlin circling his vessel as it drifted ever so gently downward. There was something familiar about that big boy, like they'd met somewhere before, but his memory was not there anymore. Lightheaded, he was sleepier than he had ever been. *Mako* nestled onto a sand bank. The marlin swam by and glanced in the porthole to stare at the human who'd released him not so long ago—near this very spot.

Still seated at the controls, Ray was quite dead, his oxygen-deprived body rigid, a sinister smile frozen on his face, his hands forever in a death grip on the yoke.

BACK ON SHORE, Willa walked to the boathouse to make sure Ray obeyed her orders. The oversized doorway to the bay was wide open, and the *Kismet* was gone, she heaved a sigh of relief. She sat on the dock smoking, waited for an hour, then called Ray's cell repeatedly and got a recording saying the person you are trying to reach is not available. Next, in an anxious voice, Willa called the coast guard to report that her father's boat the *Kismet* was missing and presumed stolen.

A polite but somber officer who took down her information called back a short time later to report the *Kismet* was spotted by the captain of the *Biloxi Belle*. She was making for the deep water at full speed. When asked if she knew who was aboard, Willa answered she did not. Her father was out of the country. It must have been a thief or somebody taking it out for a joy ride. As planned, Willa contacted her dad, who was sad about his boats but glad to be rid of the pain-in-the-ass kid.

"By the way," Dr. Braun mentioned. "At the end of the week, I'll be coming back from the island. We need to sit down and discuss the future."

Willa Rae was surprised at her conflicted reaction. Now that Ray was gone, she sensed a newfound freedom. One she'd surely lose as soon as her father came back.

ON THE LEFT COAST, true to their pact, Talley and Millie formed a company called Sister Nation, purveyors of natural products designed to keep humanity young, vibrant, and healthy. The Sister Nation business plan mirrored Amor del Sol and its predecessors in one aspect: it used minimal amounts of addictive substances absorbed into the skin to attract and lock in customers. Otherwise, they were vastly different. They employed an old-fashioned approach, whereby Sister Nation stocked their natural products in brick-and-mortar facilities that they leased up and down the West Coast. Starting with their flagship store in Napa, California.

Sister Nation's intentions were to manufacture their goods from flora growing naturally in the region. To do so, they needed an out-of-the-way place to set up production. With the connections she developed over the years and documentation Talley had on influential people who frequented Slice of Heaven, licenses and permits were no problem. No one knew the countryside better than her California boy toys, who'd explored the area since they were kids. One of them remembered an old, abandoned winery about to go up for auction. With high hopes, Talley and Millie climbed into a four-wheel-drive Range Rover and took off to check out the place. It took longer to get there than it should have; they got lost twice, even with good directions. By the time they arrived, they understood why the winery had failed; it was too remote and the wine it produced must not have been exceptional enough to overlook the inconvenience. As the only bidders who showed up the day of the auction, Talley purchased the rundown winery for a song.

Sister Nation banked that a solid Left-Coast-driven growth would gradually move the goods east. By the time it took hold on the Right Coast, Talley and Millie had the option to either go the route of the web, continue as is, or sell off the company to a large conglomerate. As Sister Nation grew in popularity, when Talley saw an opportunity, she planned to introduce relabeled Amor del Sol as a trusted new Sister Nation sun care item.

Being incognito gave them a terrific opportunity to be successful. Neither Talley nor Millie had as much as an outstanding parking ticket, and Talley virtually owned the loyalty of the local constabulary since most of them visited Slice of Heaven with regularity.

Two new manufacturing plants for cosmetics and sun care products were under construction behind the original building at the winery up the mountain. To provide an even better cover, the Sister Nation entrepreneurs carried on a meager wine production charade up front. Talley calculated the minimum effective levels of addictive substances to mix in with the ingredients for Sister Nation brand products. Millie designed labels and product descriptions to draw attention to their charming lines of merchandise for the discriminating woman. With no sense of urgency, the Sister Nation team continued to set up their business, careful to pay attention to detail. A refreshing change of pace for Millie, not to be mired under a series of unmeetable deadlines, imposed by her former male cohorts. She was pleased that Talley had an easy-going way about her, efficient and effective, without being too pushy.

CHAPTER 7

SHORTLY AFTER THE NEW manufacturing plants were up and running, Talley leased storefront properties in Northern California, Oregon, and Washington state to market their all-natural goods from the fertile soil of the Napa Valley wine country. Supplements and cosmetics, with an eye-catching Sister Nation logo on the label, guaranteed the authenticity of its contents. Now that their partnership was established, Talley brought Millie up to speed on the built-in features of the mountain cavern—if for some reason they had to hide or evacuate the farm.

Millie gawked in amazement at what Talley revealed. From the center of the main cavern, four exit tunnels fanned out like spokes on a wheel. Running down both sides of the tunnel floors were two-foot-deep mesh-covered troughs carrying fresh water pumped from natural underground springs into a water purification system. Industrial generators ran on propane tanks to filter the air.

Jack-hammered out of solid rock and centered on opposing walls in the four tunnels were a pair of voluminous stylishly furnished two-bedroom suites with full baths. Millie shook her head. It had to have cost a fortune to excavate, reinforce, and configure each of the spacious quarters that accommodated four persons comfortably. Full kitchens, laundry, and storage—all the comforts of home.

Millie's eyes lit up when she took in the spiffy oblong alcove at the end of the tunnel that offered a gaming area, food court, gym, theater room, and a business billet set up to keep in contact with the outside world. Best of all, each tunnel had its own alcove with its own escape passage. As they walked outside into the sunlight, Millie fawned over the extraordinary feat Talley accomplished in the mountain cavern.

Her Sister Nation partner shrugged. "Thanks, but I can't take full credit. Long before I took over the farm, in the days of prohibition, bootleggers dug the tunnels to conceal their stills and moonshine from rivals and revenuers. I'll admit it has been a costly process to update the hideout top to bottom, but I figured one day it might come in handy."

SELFISHLY, TALLEY KEPT one escape route secret; below all the other tunnels were two additional tunnels. The one on the right, the longest of the two, had a stream winding its way underground to the Napa River; the left one led away from the river out the backside of the mountain, exiting much lower down the mountain than the others. To date, Talley was the only living person who knew of their existence. During the rehab up above, she did her best to keep workers from discovering the entrance to the lower escape routes. Long legs and short skirts did the trick.

DURING THE SIX MONTHS it took for the Northern Cal women to establish their businesses, Trey McCall and his team at Nemesis were busy not being busy. No one heard a peep from his estranged son's criminal squad, which gave them cause to wonder. Could it be that after numerous failed attempts to force their scam on the world, the gang gave up and went into retirement? As soon as Nemesis learned Ray Cunningham, alias for Bobby McCall, had been seen with Willa Braun, she became a person of interest in the case.

The background on Nemesis's newest suspect, Willa Rae Braun, was sketchy. However, Warlock's deep-dive research discovered that her old man Wilmer Braun, was a distant cousin of Eva Braun, Adolf Hitler's significant other.

The consensus among the Nemesis elite was to send Ty Dossier to Biloxi to surveil Willa Rae. His twenty-five-year tenure as a former Dallas police detective would be invaluable. With his easy-going attitude, youthful energy, and country-boy demeanor, Ty would fit in nicely with the social demographic at the Half Shell Oyster House.

NO SOONER HAD TY STROLLED into the packed bar than Willa zeroed in on the new meat and about took out two barmaids and a busboy to get to him before anyone else could. On her way there, she undid an extra button on her blouse, exposing impressive cleavage, and greeted him with a toothy smile.

"What'll it be there, handsome? Grilled oysters are off the charts at the Half Shell, and the beer is extra cold," Willa boasted.

Smiling back, Ty scrunched up his face and cocked his head. "Hmm, how about some of those grilled oysters and an IP. Oh, and extra horseradish on the side to spice things up."

Spicy, hmm, she thought and nodded. "Coming up in a flash."

He ate his meal in silence, finished off his beer, and paid his check, noting she'd written her number, with a heart beside it, in the margin of his receipt.

On his way out, he heard her shout over the noise in the bar. "Hey, what's your name? Mine's Willa Rae, you know, just in case."

"Ty, nice to meet you, Willa Rae."

With a smile, then a wink, she said, "Same here, Ty, don't be a stranger now, you hear."

TREY MCCALL SENT TY to Biloxi to find out where his black sheep son may be hiding out. The Nemesis chairman was certain that Willa knew or at least had a good idea where he was. Ty had a knack for getting to the truth with a reserved manner about him that made people want to confide in him. After a week, Ty finally asked Willa out to dinner. They started off slow, nothing romantic, just a nice meal and small talk to get acquainted.

ON THEIR THIRD DATE, Ty decided it was time to find out more about her than she'd shared. "Seeing anyone lately? I don't want to be the rebound man, you know."

"No, not really. Well, there was this guy, Ray. Thought he was a big shot around here, but he wasn't. Promised to make all my dreams come true, but then he just up and vanished. Haven't seen or heard from him since." Willa shook her head in bewilderment.

Something in the way she said it didn't ring true. She became distant, so he went back to making small talk and asked her if the deep-sea fishing was any good this time of year. Willa Rae said it was good pretty much of the year, that he ought to go down to Buddy's Charters and book a day. She raved on and on about Bud Williamson being the best boat captain on the Mississippi Gulf Coast. If he wished, Willa could arrange a trip for him, but she'd have to pass, since she no longer relished the idea of going out where the big boys swim. *Curious*, he thought, *why would a boat builder's daughter not want to go out on the water?*

Nevertheless, he said it was a terrific suggestion, one he would check into in the morning. After a tasty steak and a bottle of delicious cabernet, Willa tried her damnedest to get Ty into bed when he dropped her at the Braun estate. True to the promise to himself, he begged out, saying he was too much of a gentleman to take advantage of a lady under the influence. After considering his chivalry, she leaned in to give him a goodnight kiss.

WHEN TY GOT BACK to his suite at the Beau Rivage, he called the Williamsons to explain he was back in town at the request of Nemesis and wondered if he could book a day on the water with the two of them. It happened they had a cancellation for tomorrow at six a.m. sharp. Ty hopped into bed and willed his mind to quiet down so he could get a few hours of sleep before the early-morning alarm.

At six a.m. they exchanged hellos, climbed aboard the *Biloxi Belle*, and departed. Bev and Ty went below to make coffee while Bud manned the controls on the bridge. The wind was up and the seas were choppy. By six thirty, they were barely halfway out to the deep water. Tired of fighting the swells, Captain Bud slowed the craft and engaged the autopilot. A few moments later, Bev and Ty arrived from below with a pot of hot java and sweet rolls.

Bud was curious. In between bites, he asked, "So, Ty, what is this all about? It's our understanding that all's been pretty quiet here in Mississippi. Is there something we need to know?"

"We're not sure, not yet, but Trey and I wanted to find out if either of you have seen or heard from Ray Cunningham in the last few months?"

"We have not," replied Bev. "We thought maybe he'd grown tired of the slow-moving lifestyle here on the coast and moved on to a more exciting place. Why are you asking?"

"You and Bud were right, Bev. Ray Cunningham was an alias for Robert McCall, Chairman McCall's eldest son. Robert has gone off everyone's radar. Nemesis is concerned, and we are pulling out all the stops to find him."

NOT EVERYONE'S RADAR. There was someone who knew exactly where Ray was at that moment. Using the GPS on Ray's Rolex to track him, Desiree Richards jotted down the precise coordinates on a notepad in her Montreal office. His position had not changed in nearly a week. There was little doubt he'd perished in the deep water of the Gulf of Mexico an hour off the Mississippi coast. Desiree poured herself a glass of champagne in celebration—she'd one-upped the McCalls— who were still searching for Trey's black sheep son. She chuckled and thought to herself, *How befitting it was that Rob attempted to escape on a boat called* Kismet.

THE SEAS CALMED as they approached the blue water. Bud took the controls and released the autopilot. Ironically, when he circled to head back to port, the *Biloxi Belle* passed directly over *Mako*, with the remains of its captain forever at the helm staring sightlessly into the dead quiet on the sandy bottom. Bud vividly recalled this was about the spot where Ray hooked, fought, and released his amazing Marlin.

It turned into such a picture-perfect day to be on the now glass-like surface of the water that they spent the rest of it trolling for game fish. The *Biloxi Belle* drifted into dock at dusk. Unexpectedly, Willa Rae was waiting as they pulled in. She acknowledged her old friends as they disembarked and gave Ty a friendly peck on the cheek before asking how their day went. Almost in unison, the weary anglers said it would have been a damn sight better if the stubborn fish would've cooperated. Bud and Bev re-boarded to clean up for tomorrow's early-morning clients while Ty and Willa Rae sat on a bench overlooking the bay to chat and admire the soft-hued colors of the sunset until the yellowish-orange ball vanished beneath the horizon. Willa Rae asked him if he was hungry and said she'd buy if he'd join her at The Rackhouse in downtown Biloxi for an early supper. She acted antsy—something was up—so he agreed.

Following the meal, she asked Ty to follow her back to the Braun estate. There were things she wanted to discuss with him in the strictest of confidence. Not quite sure exactly what that meant, inquisitively, Ty agreed. But, under no circumstances was he going to sleep with her.

When they pulled into the circular drive, Ty was astonished at the sheer magnitude of the Braun mansion. He figured since she was a waitress, things weren't going all that well for the family. She unlocked the front door and waited for him before they entered. He was astounded when he stepped into a massive travertine-floored foyer with an impressive crystal chandelier hanging from a forty-foot-tall ceiling. In awe, Ty panned the interior as he took in the uncanny reproduction of a Versailles living room with mirrors, marble columns, polished hardwood floors, and an exquisitely painted mural of an angry storm brewing on the ceiling. A massive walk-in fireplace in the center was the focal point. Leather couches and antique custom-crafted coffee tables imported from Germany were placed strategically around it. Beautiful paintings of watercraft decorated the walls, and a magnificent painting of a three-masted schooner adorned the place of honor above the mantle.

As she moved past him to one of the leather couches, Willa Rae motioned for Ty to have a seat as she went to the bar to fix them a drink. Subdued and apparently ready to be forthcoming, she was in a mood Ty had yet to witness from her. Nestled up beside him, drink in hand, with her head on his shoulder, tears welled up in her eyes. Holding her tight, Ty asked what was wrong. Deep-seated memories surfaced that she could no longer hold back. Ty gave her a squeeze, a sign she took as permission to unload her troubles on him.

Between sniffles, Willa Rae recollected, "My father is not exactly what he presents himself to be. Like his father, Gerhard Braun, he is a spectacular shipbuilder, an innovator, a visionary architect of machines above and below the sea. Gerhard designed and built some of the most destructive warships for the German Kriegsmarine in WWII. Only God knows how many human beings lost their lives because of what my grandfather built. Toward the end of the war, my granddad saw what was happening to Germany and Japan and escaped to the United States. Along with his son, Gerhard brought gold, jewelry, art, and currency worth hundreds of millions of dollars.

"He paid the captain of a U-boat handsomely to bring him, his son Wilmer, and his booty via the Gulf of Mexico to the Mississippi Coast. After surfacing near Biloxi, Gerhard rowed to shore in a rubber dinghy with his son and his spoils of war. The U-boat captain bid him a fond farewell and promised to meet him back here after the Germans won the war. A promise the captain was unable to keep. On its way back to Germany, a US destroyer sunk the German sub—leaving no witnesses to the escape. My grandfather bought this estate for cash and hid his spoils in the basement. Over the years, he established himself as a world-renowned boat builder. Along the way, he taught my father the boat-building business."

Composing herself, she wiped away a tear. "Ty, my father is a mean, deceitful monster who has preyed on others his whole life. For as long as I can remember, I've been nothing more than a pawn for him to use as he saw fit." She was no longer weeping but exorcizing a demon—her voice loud and demonstrative. "That son of a bitch had me working as his spy to gain information from some of the most despicable jerks you could find in this world. Well, the last straw was Ray Cunningham, who was really Trey McCall's kid, the dude who runs Nemesis. My old man wanted me to provide him with info about a company called Amor del Sol so he and his German cronies could commandeer it for themselves and make a big score."

Willa Rae focused on Ray. "Anyway, Ray Cunningham was the worst of the worst. By the time we got back here from an abbreviated trip to Key West, I'd had my fill of him."

Ty cocked his head and scrunched his eyebrows before he inquired, " Are you … ? Wait a second. You keep saying *was* instead of *is* when you refer to Ray. Did something happen to him?"

"Yes, it did, that's what I'm trying to tell you. Paranoia engulfed him; Ray hauled ass out of here on my dad's best boat, unaware there was a serious issue with the electrical system. I discovered the boat was missing and called the coast guard immediately. A short time later, they called back to inform me a charter boat captain saw my dad's boat heading for the deep water at full speed. My guess is the boat caught fire and exploded."

Ty stared up at the painting of the angry sea on the ceiling to collect his thoughts about what she divulged. After years as a homicide detective, he found her tale too neat and tidy. Suspects often gave partial truths in statements, mostly to prove their innocence or to provide an alibi. There had to be much more to her story about Trey's son than she divulged.

Exhausted after her revelation, Willa Rae fell sound asleep on Ty's shoulder. Slowly, Ty got up, placed her full length on the couch, covered her with a blanket, and laid a pillow under her head. He kissed her gently on the forehead, then left through the front door, locking it as he exited. On the way back to the hotel, he called Trey McCall to fill the chairman in on the latter part of the evening. Sadly, he apprised Trey of his son's likely demise at sea. There was a noticeable gasp at the other end. Swallowing hard, Trey asked Ty if he believed Willa Rae's story.

Ty hesitated. "Not all of it, sir, especially concerning Robert. Her father is a tyrant who probably used her to gather information for him. Judging by the way she first came on to me, she's no stranger to the bedroom or back seat of a car."

"I see. Very well then. Tomorrow morning I'm flying to Biloxi to check her out for myself. In the meantime, get some shuteye," instructed a father at odds with how he should feel about a missing son he never really knew.

Three hours later, Ty's cell phone vibrated. Willa Rae was in hysterics, pleading for him to please come back to the house. Wilmer Braun was coming back from Isla Segura with his army buddy Fritz to have a serious chat with her. Recognizing genuine fear in her voice, Ty threw on some jeans and a George Strait tee shirt, retrieved his vehicle from the valet, and drove back to her house. She was waiting for him outside in the driveway, and before either had a chance to say a word, he grabbed her arm and led her away from the house to talk.

Despondent, Willa pleaded, "My father is flipping out about Ray and me. I didn't know what to do … so I called you."

He stopped and turned to face her. "What can I do to help?"

"I don't know unless you know a super-secure hideout." She wept.

He sighed. "I do, though my guess is that you aren't going to like it."

"Try me." Willa Rae cringed in anticipation.

Ty laid it out for her. "Okay, here goes. My boss is flying over here tomorrow in his private aircraft. But he's not only my boss, he's also my best friend. His name is Trey McCall, Robert McCall's father, and his ranch, The Circle M, is probably the most secure place on the planet for you right now."

Taken completely by surprise, Willa Rae glared at him. Not knowing whether to slap him or thank him, she chose the latter. Ty explained the particulars in black and white. By agreeing to take refuge at The Circle M ranch, she would have to provide indisputable evidence to back up her accusations against her father. Either that or remain in Biloxi and be at the mercy of her father's mercurial moods. Her only real chance to come out with any kind of life, was to agree to come clean and leave with Ty and Trey. Willa Rae left her clothes, cosmetics, and luggage at the mansion to give the outward appearance that she was coming back. On the way to the Beau Rivage, she pouted when she learned the sleeping arrangements.

"She must be a very special woman," Willa Rae uttered under her breath.

Ty overheard, slowly nodded, and remarked, "My wife, Miranda, is the most incredible woman I have ever known in my life, and I love her more than life itself."

Willa Rae smiled. That was all she needed to know. She thought over her options during what was left of the night, tossing and turning in the spare bedroom of Ty's suite at the Beau.

TREY MCCALL KNOCKED ON the suite door at eight a.m. Following introductions, Trey got straight to business. He asked Willa to recite her story, leaving nothing out. If he bought her story, Trey promised to give her sanctuary at The Circle M. She spun her convoluted tale, after which Willa Rae begged for his help.

Trey carefully considered his response. "Young lady, I find your explanation quite interesting; littered with very few facts, sprinkled in with a whole lot of fabricated bullshit. Now, if you want the security I have promised you, might I suggest you give me the truth, not a bunch of crap absolving you of any guilt."

On cue, her eyes watered. She saw the knowing glint in Trey McCall's eyes, turned off the faucet, stared down at the floor, then leveled with him with no embellishments.

Wearing a scowl, Trey cocked his head to make eye contact. "Let me get this straight about my son Robert. You say the plan was for him to scuttle the host boat and escape in a mini sub, is that right?"

She nodded.

"And you knew ahead of time the sub had been sabotaged and that whoever attempted to go any reasonable distance would most likely suffocate from lack of oxygen as the mini sub settled to the bottom of the ocean?"

Again, she nodded.

Staring at her for an inordinately long time, teeth clenched, Trey tried to visualize what his son went through in his last moments. "Thank you, I believe we now have an accurate set of facts. As promised for the time being, Nemesis will give you sanctuary until I figure out what is best to do about the situation. By no means can I condone any of what you did, although, to some extent, I understand it. Robert went off the rails for a lot of unfortunate reasons, which in no way excused his decisions and reckless behavior. He hurt a lot of people in his life, both physically and mentally. I'm not so sure he had to die for his transgressions, but I do believe the world is a better place without him in it. Enough for now. Wheels up in two hours."

Ty drove them to the FBO in Gulfport, dropped them off, and went back to the Beau Rivage. Trey's orders were for him to stay in Biloxi and keep an eye on the Braun Estate for the return of Dr. Braun and his German friend, while continuing their investigation into the baffling theft of Amor del Sol products from the warehouses near the docks.

ON THE LEFT COAST, Millie and Talley, were wheeling and dealing, sending Sister Nation goods to replenish their stores at a record pace. Unbeknownst to them, Nemesis's supercomputer picked up on the abrupt upsurge of Sister Nation. As standard operating procedure, Warlock vetted any and all such ventures that generated as much sudden success as Sister Nation. A useful precaution against being hoodwinked by scam artists.

Following protocol, Tara McCall ran a cursory check on the company. Everything seemed to be in order. It *was* interesting that the company also owned and operated a winery, but, after all, it was California, and Napa Valley at that. The owners, two college roommates and sorority sisters, were making a big splash in the wine country. It was nice to see the free enterprise system work its magic.

Up the mountain at the horse farm in Napa, Talley and Millie carried the free enterprise system to the extreme. The Slice of Heaven bordello was in full swing on the weekends and the second batch of Sister Nation merchandise, dosed with an increase in narcotic additives, was on the way to their stores. Things were a far cry from legit at Sister Nation. The popularity of the products was trending east, and unexpectedly, the wine business was flourishing. Sales were going so well that the founders of Sister Nation decided to hold off until after the expansion to introduce the stolen relabeled Amor del Sol sun products. Now their objective was to remain calm and avoid the two things that destroyed the Richards's master plan in the past—greed and paranoia.

UPON THEIR RETURN FROM MISSISSIPPI, Trey escorted Willa Rae to a cottage to get settled in, then moseyed down to the golf range to find his son. A most unpleasant task lay before him—something he'd dreaded on the flight home. Before they got into a discussion about golf, Trey said he had some sad news he felt Jefferson ought to learn from him.

They sat on the perimeter rock wall on the back patio. Trey bowed his head reverently "Jefferson, your older stepbrother was met with a terrible accident at sea. We don't know all the specifics yet; but it's safe to say he perished in a boating mishap near Biloxi, Mississippi."

It took a second for the news to register with Jefferson. "I'm so sorry, Dad. Robert never gave us much of a chance to get to know him or vice-versa. He'll be in my prayers tonight. You know there is a silver lining for all of us in this. He is freed from the demons that tormented him, and we can breathe a sigh of relief that he will no longer be a threat to our family.

"I have an idea. What say we take the rest of the day off and go fishing. I heard there's a huge ole bass lurking in the shade of that cypress near the bend of the lake. Bet I hook him before you do."

As they made their way to the lake, Trey put his arm around his son to let him know how much he appreciated the deflection. Funny thing, there just happened to be a big bass sleeping in the shade of a cypress tree limb overhanging the shore. As soon as Jefferson's lure landed on the water's surface, the largemouth hit it, dived down, and ran for the deep water in the center of the lake. A fighter all the way, the old bass tried his best to dislodge the fake minnow. It leaped out of the water and tail-walked a couple of times before it finally gave up. Jefferson reeled in his catch, grabbed it by the mouth, and removed the hook, before he gently released the fish back into the lake. Neither McCall wetted another line. Instead, they sat on the shore and talked—about life and family—until darkness drove them inside.

THE WORLD WILLA RAE LEFT was one of deceit and apprehension. For her defection to work, there had to be mutual trust between her and Nemesis. Tara and Miranda did their best to make Willa Rae Braun feel at home, to help her fit in. They brought her basic clothing items to get her by until they could take her to town for some heavy-duty shopping. After the first week, Willa Rae glanced around at her surroundings and the folks at The Circle M—and wept. But this time they were tears of joy. The wide-open spaces and smiling faces gave her a sense of freedom that warmed her heart. For the first time ever—she felt wanted. This was her chance to change her life for the better. It would not be easy.

FRITZ GRUBER AND WILMER BRAUN arrived at the Braun estate to find an empty house—not a sign of life inside or out. Irate, Wilmer stomped around the place like a caged animal cursing in German, frothing at the mouth. Never had Willa Rae so blatantly disgraced him. Not so much as a note or phone call to explain. What if it was something else? Maybe there had been an accident and she was hurt. He hurried to the boathouse. She wasn't there either. His anger returned. Such insolence could not and would not be tolerated, period. With no idea where Willa Rae was and the Biloxi warehouses emptied of the Amor del Sol merchandise, his plans for easy money slipped away. The smart thing for him and Fritz to do was skedaddle back to Isla Segura and work up a new angle. If they could find Boris or Natasha, they might be able to salvage something. One or both of them surely knew the location of the stolen goods.

THE GERMAN DUO had no way of knowing that Boris was less than ten miles from the Braun estate in his beach bungalow. After a short stint in New Orleans and several round trips to Montreal to see Desiree, he assumed the life of a young man lucky enough to spend his days enjoying what Biloxi offered him—anonymity. Now sporting a buzz cut, a mustache, and an enviable tan, he committed to a daily exercise routine that altered his physique by twenty extra pounds, mostly muscle. Far from the image he left behind as "Boris the nerd." Even though he went by another name, he would always think of himself as Boris.

To be on the safe side, he kept to himself. Many a night, he reminisced about his Natasha as he strolled along the beach and bathed in the moonlight, listening to the ocean waves breaking and rushing onto the beach. He wished they could be together, and maybe one day they would. For now, they would have to depend on technology to communicate.

Because Desiree believed in them from the beginning, Boris and Natasha remained indebted to her for the opportunities she continued to provide them. All three wore spycam jewelry, more sophisticated than what Boris gifted Ray Cunningham. Desiree and Boris sported stylish watches while Millie (Natasha) wore a black opal choker around her neck, synced to allow them to communicate verbally and visually; they were the means by which Desiree in Montreal, Boris in Biloxi, and Millie out west learned of the demise of Ray Cunningham in Davy Jones's locker.

PATIENCE PAID OFF for Sister Nation. Instead of forcing growth, they'd waited for it, and now the public demanded it. Although Sister Nation had the capacity to manufacture, store, and ship up to three times the amount of product, it was too soon to expand. With summer right around the corner, Sister Nation would introduce the summer line, which included the seized Biloxi merchandise they'd relabeled and kept in storage. They'd consider creeping eastward if the new line was successful. It wouldn't be prudent to get ahead of themselves now and risk being found out.

Most baffling of all to the founders of Sister Nation was the unexpected success of the winery. Set up as a front for the sun product business, it prospered in one of the toughest wine markets in the world. Credit belonged to a bright, young vintner who was not afraid to step out and be inventive—Ramon Santiago, from Barcelona, Spain. A dashing figure of a man with all the flare and fiery spirit of a Spanish matador. Ramon introduced a daring blend of grapes to produce a robust red that flew off store shelves in the valley and gained popularity in the snobbish wine community.

Talley took a shine to the debonair Casanova. They'd been seen dining and dancing together in some of the plush night spots around the Napa Valley during their on-and-off affair. For the moment, it was off. Believing him to now be free game, Millie made her move on Ramon, who was pleased to oblige her pursuits. Soon she and Ramon were an item. Talley took offense, maintaining that Ramon was her property to do with as she wished. Each day Millie and Ramon were together, Talley's hatred for her business partner grew. It all came to a head one day in her office when Talley flew into a rage. She screamed at Millie that she'd had enough and produced documents she'd recently prepared to dissolve their partnership.

MILLIE WATCHED TALLEY light a cigarette and stew, mumbling obscenities under her breath, then Millie stood up and abruptly left the office to take a stroll outside to gather her thoughts and curb her emotions. A short time later, Millie reentered the office, grinning, and plopped down in the same chair she vacated half an hour ago. Offended by her lackadaisical attitude, Talley glared over at her. Millie blew her off and calmly asked her for the legal documents, which Talley aggressively slid over. After she glanced through them, Millie took out a pen, signed, and initialed where required, then handed the papers back to Talley. Coolly, Millie went to her quarters, packed her belongings, and left in her SUV to join Ramon down the mountain.

When she pulled into his driveway, Ramon was anxiously pacing the floor of his condo.

"It's done," Millie squealed in excitement as she burst through the front door. "Can you believe it? We're free at last."

His smile filled the room as he picked her up and twirled her around. "Unreal, anybody ever told you, you're the best ever. Oh yeah, guess what else happened today. One of the most progressive wineries in Sonoma offered me a position in their winery at twice the salary of Sister Nation. And they want you to handle their ad campaign."

Millie swooned and hugged him with all her might. "What an awesome way to embark on a new beginning."

IT TOOK A FEW DAYS before it sank in. Talley was in this all by herself. Monetarily, she'd made out fine. Splitting the assets with Millie left them each with enough money to live anywhere on earth they wanted or buy a yacht to sail around the world. During their partnership at Sister Nation, Talley handled logistics, while Millie was in charge of computer software for the company. Her computer programs were complex, password protected, and stored in a cloud. Rather than personally hawking the marketplace every day, her apps did it for her. By design, her programs were nearly impossible to hack. Each program had its own specific job. For instance, one directed an automated sensor along the assembly line to increase the amount of addictive drugs added to the formula, another calculated the proportions of non-addictive ingredients to decrease in order to make weight specifications, and so on throughout production. All Millie had to do was enter a command from her computer. Unfortunately, Millie never formally wrote her passwords or calculations down—just a scribble here or there. All the critical information took residence in her genius mind. Talley, with her other responsibilities, never gave it a thought to check and see if her partner kept records. She just assumed she did.

CHAPTER 8

WHERE COULD TALLEY GO to find a replacement with such a unique talent? She did not want to appear anxious even though without Millie and her passwords, Talley was screwed. *Just maybe . . . there was a way . . . Ma's chronicles of all the regular clients of the Slice of Heaven brothel may hold the answer.* There had to be someone in that conglomeration of misfits, who she could coerce into finding a cyber geek to fill the position. The acting madam of Slice of Heaven searched through the records.

One by one, she eliminated the possibilities until she found the right person, Judge Anton Gleason. A gruff old litigator who presided over the most egregious criminal cases in the county; a twisted soul with a particular hankering for a sweet little coed named Bambi, who played all sorts of sordid roles to placate the old man's fantasies. With a bit of coaxing, Bambi divulged some of the judge's wildest desires to her boss. Talley shook her head in disgust. With the resume of perversions, she had him; hopefully, the judge could help her. Talley summoned the judge to a meeting the following day in her office.

Without a clue as to why he was summoned to the Sister Nation horse farm, Judge Anton Gleason waltzed into Talley's office with a huge smile on his face—which quickly turned to a frown when confronted by Talley about Bambi's allegations. Like a delinquent child sent to the principal's office, Judge Gleason balked, then rebelled and threatened to shut her down. Talley sneered at him and stood her ground. She let slip a few examples of his warped fantasies to show him she was dead serious. Judge Gleason fought her all the way until she sweetened the pot with an offer to make him a partner in Sister Nation. All he had to do was provide a favor. As soon as she showed him the revenue already generated on the West Coast, *his honor* was all in, and eagerly signed a contract.

Back in his office in town, the crooked judge tore through his files in search of a fitting prospect to fill the void Millie left behind. Judge Gleason found five ex-convicts who had the necessary credentials that Talley required. Each spent time in prison, although much less than they deserved, thanks to the generosity of the judge who doled out minimum-length sentences to them all. Two of the five were college grads, familiar enough with computers to have cyber theft on their rap sheets.

First was a guy with a wife and a newborn, well on his way to estab-lishing a responsible position in the public sector.

Second was an ex-con who had just finished a few days in jail for being drunk and disorderly, obviously having trouble adjusting back into society. *Gary Edington was just the man for the job,* thought the judge—a computer science expert and a whiz at chemistry.

While in graduate school at San Francisco State University, Gary had been duped into creating a hypothetical computer program to move contraband goods on the internet, supposedly as an exercise for his friend's class in criminal justice. Gary had designed the program for his pal only to find out later he'd been scammed. He had been arrested along with his buddy for selling illegal drugs online and appeared in front of Judge Gleason. After his honor had reviewed the evidence, and being that it was the young man's first offense, the judge had gone easy on him. In return, Gary had given him the old, *If there is ever anything I can do for you, just call* promise. Time to find out if the ex-con was a man of his word.

THANKFUL FOR SUCH AN UNEXPECTED opportunity, Gary made himself a promise to not screw it up, no matter what. After his release from jail, he'd tried his very best to go straight. Sadly, due to his criminal record, he'd found decent jobs difficult to get. With his advanced skill sets, Gary was overqualified for the work that was available to him. Soon he lost interest, which led to termination. Finally, he gave up on permanent employment and did odd jobs to make ends meet. Then out of the blue, the judge had called.

JUST BECAUSE THE SISTER NATION cofounder and the judge were going into business together didn't exactly mean there weren't trust issues both ways. With an ex-con in the picture, Talley was even more uncomfortable and made up her mind to find a reason to reject this guy no matter what. Talley brought some of Millie's old undecipherable notes with figures and symbols scribbled in margins—sure to stump the jailbird. Much to her dismay, Gary deciphered the notes in no time, validated the results, then explained them to the other two in laymen's terms.

Impossible, she thought. To her way of thinking, the man just performed a miracle, even figured out the passwords from the scribbled mess in the margins, and brought everything back up and online. All of a sudden, Talley saw the man in an entirely different light.

Gary *was* attractive—handsome, to be more accurate—and had an engaging yet calming manner with a special twinkle in his eye that got her attention. As if he sensed her approval, he flashed her a devilish smile. It had been a while since the boys down the mountain had paid her a visit, and she was aching for some reckless love. Maybe a little wicked sex would ease her current angst.

HALFWAY ACROSS THE COUNTRY at The Circle M ranch in Texas, Noah Bouchard and Warlock concentrated on Willa Rae Braun and the missing Biloxi warehoused goods. No one would steal that amount of product without having something in mind for it. Chairman McCall summoned Willa Rae to his office to find out more from her about the maître d' Lorenzo, who caused her and his son Robert to vacate their rental in Key West so abruptly and what ensued thereafter.

As if it were the night before, Willa Rae laid out what happened for Trey. The evening was divine until they exited the restaurant and Lorenzo called Ray "Mr. McBride." It was like a switch went off in the boy's head. Ray went berserk and took his frustrations out on her the same way her whacky old man used to do. Later back at the Braun estate, Ray's paranoia heightened. She'd had enough and devised the faux escape plan. For the first time since Ty and Trey talked to Willa Rae in Biloxi, she told the whole truth.

At the same time Trey and Willa Rae were discussing the tribulations of Robert McCall, Nemesis picked up on some heavy-duty chatter from the mob. The syndicate had a mounting concern over upstarts using propaganda in the marketplace to undermine the mob's most lucrative pharma enterprises. Specifically, the ones that adopted the *Richards method* to acquire repeat customers through addiction. It wasn't as if the giants in the pharmaceutical business didn't do the same or worse—they just didn't want attention drawn to the practice.

To sabotage the trend, pharma hired passive mercs like Lorenzo to keep an eye out for the little guys trying to elbow their way into the market. A prime example was Ray Cunningham whose conduct in the Florida Keys suggested he was either responsible for the theft of narcotic-laced goods in Biloxi or knew the parties who were. Since Ray was no longer a factor, Boris or Natasha were the most likely candidates. They'd disguised their identities so well, the chance of finding them was slim.

Except for Desiree who monitored them via spycam from her lair in Canada, patiently biding her time—for precisely the right moment to strike.

BACK AT THE SISTER NATION BASE in Napa, the hijacked Amor del Sol stored inside the mountain presented an unforeseen complication for Talley. Every run of a product contained its own chemical fingerprint—the proportions of addictive narcotics in its formula at the time of manufacture. Talley and Gary overlooked that little detail when they decided to put the stolen goods on the market rebranded as Sister Nation goods. It was such a small thing—so seemingly inconsequential, neither considered it. Instead, Talley went about business as usual. The success they had in brick-and-mortar stores was phenomenal. Soon the stores were clamoring for more. Sister Nation increased their production to keep up with demand, unaware the most recently manufactured products were far less potent than the rebranded Amor del Sol that was so popular.

As if she didn't have enough going on, Talley experienced buyer's remorse having to do with the judge. The man was unconscionable and considered himself to be a knight in shining armor who saved Sister Nation from certain collapse. His arrogance overshadowed his incompetence. Of the three partners in Sister Nation, the judge was by far the weakest link, a huge liability if investigators began to snoop around.

Realizing she'd made a grave mistake in a moment of weakness, Talley met with the truckers down the mountain. In the event the judge compromised their operation in any way, Talley's boys had no problem taking care of the crooked judge permanently. He'd been nothing but a royal pain in the ass for the whole of Napa Valley with his condescending attitude. Not to mention his total disregard for the law when it came to what he wanted. It would be a pleasure to be rid of him.

AT THAT MOMENT, Sister Nation was the furthest thing from Trey McCall's mind. In the peaceful calm of his office, a low, melodious whoosh of the ceiling fan kept a constant beat. Trey leaned back in his desk chair about to drop off for an early afternoon nap when his wife Tara knocked gently on his office door. In her hand was an intercepted post Judge Gleason sent out on social media. Warlock tagged the correspondence because of the watchwords *Sister Nation*. "So much for a nap," mused Trey as he scanned the message. Mainly it was an egocentric word salad with the judge patting himself on the back. The Nemesis chairman was taken aback at how pompous the judge must be to assert that the recent boom in sales at Sister Nation was due specifically to his coming aboard. To Trey's knowledge, the man was not known for his business acumen—quite the opposite. It gave him pause to consider that maybe Nemesis missed something in their cursory investigation of Sister Nation.

Gary Edington was in his office at the Sister Nation headquarters checking his personal social media sites, when he stumbled across a series of the judge's brazen posts and called Talley immediately. During a hastily arranged meeting, Talley ripped into the judge while he smirked and argued that he could do whatever he wished online without their permission. That was not the apologetic response Talley and Gary expected to hear. Without another word, Talley adjourned the meeting, sent Gary to town on an errand, and after a rather nasty verbal exchange with the judge about loyalty, dismissed the disdainful louse from her office.

AS SOON AS *his honor* got in his shiny black BMW and drove away, Talley picked up her cell phone to call her trucker allies who were up top loading and unloading goods at the Sister Nation winery/factory— it was time to dispose of the package that was currently in transit down the mountain in a stately black luxury Beemer. Gary was already on his way into town on a mission to check the judge's devices in his office for his most recent entries on social media, make copies, then erase any unsent messages.

With her plans in motion, Talley grabbed a beer and a pack of smokes and relaxed in her favorite leather recliner. She leaned back and pictured the judge feeling all full of himself for standing up to his partners, listening to his favorite tunes as he cautiously wound his way down the mountain, muttering to himself how stupid it was that they weren't touting Sister Nation on social media. For all he did for them, they should be proud of him for taking some initiative. But no, they blew up, insulted his actions and his intelligence. Well, screw them, he would just go on about his business despite them.

She could visualize it all. Judge Gleason reflexively checking his rearview mirror to see a big semi bearing down on him, not an unusual occurrence in this neck of the woods. A quick second glance and the truck was on his bumper—a menacing, sinister grin on the driver's face. In full panic mode, he'd have to chance the hairpin curves ahead at dangerous speeds or risk being run over by the truck. His frazzled nerves unable to handle the pressure, Talley envisioned him sailing off the mountain. Safely tucked into his BMW, with his seatbelt buckled, ricocheting off boulders for several thousand feet down the side of the mountain, the judge screaming all the way until he couldn't anymore. And the semi skidded to a halt before the abyss.

The phone startled her out of her reverie. It was her truck driver accomplice reporting in. The package had been delivered. He went on to describe the details of the *accident* almost exactly as she'd viewed them in her mind. Even the screeching and gripping of pavement as the air brakes brought the semi to an abrupt stop well short of the precipice with a loud hiss and the smokey stench of burning rubber in the air. As a final tribute, he got out of his truck and walked to the edge to pay his respects to the departed judge with a one-fingered salute.

Meanwhile, at the judge's office, Gary meticulously copied all the man's unsent emails as Talley ordered, then deleted them, and gathered up the computer along with the judge's laptop and iPad. To mimic a burglary, Gary ransacked the office and removed some of the files, hoping the cops would assume it was a bitter parolee getting revenge on the judge for putting them in prison.

As soon as Gary got back up the mountain, he walked casually into her office. Talley handed him a beer to toast the sad demise of their partner, poor old fella lost control of his car and drove right off the mountain. Gary smiled and clinked his bottle to hers. Most unfortunate for the judge, all was going so well, what a pity. To complete the coverup, they loaded the equipment from the judge's office into a four-wheel Range Rover and drove to the furthest pasture with the deepest pond, piled it all into a boat, rowed to the middle, and heaved the evidence overboard.

Neither had anything to say on their way back to the main house. It had been quite an eventful day, one they would never forget. Once inside, with a deep sigh of relief, Talley settled back into her recliner with a bottle of Budweiser and a cigarette. Gary slid off his shoes and stretched out on the comfy leather couch across from her with a Dos Equis beer tucked in the armrest beverage holder. He sipped his brew while he reassured her that he'd messed up the judge's office real good to feign a burglary and deleted all the unsent messages on the old fool's devices. He chuckled before he added that it was a good thing he did. The old buzzard was about to disclose their plans to the world. Talley grabbed a couple more beers from the fridge, handed him one, and plopped back down in her seat, content for the moment. Or so it seemed, until one serious issue crept into her mind: what if he missed an email and it snuck out?

NEMESIS WAS ABOUT TO CLOSE THE BOOK on their surveillance of the California company. Nothing of any real consequence surfaced, no more unusual communiques to raise a red flag. While Tara was on the phone with Trey about to shut things down, news of Judge Gleason's unfortunate accident broke. She put the phone on hold to listen to the particulars and thought it sounded fishy. How could the judge lose control of his car in perfect weather on a road he drove nearly every day? According to reports at the scene, the judge had not been drinking, so why was he driving so fast into a curve he'd negotiated so many times before? Perplexed, she revisited the judge's most recent cyber activity. There it was, his last sent message on social media. Good old Judge Gleason bragged about Sister Nation's reintroduction of sun protection products it had obtained and rebranded from a tried-and-true formula from the past, a guaranteed winner. Could it be that Sister Nation had somehow obtained the stolen Amor del Sol merchandise and were marketing it as their own?

IN AN INSTANT, the cyber lab was awash with activity. Agents tore through any documents relative to Gleason's life. Nemesis agents searched specifically for anything that pertained to businesses under the Sister Nation umbrella. They put Warlock on full search mode to work on the project; in minutes, they had all the files even remotely tied to the northern California property. Warlock separated the files into specific categories. In a file labeled *Sister Nation Startup*, Miranda noted the names of the two original partners on the documentation for the organization, Talley Marsh and Millie Snowden, neither one had a criminal record.

What was behind all that, and why did Sister Nation bring a felon aboard as a partner in the Sister Nation conglomeration? Miranda made a note to find out. And who was Millie Snowden? Would it be too farfetched to consider that she and Natasha might be one and the same person?

STRANGELY ENOUGH, Talley was thinking about Millie, but not in the same way as Miranda. Caught in a quandary, Talley paced the floor chain-smoking in her living room at the farm, fully aware that Millie was far more computer savvy than Gary, much better equipped to deflect and circumvent potential cyber activity directed at Sister Nation.

Paranoia settled in. Talley brought the boys from down the mountain up top to ready the storage bunker in case of attack. At best, that gave her some peace of mind. Even if she and her outfit were under siege, they'd have multiple options to slip away undetected.

While Talley was busy outside, Gary Edington was inside checking the internet and his cyber-hacker sources for any indication Sister Nation was under investigation. Nothing showed up on official government or law enforcement agency sites. Unfortunately, it was impossible to find out if independent organizations like Nemesis were nosing around.

FROM THE LATEST INFORMATION, Miranda figured out that Judge Gleason gave Gary Edington a light sentence. On Miranda's orders, all inquiries Gary sent and replies he received were stealthily intercepted and filed by Warlock. It seemed the man was worried about being surveilled. If Sister Nation was legit, why would it matter? Time to double down on Sister Nation.

CHAIRMAN MCCALL DECIDED to send a couple of agents to California to get a firsthand look at the company. Tina Tremblay and Rose Conner were closest, currently in western Canada. Both had experience with criminals working the same scam Sister Nation appeared to be running. Besides logistical proximity, Canadian women would be less suspicious. As cover, Tina and Rose posed as a couple of female entrepreneurs touring the wine country, venturing out to explore some of the newest entrepreneurial undertakings. Their mission was to work their way into the Sister Nation family, either as investors or distributors under the premise they admired the diverse approach the company employed.

Through his connections in Napa during his pro golf career, Trey arranged for his two agents to base their operation out of the Silverado Resort. The complex was less than a forty-five-minute drive to the Sister Nation Enterprises headquarters. Silverado held a special place in Trey's heart from his playing days on the PGA Tour when he tied the course record held by John Mahaffey on the South Course during his rookie season. Because their boss had been such a successful player, both women took up golf and reached the point where they truly enjoyed the game. Hopefully, they could find the time to play a few rounds, to rub it in, when they talked to Trey.

Flying commercial from Calgary, they arrived at SFO midday on Friday. An hour and a half later, they drove into the resort and immediately understood why Trey thought so highly of Silverado. The mountains in the background, two beautiful golf courses with mani-cured tree-lined fairways, and the crisp, clean mountain air blending with the lingering smell of wood-burning fireplaces made for a sensa-tional setting. Delighted with their accommodations, Tina and Rose unpacked and settled in. Before it got too late in the day, Tina made a call to Talley Marsh to set up an appointment for the next morning first thing. Talley did not seem all that interested in having a meeting but gave in when Tina said they had come all the way from Canada.

After dining in the main clubhouse on grilled artichoke, New York strip steaks, green beans almondine, scalloped potatoes, and bananas foster for dessert, the two undercover entrepreneurs walked back to their condo to get a good night's sleep before heading up the valley in the morning to visit the Sister Nation Enterprises main office.

At 6:30 a.m., they were out of bed, and they were finished with breakfast by eight, anxious to get going on what could prove to be an endless day. It took a bit over forty minutes to get to the winery, arriving early at the big gates to the winery that officially opened at nine a.m. To kill time, they toured the perimeter of the farm, checking out the landscape and winding their way back to the gates as they opened— perfect timing. One of the original partners of Sister Nation greeted them at the front door and ushered them into her office.

NOT IN THE MOOD FOR SMALL TALK, Talley Marsh asked dismissively, "Okay, ladies, I've got a busy day ahead. What is it that I can help you with today?"

Tina replied, "Well, Ms. Marsh, we recently sold one of our businesses in Alberta, Canada, for a respectable profit and want to branch out by investing in new and promising bucket-list endeavors. Your successful diversification between the horse farm, the winery, and specialty products for discriminating women—intrigues us. We wondered if you'd be interested in selling your growing enterprise? If so, for how much? If not, are you open to taking on new investors?"

Piqued by Tina's proposal, Talley responded amicably, "Please call me Talley. At this time, we have no interest whatsoever in selling, period. However, we may be interested in the latter. Do you have an amount in mind as an investment?"

"Well, Talley, initially, we'd like to invest two million dollars US, more to come if we see profits rising in the future," Rose announced without blinking an eye.

Talley gulped and exclaimed, "That's a substantial amount of money. Why would you commit that much cash to a business you know nothing about—sight unseen?"

Tina fielded that question, "Because we believe women deserve a larger presence in the world of high finance; your company is trending in that direction. We want to get in as close to the bottom floor as possible to enhance our profits. You are still a West Coast undertaking, we figure it won't be long before you are nationwide, then international. We want in now, while you're growing."

Overwhelmed by the offer, Talley sat back in her chair and lit a cigarette to calm her nerves as she contemplated her next move. It would not be in her best interest to appear too eager, so she agreed to give their proposal some thought after she ran it by her partner Gary and would let them know tomorrow. At Talley's suggestion, they arranged a noon lunch meeting in the main house at the horse farm. Assuming that as a polite dismissal, the Canadians left the winery to return to Silverado, encouraged they were not turned down flat.

IF TINA AND ROSE BECAME INVESTORS in Sister Nation, given their multimillion-dollar commitment, Tina felt they could push the envelope. She was anxious to stir the pot by proposing the company move into cyber-marketing via the internet and social media—a logical step to increase revenue. It would be worth it to hear Talley's and Gary's reasons for not already pursuing that avenue.

CHAPTER 9

TINA AND ROSE WERE ANTSY as they drove up to the horse farm for their noon lunch meeting, filled with ambivalence at the unpredictability of dealing with Sister Nation. Talley's body language the previous day gave them no clue about what to expect today. They fretted as they walked up the path and hesitated briefly at the front door before Tina rang the doorbell. Gary and Talley greeted them at the door. Talley, much more amenable than yesterday, welcomed them to the farm and thanked them for their interest in Sister Nation, then ushered them into an elegant boardroom. Rose took it all in, the dark wood paneling, Brazilian hardwood floors, the elegant Persian rug covering the floor underneath an enormous antique table that easily seated twenty people. Paintings and photographs of prestigious horses filled the walls around the room, a portrait of an Arabian stud named Moonshine decorated the space above the mantel of a massive fireplace. While the group took their seats at the table, Talley explained a little about the company mission.

"Sister Nation is the brainchild of mine and Millie Snowden's. Our quest remains to bring the little piece of heaven we know as the Napa Valley to the outside world. Naturally, I was devastated when Millie resigned and decided on a different life. And then, by the regrettable tragic loss of another of our valued partners, Judge Gleason, in a freak accident. Two heartbreaking events, to be sure. Thanks to Gary and his tenacity, we're back up and running at full capacity. Quite honestly, we hadn't thought about taking on investors. However, after you two showed up yesterday with your proposition, it made us rethink our strategy. Before we eat, if it's all right with you two, we'd like you to join Gary and me for a spin around the place—to give you an opportunity to see just what you'd be investing in."

All agreed and were soon on their way. Gary drove, and Talley acted as tour guide.

Early on the tour, they passed some cabins with a sign in front that read Slice of Heaven, and Rose asked, "What pray tell are those?"

Gary stopped the vehicle while Talley fielded the awkward question. "Oh, those are our guest cabins we keep up for die-hard horse enthusiasts. It used to be a bordello during the prohibition days, hence the name. The cabins add a bit of nostalgia to the whole place, don't you think?"

It seemed a reasonable explanation to Rose, but Tina didn't buy it.

After a cursory tour of the farm, the winery, and the factory, the quartet returned to the ranch's main house for a late lunch and discussions about what the new investors' role would be within the company. Gary laid out what he and Talley foresaw as a workable arrangement if they were to join forces. After his presentation, he asked Tina and Rose to consider the proposal and get back to them within the week.

AT THE HOUR MOST FOLKS are pouring their first cocktail of the day, Tina and Rose were back at Silverado, sitting in a steamy whirlpool at the spa, reviewing their lunch meeting.

Rose wiped perspiration from her brow before she asked her partner, "What was that weird glance you gave me when Talley explained away the cabins on the hill? I bought her story, but I guess you didn't. What gives?"

Tina sighed. "Talley said the cabins were guest quarters for horse enthusiasts, which struck me as odd. Remember, before we went on the ranch tour, when we were sitting in front of the fireplace at the farmhouse? By chance, did you spot any current pictures or paintings of their horses? I didn't. On our tour of the horse farm, I didn't see as many horses as I expected to, and no Arabians at all. Why would any respectable horse enthusiast take a second look at the horse flesh we saw today? Nice healthy animals, but not a thoroughbred among them. No doubt in my mind, those cabins are being used for other purposes. It's a distinct possibility they're still used as a bordello.

"What if the local constabulary is aware of its existence and is turning a blind eye? Could be some of them are active participants. If so, what else are they willing to ignore? All kinds of scenarios come to mind, the worst being it's a community conspiracy with all in the valley profiting from Sister Nation. My guess, we are dealing with some sly characters. I don't trust them at all."

THE REPORT FROM TINA did not surprise Nemesis execs, given the disturbing data emerging from another source in regard to Sister Nation company's resounding success. Intercepted discussions between pharmaceutical conglomerates and their subsidiaries showed their concern about government agency intervention caused by Sister Nation. For decades, the drug industry worked diligently, lobbying Congress and working the media, to convince the public that their products were safe and performed as advertised. Many products were the darlings of the internet and social media—making companies and the media billions. Almost overnight, this nouveau riche Left Coast collection of Sister Nation products had encroached on pharma conglomerates' profits by implementing the pharma goons' own modus operandi: slipping addictive substances into their products. And these shady manufacturers of over-the-counter remedies were pissed off. A few had already sent spies to California and put their private mercenary forces on alert.

Within the week, truckers from down the mountain alerted Talley that strangers were milling about asking questions about Sister Nation. Not the investor or government types. These were the rough-and-tumble dudes. When Talley asked her men if they were up to the task of taking these intruders on, the truckers grinned and nodded.

TO PREPARE FOR A CONFRONTATION, Talley had the boys in the valley come to the farm and reinforce the place. With the promise of some excellent weed and female interaction, the road warriors were there within the hour, in force with weapons, ammo, and a few explosive surprises. Most of them were hunters and trappers, who knew the property well from hunting there since they were kids. A few were retired military special ops veterans adept in guerrilla warfare, trained to arm and set landmines, skilled in the art of building and disguising devices to snare, entrap, and incapacitate intruders. Careful to map out the locations of the deadly camouflaged booby traps and tripwires to hand out to the personnel on property. The boys concealed their surprises for unwelcomed guests and moved the livestock to the outer pastures to avoid any possible danger to the animals. When they finished, everything appeared normal to the naked eye.

THE MOMENT CHAIRMAN TREY MCCALL was informed of the activity in Napa, he called an emergency meeting with Nemesis directors to brainstorm the situation confronting Sister Nation.

"Thank you, ladies and gentlemen, for joining me this morning. We just received confirmation from Tina and Rose that fringe-pharma mercenaries are circling Napa like vultures, anxious to take care of business up the mountain at the Sister Nation compound. We've also learned from our agents on the ground that Sister Nation reinforced its headquarters at the farm. If we hang back and let these factions attack each other, there's a good chance all we'll have to do is go in later and pick up the pieces. We are fortunate to have two of our best agents, Tina and Rose, in position on site. If or when there's an altercation between the adversaries, we will know within seconds. At that point, Tina and Rose have orders to clear out immediately. That is all I have so far. Any questions?" There were no questions, and he adjourned the meeting.

It was times like this that Trey appreciated the unique reach of Warlock. Thanks to a cybercrime computer program, second to none in the world in speed, accuracy, and anonymity, he now spent more time enjoying golf with his boy. Instead of pouring over random reports like the old days, all his agents did was plug in trigger words like Sister Nation into the program. Warlock sorted the info that pertained to those flagged words and organized it into files. Anything pressing was sent to Trey within seconds. While he helped Jefferson prep for the US

Open held at the famed Winged Foot in Mamaroneck, New York, Trey could be away from The Circle M but never out of touch.

SOMETHING BIG WAS GOING DOWN, Jefferson could feel it. His father had been preoccupied the last few times they had been working on their golf games. When Trey walked up, Jefferson asked him if anything was wrong.

Trey shook his head. "Not anymore, son. What say you and I play some golf with the boys around Dallas this week? It's been a while for me, and you need to sharpen up after your mini vacation from the Tour. I want you to be as keen as possible; Winged Foot will test every aspect of your game."

DURING HIS PGA TOUR CAREER, Trey McCall had played in two US Opens at Winged Foot. In the first, he missed the 36-hole cut, and in the second, he tied for seventh. There were lessons to be learned from both showings. In the first, Trey hadn't listened to the experienced players about the importance of local course knowledge at Winged Foot. For his second appearance, he soaked up as much course knowledge as he could from members and veterans in practice rounds. Highly acclaimed golf architect A.W. Tillinghast designed the east and west course at Winged Foot. Both required exceptional skill, shot management, and patience in order to score well. The west course hosted the US Open, viewed by many as the epitome of major championship venues with narrow, sloping tree-lined fairways; thick, gnarly rough of blended fescue and bluegrass; deep greenside bunkers; and sloping, lightning-fast greens that took their toll on low scores.

Trey and Jefferson arrived at Winged Foot on Thursday evening, a week before the championship began. Jefferson's caddy, Moondance (Dance) Johnson, was already there to map out the course in advance of their arrival. Trey learned his lesson years ago about how much local knowledge came into play to save shots on the demanding prestigious layout. Pierce Talbot, a longtime friend of Trey's and a member of Winged Foot, was kind enough to invite them to stay with him at his home near the course for the championship. Their host arranged tee times for them to play the next few days. As a two-time club champion at Winged Foot, Pierce was an excellent source of information on the subtleties of the course.

Just after noon on Sunday, while Pierce, Trey, and Jefferson were playing the par three tenth, an unkept bloke in a grey jacket, white button-down shirt, USGA club tie, and scuffed-up black shoes desperately in need of a polish drove his golf cart up to the green. With great difficulty, the bloke got out of the contraption and shuffled toward them.

Lawson Skiles glared down at Jefferson in a massive deep bunker left of the green and yelled, "Hey, you, dumbass down in the bunker, what the hell do you think you're doing?"

Surprised by the sound of an unfamiliar voice, Jefferson glanced up. "Playing a very difficult bunker shot."

Skiles sputtered and fumed. "No shit, smartass, do you know who I am, and for that matter, what I am?"

Now a bit annoyed, Jefferson shook his head. "No, I don't know who you are … however, I do know *what* you are."

Before the exchange went any farther, Pierce Talbot intervened. "Excuse me, gentlemen, is there a problem here?"

Furious at the interruption, Skiles's face turned beet-red. "There most certainly is, and by the way, who in the hell are you?"

"Pierce Talbot, a member and two-time club champion here at Winged Foot. My family and I have been members of the club since my great-grandfather joined decades ago. And I resent the way you are insulting my guests."

The man tried in vain to stare Pierce down. "I don't give a flying flip about you or your family. My name is Lawson Skiles, and I am on the executive committee of the United States Golf Association. You know, the one's putting on the US Open here this week. Your guest is breaking our one-ball-only rule for practice rounds. I saw him play several shots out of the bunker over there, and I *will not* stand for it."

"Let me get this straight, you say you are a member of the USGA Executive Committee who wrote the rules and regulations for the upcoming competition *next* week, am I correct?"

"That's right, bud. And we expect those rules to be obeyed to the letter. Got it, there, sport?"

"To the letter, you say?" Pierce chuckled.

Now an irate Lawson Skiles screamed, "To the letter, bozo, to the flipping letter!"

Trey McCall strolled over to find out what the commotion was about. Skiles instantly recognized Trey, and his face turned even redder. It so happened, Lawson Skiles was the apathetic referee who magically found McCall's opponent's ball on the final hole of a US Open years ago. Before Trey said a word, Pierce held up his hand and nodded to signal that he had this.

"So, Mr. All Important, USGA Executive Committee Member, who wrote the policies for the upcoming competition, might I suggest you read what you say you wrote before you go about throwing your considerable weight around. As a member here, I read the covenants thoroughly. Inasmuch as my good friends Trey and Jefferson McCall were coming up to stay with me for the championship. I made tee times for us to play this weekend, following to the letter the rules and policies you and your associates were so kind to provide to the club in triplicate. Please note your association does not officially take over the golf course until three p.m. *this* afternoon. According to my watch, it is nearing one p.m. Sir, you have no say for two more hours. By that time, with no more interruptions from you, my friends and I will be long gone. Have a nice afternoon, Mr. Skiles. It was a pleasure to meet you in person and witness you live up to your sordid reputation." With that, Pierce tossed a golf ball into the bunker, encouraging Jefferson to hit another shot.

FOR THE MAJORITY OF THE CHAMPIONSHIP, the McCalls did not see Lawson Skiles—until Sunday afternoon. For the first three days, Jefferson played splendid golf: the only contestant under par with a five-shot lead going into the final round. As Jefferson made his way to the first tee, he noticed Lawson Skiles standing by the starter tent with a wry smile on his face. However it came to be, Lawson was the referee for the final pairing, just like back when his dad had a chance to win the US Open.

As Jeff brushed by him to get his playing partner's scorecard, Lawson whispered to him, "I'm going to watch every move you make today, so be aware. I wish you the same fate as your father experienced years ago."

When Jefferson tried to squeeze by, the man stuck out his foot to block him. Jefferson motioned with his head for the man to gaze down as he was about to put a shoe full of steel spikes through the top of the jerk's foot. Lawson quickly retracted his foot and hoofed it out of the tent with a scowl. Throughout the round, Lawson did everything he could to distract Jefferson by standing in his peripheral vision, jingling change, or deliberately moving during his swing. None of it worked. Jefferson birdied the last two holes to shoot one under for the day and secure a six-shot victory. It took an unusually long time for the winner to come out of the scoring box, leading folks to believe there might be some irregularities on the scorecard.

But it was nothing like that. Jefferson gave the referee a tongue-lashing that many in the box thought was long overdue. Lawson began to read out McCall's hole-by-hole scores, and Jefferson said he did not need him to do so. He ignored Jefferson and read them out anyway. Jefferson listened patiently but handed in his card at the scoring table before Lawson finished. Jefferson got up to leave, and Lawson grabbed him by the shirt. Martial arts automatically kicked in and before anyone else could react, Jefferson pinned Lawson against the wall.

Seething on the inside, Jefferson spoke clearly and decisively, "My family and I have had all we're going to take from you. After your actions the last two Sundays, one would imagine you'd feel awkward and embarrassed right now. Yet you're neither. In my book, you're nothing but an insignificant buffoon, a disgrace. You give a bad name to the others in your organization who genuinely promote and love the game of golf. My father never talks about the year he was runner-up in the US Open; you're probably the reason for that. I'm guessing if not for you, there would be two US Open trophies in the McCall trophy case."

Quietly, Jefferson released the terrified relic and left the scoring area to the applause of those inside the box and the mob of well-wishers waiting outside. Lawson Skiles sulked about inside until the crowds diminished, then left the golf course as quickly as possible. A few days later, Pierce Talbot informed the McCalls that Lawson Skiles resigned from his executive post at the USGA.

CHAPTER 10

WHILE JEFFERSON WAS BUSY winning the US Open in New York, things were stirring in Northern California.

Tina and Rose announced their mounting concern to Talley who noted that she and Gary heard the same rumblings from the boys down below. Preparations were already underway at the farm. The boys from down the mountain moved into the brothel cabins. They checked and rechecked their weapons and ammunition caches before they moved the last of the provisions into the mountain stockade.

THINGS CAME TO A HEAD when radical pharmaceutical factions overseas lost patience with their reps in the United States. Each day Sister Nation stripped them of more profits, which predictably initiated their directive to demolish Sister Nation. Nemesis immediately picked up the transmission and contacted Trey, who was in mid-celebration of Jefferson's US Open victory, surrounded by a multitude of their best friends at the ranch in Texas. Graciously, he excused himself from the festivities and made his way through the crowd to his office. As he entered, Tara and Miranda showed him a transcript of what the foreign consortium sent and received. Immediately he got in touch with Tina and Rose who, at Talley's request, moved into the Slice of Heaven cabins at the horse farm supposedly to get the feel of Sister Nation—from the ground up. Tina stepped outside and took the call on her cell.

"What do you two think, Tina? Should we have you and Rose vacate the premises?" Trey asked anxiously.

"Not yet, sir. Rose and I talked it over and feel we ought to stay and ride out the storm to see where it leads. We believe Talley bought into our identities and now considers us valuable allies."

LATER IN THE CABIN, Rose inquired, "So Tina, have you picked up on the friction between the head Sister and Gary? What's that all about, I wonder?"

Tina shrugged her shoulders. "I have no idea, but there is definitely an issue of some kind. Maybe she's overwhelmed with the outside pressures or she's lost faith in Gary. Whatever it is, she's distancing herself from him."

HE HADN'T IMAGINED IT. For some ungodly reason, Gary couldn't fathom why he became the brunt of Talley's wrath. He sensed a bitterness escalating in Talley that made him extremely uncomfortable. He'd already made a pot full of money, more than he would ever need. At a convenient time, when Talley was preoccupied with something away from the farmhouse, he planned to clear out his bank account and leave for good. Sooner than he expected, just after lunch the next day, Talley went to the winery to check on a production issue. Gary seized the opportunity and attempted to drive off the property. As he approached the first of two security gates, he pushed his remote device to open it. Nothing happened. Again and again, he pushed the button with no response.

Frustrated, Gary got out of his vehicle to work the keypad manually. Abruptly, a bush moved in front of him and pointed a .45 automatic at him. Then a voice came out of the bush and asked him what he was doing. He recognized the familiar voice as one of the boys from down the mountain.

Gary replied calmly that he was just going to town to pick up some office supplies for Talley. No reason to raise suspicion by acting hostile or appearing anxious.

The guy in the ghillie suit checked his phone for messages, "Nothing here. Sorry, sir, my orders are that no one leaves the compound without clearance from Talley Marsh."

Gary attempted to joke with the man, who stood his ground and ordered Gary to turn around and go back to the farmhouse before he reported him to HQ. Wondering what in the hell was going on, Gary got back in his jeep as ordered and drove to the farmhouse. As soon as he turned into the drive, Gary encountered all sorts of commotion with folks running willy-nilly moving out of the house and cottages over to the mountain stockade.

BACK FROM THE WINERY, Talley was directing traffic and saw Gary out of the corner of her eye. "Gary, word came up from the valley that a large group of armed men are headed our way."

"So, that's the reason for all the commotion."

"Yep, time is of the essence. Better head into the mountain."

At first, Gary was skeptical until he heard an explosion in a nearby pasture. Apparently, they were here and closing in. Scared and now motivated, Gary hurried into the mountain fortress as the door was coming down. Inhabitants inside gathered around television monitors to observe the merciless seek-and-destroy mission taking place on the farm. Judging from what they saw, the local boys held off the enemy best they could, until they were forced to retreat as the size of merc force increased. Remarkably, not a single local was killed or wounded.

Viewers found it sad to watch so much history go up in flame, although Talley did not seem all that upset. It soon became apparent to the leaders of the attack force that there was a problem. Other than the minor force they encountered early on, there was no one around. Where was everybody, since they weren't at the winery, the factory behind it, or here at their headquarters?

Gary, Tina, Rose, and Talley assembled in the Sister Nation exec. cubicle, at the end of the first tunnel on the right, supposedly to organize a routine for the group to follow while in hiding. The true purpose was for them to leave by the private underground tunnels. Talley sent Gary to fetch essential Sister Nation company papers from the wall safe across the hall.

AS SOON AS HE WAS OUT THE DOOR, Talley lifted the concealed hatch and led Tina and Rose down the ladder to the lower cavern housing two tunnels, instructing them to take the right tunnel and wait for her at the end by the water. When she went to remove the ladder, to her surprise, Gary was standing by the hatch with a satchel of papers in his hands staring down at her with a questioning expression on his face. Recovering quickly, Talley hurried him down the ladder. Then scurried up to close the trap door and tightened and locked it down.

Observant as ever, Talley improvised. "Relax, partner, I thought this little surprise might come in handy someday. These tunnels were built by the bootleggers who used them to smuggle in their booze and doubled as an escape route. I sent the girls up ahead. You and I should split up just in case. You take the right tunnel to meet up with them, I'll take the one on the left. We can all rendezvous later."

She wondered if he would take the bait. He did. "Tell you what, you take the right one—and I'll take the left tunnel."

Boy, was that easy. She snickered to herself as she took the right tunnel that wound gently downhill to a cavern roughly the size of a high school basketball court, fifty feet wide and eighty-four feet long, where she found Tina and Rose sitting on the shore dangling their feet in a collection reservoir that fed the Napa River from an underground spring. A motorized rubber raft tied to a small dock provided transportation out. Two heavy-duty waterproof duffels covered by a tarp were tied down securely in the stern of the craft—one was full of money, the other contained Ma's incriminating journals plus other miscellaneous documents of importance. The girls hopped aboard. Talley casted off and manned the small outboard motor. The trio puttered down a man-made stream cut into the floor of the cavern that led out to the river.

In less than an hour, they rounded a bend in the river where she guided the vessel to shore and secured it under cover of low-hanging tree limbs. Parked a hundred yards away was a Ford F-250 truck with a powerful motorized winch screwed down on the steel-reinforced rear bumper. A titanium sled was attached to the end of the woven heavy-duty wire rope on the winch to transport the duffels from the rubber boat into the bed of the Ford, one at a time.

After the duffels were loaded, Talley took a smoke break and made a phone call on a cell phone stored in the truck's console. Not long after, a GMC Yukon pulled up beside the Ford. Out popped Ramon Santiago and Millie Snowden, who greeted Talley with a hug and kiss on the cheek. Introductions between Tina and Rose and Ramon and Millie ensued. Their intricate ruse was more successful than they could have ever imagined. The whole world believed that Talley and Millie dissolved their partnership over Ramon—a brilliant sting. How gratifying.

MILLIE SQUINTED HARD at the Canadians. "Tina, you look familiar. I feel as though we've met before. You don't happen to know a family in Texas by the name of McCall do you, in the oil and livestock business, among other things?"

"Why yes, I do. As a matter of fact, Rose and I have even done jobs for and with them in the past. You see, for years we worked in a private investigation agency out of Montreal. Until we got tired of that rat race and retired with enough money to open our own operation. Luckily, we caught the business cycle at the right time and turned quite a profit. We got fed up watching criminals walk away with huge cash profits, monies you don't pay outlandish taxes on. So, yes, we know the McCalls, but haven't seen them in years."

Millie watched her body language and paid close attention to every word. "And now you two want to cash in big with the three of us. Am I right?"

Rose thought quickly and spoke up. "Yep."

As a last piece of business, Ramon set the rubber boat adrift to seek its own destination along the Napa River. Tina, Rose, and Talley climbed into the Ford truck, Ramon and Millie into Yukon, and started on their way to Sonoma. During the trip, there was not much conversation in the Ford.

Not so in the GMC, Millie wondered if Tina and Rose were on the up-and-up and asked Ramon what he really thought.

The debonaire vintner said it was too soon to tell. But if they were there under false pretenses, it would not be long before they exposed themselves.

NEXT TO NOTHING was left standing at the Sister Nation facilities in Napa. Fortunately, the animals in the back pastures escaped without injury. The mercenaries located the elaborate hideout in the side of the mountain, thanks to detailed sketches and architectural renderings, including escape routes *carelessly* left behind in the top drawer of Talley's desk. Beside them was a handwritten clue to help remember the combination. Three words—double the devil. On the first attempt, they tried 666666 on the keypad and waltzed right in to find the space totally deserted even though there were enough supplies to last for months. It was as if the former occupants chose to abandon the farm and forgo defending it.

GARY CAME TO THE END OF HIS TUNNEL and found it boarded up; he thought about turning around until he heard echoed voices from the cavern foyer. There was no turning back—he had to get out and fast. With no tools available, he ripped and tore at the boards, pulling them apart with his bare hands, which quickly bloodied and became slippery. To stem the flow of blood, Gary tore the sleeves off his shirt and wrapped them around his hands as gloves for a better grip. Using the sturdiest torn-off planks to pry boards apart, he created a hole large enough for him to squeeze through and scramble part-way down the mountain. Voices from above and below carried in the still air. They were looking for him. In a panic, he squeezed into a saucer-like depression under the lip of a ledge hidden from searching eyes. Exhausted and still bleeding, Gary remained under the ledge until sunset. He waited until he could no longer hear the voices and moved down the mountain before he became dinner for a pack of coyotes.

Fear pushed him to his limit. He slipped, slid, and tumbled his way down as the last slivers of daylight disappeared over the horizon. Rocks and thorny brush tore the skin on his bare arms and ripped his pants to shreds in his uncontrolled race to the flat land below. Miraculously, he burst through the brush, and in a bloody heap, spilled out onto State Route 29 to Napa. Seconds later, he heard the screech of brakes and then caught a whiff of burning rubber as a car stopped just inches from his blood-covered head. In a flash, the door of a police cruiser flew open, and Deputy Sheriff Dewayne Rogers ran over to him.

"Holy shit, man. What the fuck? I could have killed you. Oh man. What a mess, we need to get you to a doctor, pronto."

DEWAYNE CAREFULLY LAID GARY in the back of his patrol car and rushed him to an emergency clinic only a short distance away. Luckily, Gary's wounds were mostly superficial. The doctor sewed up his head wound, cleaned and dressed the other cuts and abrasions, and gave him a tetanus shot before he released him. While Officer Rogers waited, he called the sheriff to fill him in on the man. With so much blood covering Gary's face, Dewayne hadn't recognized who it was that he'd rescued. On their way to the sheriff's office from the clinic, neither man spoke.

Sheriff Medford got down to business. "Gary Edington, ex-con and partner in Sister Nation. We met casually when you first got here, but in case you forgot, my name is Sheriff Gwilym Medford. Appears you've had a pretty bad day so far. I won't keep you long. Just need to ask you a few questions. Do you know anything about what happened up the mountain today? Specifically, who or what was responsible for the demolition of Sister Nation farm?"

Without sentencing himself to a long term back in prison, Gary could ill afford to tell the man the truth. Gary's hesitancy to answer elicited an unexpected follow-up from the sheriff.

"We believe there was a malfunction in the gas line connected to the structures at the ranch and the winery. Most of those lines were old and rusty. Could be they developed undetected leaks over the years—a disaster waiting to happen. As soon as one went up, they all did, leveling the buildings. What puzzles me, with all the rescue crews and state law enforcement agencies searching the property, why they didn't find any casualties? What do you make of that? Before you answer, my guess is there must have been a company retreat or holiday and the usual personnel on the premises were away for the day. All except for you, that is. Why is it you were the only one there?"

Thinking on his feet, Gary replied, "We gave the employees a day off in our appreciation of all the hard work and overtime they'd put in over the last six months. I came in to tie up some loose ends with a couple of new products we were about to introduce. All at once, it sounded like WWIII. My only exit was a path down the mountain behind the corral. It was so smokey, I found it hard to breathe, and I lost my balance several times before I scrambled out on the road and your deputy rescued me."

Scratching his chin as he contemplated Gary's explanation, the sheriff asked, "So what happened to your hands and your shirt sleeves?"

"It's quite simple. I slipped on the rocky path and skidded down the mountain. Desperately, I grasped onto anything that would slow me down. Thorny limbs on scrubs and small trees shredded my hands and arms. In due course, I tore off my sleeves to wrap my hands for a better grip."

"Makes sense, you look like hell. Lucky to be alive. You're free to go, get outta here, and take care of those wounds so they don't get infected."

A MAN KNOWN THROUGHOUT the criminal world as Mr. Xen waited eagerly for an important phone call. Xen manufactured, packaged, and distributed addictive mixtures to pharma concerns worldwide. Sister Nation manufactured their own addictive blends; hence, they were in no need of his products. Not a big deal until the dramatic increase in demand for SN goods skyrocketed and severely impacted Mr. Xen's bottom line—something he took personally and vowed revenge.

Gwilym Medford was on the phone the minute Gary Edington left his office. A foreign-accented party on the other end seemed most pleased with the police officer's explanation and the ease with which the cop maneuvered Gary Edington away from the truth. With today's news, it appeared Mr. Xen's worries about Sister Nation were history.

Pleased with himself, Gwilym Medford hung up, then made a second call, this one to a woman in Sonoma: Talley Marsh.

"Well, ma'am, so far, everybody is buying into our story, just like you said. Sorry Sister Nation is no more, but it had to be that way. Too many forces were converging on it for the company to survive. A few folks with cuts and scrapes are a small price to pay for a fresh start. 'Cept for around here, people are partial to having the extra cash that comes to them every month from you and the businesses. You plan to keep that going?"

Talley replied, "Yeah, we took a big chance. From what I hear, all our people escaped and no one was seriously injured. Wonder if we got any video of the mercs' faces when they found the whole place abandoned. As for the loyal citizens down below when we kick off our new production line, I hope to be able to match the goods and services we provided in the past."

Chuckling to himself, the sheriff commented, "Glad to hear it. As a side bar, a few solid citizens wondered if certain documents were perhaps destroyed in the fire."

The former madam of Slice of Heaven snickered. "Tell them quite a few of our records were completely destroyed. However, the archived ones with personal data were kept in a different location. Those are all intact and in safe keeping."

As a native of Napa, Medford knew the personal chronicles to which she referred had the names and preferences of the clients who frequented the bordello at the farm—as far back as prohibition days. Cognizant of that, he laughed, then frowned, and said, "That ought to keep 'em in line, don't you think? Lots of juicy blackmail material in those journals." Him included.

THE LIFE DESIREE RICHARDS imagined for herself in Montreal lost its pizzazz in comparison to the adrenaline rush of being in the middle of the action like in the old days. On her afternoon call with Boris, she hinted to him how she missed being in control. Although it was nice to be kept in the loop with the spycams, it wasn't the same.

Desiree confessed. "Tell me honestly, my friend, don't you miss all the excitement of the old days? Wouldn't it be fun to jump back in and get our feet wet one more time? If there was only a way, I would do it in a heartbeat."

"I guess I do miss the challenge. What I don't miss is glancing over my shoulder all the time running from the authorities."

FOLLOWING THE REVELATION they had history with the McCalls, the renegade Napa faction searched the dark web for interactions Rose and Tina had with Nemesis. Thanks to Trey McCall and Warlock, there were only a few cases where the girls collaborated with the McCall's cyber-crime organization, none of which amounted to much. Talley snickered, raised her eyebrows, and nodded her approval at the good news.

NEMESIS AGENTS SENT BY TREY MCCALL were not surprised by the devastation they witnessed at the Sister Nation site. The people responsible left no doubt they meant business. The local constabulary determined the mishap was due to faulty gas lines. Nemesis found evidence to the contrary, since the remote Winery complex, miles away from the farm, burned down as well. Veterans of foreign wars knew a scorched earth mission when they saw one. Sheriff Medford stood his ground. There was nothing Trey or his people could do to change his mind, so they left it to the locals to sort things out and flew back to Texas.

Stymied in Napa for the present, Trey took advantage of the lull in the action to play golf with Jefferson, the reigning US Open champion.

As per usual mid-summer in Dallas, the sun beat down like blue blazes, weather Trey preferred when he played nowadays. It kept him loose, especially his reconstructed shoulder. As soon as he rounded the corner of the clubhouse at their driving range, he spotted Jefferson working on his pitch shots in the short-game area.

He was about to say something when Jefferson pitched one into the hole, grinned, and quipped, "You up for a little closest-to-the-hole around the green?"

Trey shook his head. "No chance. I'm not falling into that trap. Instead, how about a few holes of call-shot to sharpen up the old game?"

In Trey's experience, there was no better way to expand one's shot-making ability than to call your shot before you hit it, then have your opponent attempt to replicate the shot.

Jefferson leaped at the challenge. "You're on, old man. Hope you brought your checkbook."

Caught up in their rivalry, they played an entire nine. The duo jabbered the entire way around, needled each other before each shot, and laughed, having an awesome time. After the men finished their match, they sat outside the grill and bar area in the shade under the spreading oak trees to sip iced teas and talk about the future. Jefferson had accomplished so much, in such a short period of time. It was a certainty Trey's son would be a member of the US Ryder Cup and World Cup teams, along with a five-year exemption to all PGA Tour–sanctioned events for winning the US Open. Proud of his boy for all he'd done, Trey asked him if he'd re-evaluated his goals for the future. Without hesitation, Jefferson announced that he wanted to be the best player ever.

Just the answer Trey hoped to hear. "At about your age, I had the same aspirations that you have right now and believed I had the potential to fulfill my goal. So did my mentor Don January who shared his vast knowledge of golf with me. Not all of his wisdom resulted from hard work, most of it came from a man who understood the golf swing better than maybe anyone else ever did, Ben Hogan."

Trey let that sink in before he continued. "Don made me promise to never give away any of what *the man himself* showed him unless that person was truly worthy of it. On a day I will never forget, Don took me to Shady Oaks to meet Mr. Hogan and watch him hit balls. It was spellbinding to see the control Hogan had with every club, something I'd never seen before nor since—until recently. What amazed me most was the crisp sound of impact on every shot. It was incomprehensible to think how many hours of practice and attention to detail it must have taken to develop such control. Talent like that was special and earned through dedication. In the wake of such an impressive demonstration, I knew why Don January swore me to secrecy.

"I must confess, I fudged a little when it came to you. By subtly incorporating the knowledge entrusted to me in the form of suggestions, I taught you how to play the game. I intentionally held back where the wisdom and solid fundamentals came from until the right time. Which I feel is now. I trust you will abide by the same promise that I made to Don January and be especially careful to not share what we know with just anyone. Although if you did, most of it is so simple no one would believe you."

Trey reiterated how he'd kept golf uncomplicated and consistent for Jefferson from day one. There were fundamentals to which every great player adhered—all of which were put to the test of time in competition. Over and over, Trey stressed them to his son to instill them in his brain. He gave Jefferson a checklist to tick off in his mind before each shot. Make sure the grip is proper with the left thumb positioned on top of the shaft slightly right of center with the handle of the club held lightly in the fingers of both hands to reduce tension. Adjust alignment to fit the shot shape, weight distribution, and ball position to fit the trajectory. Use the ground for balance and spring. Create width with a deliberate backswing, allow the right hand to lag and set at the top, then clear the left side with careless disregard for consequence while the hands and arms fly through to the finish.

His father had Jefferson's full attention. "Things are so different in today's world. If you don't have a boatload of so-called pundits, scientists, and statisticians dissecting and evaluating with endless testing and posturing, then it must not be worthy of consideration. If it's not contrived, complex, and confusing, they won't buy it. My point is this, the axioms we have worked so hard to perfect do not belong in the hands of those who have not, or will not, lift a finger to understand how they work or attempt to apply them. There are no shortcuts to greatness. End of sermon. What say you and I go another nine, double or nothing."

IN A HOTEL SUITE IN HONG KONG, Mr. Xen and a few of his confederates toasted to the destruction of Sister Nation in Northern California. None were aware that Talley Marsh had a plan to shake up the international drug trade on a much larger scale with a masking agent that camouflaged the chemical footprint of addictive substances. It would create a brand-new market for Talley and Millie to explore without having to worry about illegal drugs, Mr. Xen, or his cronies. All the manufacturers had to do was add a pre-calculated amount of masking agent to the drug-laced supplements they hawked. Talley and Millie could operate the business from anywhere without a permanent headquarters.

Millie liked her partner's idea but took it a step further. It was Millie's contention that somewhere lost in centuries-old ancient tribal cures was a natural catalyst that would stimulate the flow of endorphins and dopamine and release an intense sense of euphoria in humans. By replacing the drug-laced additives with an indigenous product virtually unknown in today's world, she could offer manufacturers an alternative to illegal drugs. There was only one problem. So far Millie had turned up nothing.

One evening at her wits' end, Millie ran across a reference to an ancient remedy the Mayans used for anxiety and depression. The natives gathered light-green oblong-shaped leaves from a small shrub they called Le Serena. In a two-day process, the ancient pharmacists pounded the leaves into a fine paste which they let dry in the sun, then ground the hardened compound into small granules they poured into jars and stored in a cool, dry place. When needed, they mixed a thimble-size quantity with hot water and administered the brew to the ailing party in a tea. According to the study, the results were remarkable, in a short time, the patient was free of all symptoms and experienced a heightened state of euphoria.

Energized by her discovery, Millie was anxious to obtain a sample of the mystical Mayan plant. She didn't know any Mayans, but she bet an old college chum of hers just might. There was this wild-as-hell chick Millie ran into in college at MIT. Esmeralda something … Barbarossa, that was it. She went by the nickname Izzy and was into all kinds of exotic drugs. There was a good chance her friend heard of this Le Serena leaf. If memory severed her right, Izzy was into archaeology, mainly ancient Mesoamerican cultures, and had been on several excavations in and around the Yucatan. Using her computer hacking skills, Millie found a current address and unlisted number for Esmeralda (Izzy) Barbarossa.

A disgusted-sounding individual answered the phone almost immediately. "Whoever this is, you better have a damn good reason for calling me on my private number. I don't recognize your digits, if this is a joke or a solicitation, be aware I have software programs in place to seriously fuck up your world."

Millie calmly responded. "Whoa there, Izzy, Millie Snowden here. Sissy from back in our college days. You might recall we used to take some interesting flights back then—without leaving the ground. Listen, I'm touching base about something I ran across in my research on the Mayan culture and thought you might be able to lend me a hand."

"Yeah, I remember you, Sissy. We did the *Star Trek* thing together, going where no man has ever gone before. What part of the Mayan culture are you interested in?"

"I ran across a Mayan reference to Le Serena and wondered if you heard or knew anything about it."

There was a long pause at the other end of the line. "You aren't by chance referring to a shrub with oblong-shaped leaves of different shades of green?"

"I am."

For twenty minutes, Izzy filled Millie in on her first MIT expedition to the Yucatan, where one of the Mayan guides, by the name of Kisin, introduced her to a local medication with an unusual calming influence. Supposedly, it was a remedy discovered by his forefathers centuries ago and used to soothe minor aches and pains as well to declutter the troubled mind. In the same fashion as his ancestors, Kisin mixed a thimble full of green granules he called *caida libre*, "free fall" in English, with boiling water and gave it to Izzy to sip. Half an hour later, she experienced a peaceful state of clarity combined with a noticeable surge of energy and a hyper sense of euphoria she had never felt before.

She was ready to take on the world. Izzy worked tirelessly through the day with plenty of energy in reserve to party half the night. Even more amazing, she was insatiable in bed much to the chagrin of her partners who couldn't keep up.

When the effects of the potion wore off, she slept like a baby and woke up the next morning refreshed and ready to take on the day. For the rest of the dig, Izzy pretty much lived off the magical elixir and found that even though she ate constantly, she lost weight but gained stamina. Izzy had one of the lab dudes on the project analyze the granules and work up a chemical blueprint she stored on her computer. At the end of the expedition, she attempted to bring some Le Serena cuttings back to the States. Unfortunately, the border agents confiscated them. Lacking in chemistry skills, Izzy never bothered to peer at the blueprint on her computer.

Millie was so excited she could hardly speak. "Is that blueprint still on file in your computer?"

"Probably, let me check. Yep, sure is. I just sent it to you in an attachment."

"Izzy, you've made my day. Can I pay you anything for it?"

She stretched, yawned, and answered in a mischievous tone. "No thanks, Sissy. Consider it a favor for old time's sake. Say, if you're ever in the mood to explore the universe again, let me know. Here's my private number if you ever need anything at all. My old man is loaded. As long as I keep him happy, I have carte blanche to do as I wish. Take care, girl. Ciao."

THIRTY MINUTES LATER, Millie was mulling over the blueprint, more like a formula, of the exact percentages of elements in the granules derived from the leaves of Le Serena. Her expertise was computer science, but Millie also had a firm grasp on chemistry. By nightfall, working meticulously in her private lab, she'd duplicated the ancient Mayan remedy Izzy referred to as caida libre. Now came the scary part. Before she introduced her discovery to her partner, Millie had to make sure that it worked. The question was, did *she* have the courage to sample a cup of the magic mixture? She'd gone too far to turn back now. Millie boiled a kettle of hot water, filled a teacup, and mixed in a thimble full of granules.

She went outside on the porch and plopped down in a rocking chair to enjoy the cool, clear evening while she sipped the contents of the cup. It had a slightly bitter taste, not overpowering, but enough to give it some bite. The more she sipped, the more she grew used to the taste. Before she knew it, Millie had finished the cup. Groggy, she leaned her head back and closed her eyes for only a minute, or so she thought. When she opened them again and looked at her watch, she was surprised to find she had been out for almost an hour. She felt totally at peace, in complete control, with a noticeable increase in energy, plus an unusually strong desire to have sex. Time seemed to float by nonchalantly rather than fly by at break-neck speed. Never before had she achieved this level of focus—so clear and bright. All of her senses were at their peak, and her overall state was one of complete and utter euphoria.

Star Trek Snowden was flying again, only this time totally cognizant of her surroundings. Empowered with a sober functioning mindset that kept her up most of the night, Millie compiled, sorted, computed, and prepared a presentation for Talley to peruse in the morning. After only two hours of sleep, Millie woke up refreshed and ready to go. From what she could tell, there were no adverse side effects.

AS SOON AS TALLEY WALKED into Millie's office, she detected a change in her colleague. First of all, the office was neat and tidy, a vast improvement over the usual files and papers scattered about among old pizza boxes and half-filled Styrofoam cups. The most shocking feature was Millie seemed in good spirits, a definite deviation from her normally sluggish morning self.

Talley glanced around. "What's up with you, sunshine? Why such a glowing demeanor at this hour of the day?"

"You are not going to believe this shit. It's like way far out there but stay with me. Late last night I found a reference to a Mayan drug from a Le Serena bush called caida libre. Anyway, I called Izzy, a schoolmate from MIT, who was into archaeology and went on a dig at some Mayan ruins. She knew what I was talking about because a Mayan guide gave her some of it to try. Said it put her on cloud nine and juiced up her senses with no side effects. Sooo, she gave me a blueprint of its ingredients, and I whipped up a batch. Hang on, it gets better. It drank some in a tea, and the results were un-fucking believable."

Talley interrupted. "You are some kind of batshit crazy to try a stunt like that. I mean, why would you go to all that trouble when we're on the verge of creating a masking agent?"

Millie totally ignored the interruption. "Everything was crystal clear, like in HD, and my energy level was off the charts. And guess what, I don't think I've ever been so horny. Two hours sleep, and I'm fresh as a daisy."

"Okay, okay, I get that it's really good shit. What about the masking agent we are working on?"

"Shit, can it. This stuff is way better, trust me. The Mayan remedy is natural. Its existence has been kept under wraps for centuries by the descendants of the ancient civilization."

"So."

"So this. Pharmaceutical companies worldwide are familiar with and use variations of what we use now. If this caida libre, Mayan for "free fall" by the way, pans out to be as addictive as I believe it is, we wouldn't have to deal with illegal drugs and all the intangibles they impose. We would have a simple natural additive that we alone manufacture that performs the same function as narcotics—only ours is legal. No more 'John Law' to worry about.

"More importantly, we get a refined, quality-controlled product in every batch. To be absolutely sure, I'll need to do more testing before we take the leap and go out on our own with our tranquility tea."

Convinced and fully engaged, Talley asked, "How about I join you in your testing phase? That way we can get two points of view. I'm pretty well convinced already, seeing how quickly you cleaned this place up and how terrific you look after only two hours' sleep. And I am looking forward to the enhanced sexual desire part. That could be fun."

Millie smiled and welcomed her aboard. "Sure, come on along. It'll be good to get your input."

THREE WEEKS INTO THE PROGRAM, neither Millie nor Talley suffered any side effects. Without any increase in dosage, they experienced the same remarkable boost in energy, maximized focus, and enhanced productivity. Caida libre surpassed their wildest expectations. Millie filed a patent on her formula to make sure sly copycat product manufacturers could not blindside them. A platoon of long-distance truck drivers and a host of working girls from the old Slice of Heaven joined their ranks. Truckers gave them transcontinental logistic capability to shipping concerns all over the States and the world. The girls were there for moral support, to relieve tension, and to entice new prospects. With little deliberation, they named their new outfit Nomad, a fitting name for a mobile business. A moving target was much harder to locate than a stationary one. They converted oversized RV coaches into rolling labs to produce the caida libre granules. While RV conversions were in progress, the Nomad founders set up their new network in what were often referred to as *fly-over* states. For decades, the federal government scammed members of family-owned farms and ranches with broken promises and bold-faced lies. Hard-working folks were foreclosed on by the same government that supposedly had their backs. Gutted so deep by regulations, farmers and ranchers were forced to develop cooperatives to survive. Middle America was anxious to even the score on greedy self-centered half-assed politicians who'd played them for fools.

What made the prairie states so attractive to Talley was less population, more open spaces, tornadoes, disgruntled inhabitants, and root cellars. Each of which had little consequence on its own; collectively, they were exactly what Talley was after. Resentment grew among landowners with every new tax levied or mandate enforced on them, which sought to break their backs physically and monetarily. Desperate people were not opposed to desperate measures when their children were starving, their farms were confiscated, and their dreams were shattered. To relieve some of the financial burden placed on the farmers, Nomad paid the agricultural combines handsomely to conceal cleverly disguised caida libre goods among their agricultural produce? A win-win for both parties.

A solid concept. Only, how, when, and where could they safely transfer caida libre to the trucks? Easy. Nomad purchased strategically located truck stops on major interstates. Then upgraded the facilities to offer fuel, food, and lodging for truckers on long hauls, as well as RV parking and hookups for road warriors. Existing root cellars and storm shelters were converted into underground laboratories and storage to produce and stockpile caida libre.

Under cover of darkness, crates of caida libre labeled *Eggs* or *Fresh Produce* were loaded into refrigerated trailers parked nearby and transported cross-country to container ships leaving from US ports to foreign destinations around the world. It took a solid year to complete everything that had to be done. Which gave the world plenty of time to forget about the now defunct Sister Nation. On a lark, Millie thought of a witty name to call their roadside establishments, Nationwide Overnight Motels and Diners. Acronym, NOMAD.

IN AN EFFORT TO KEEP caida libre top secret, Talley chose not to divulge Millie's re-creation of the elixir to Tina and Rose. It was too important a discovery to entrust to anyone else, not a hint of its existence could be allowed to leak out. An admirable gesture had it not been for the micro spycam that Talley was not aware of—located in the choker Millie wore around her neck. Boris and Desiree saw every move and heard every word. A twinge of guilt penetrated Millie's conscience; she hated to deceive Talley—but her true loyalties lay with Desiree and Boris. In the long run, Talley would be all right—rich beyond her wildest dreams, Millie would see to it.

Believing the old adage that two people can keep a secret better than three, Talley kept Ramon out of the loop as well. To keep him occupied, she put him in charge of logistics, a position that did not require him to know exactly what was in the shipments he sent out, only that they got there safely and on time. Ramon was the right man for the job and developed a sound rapport with the truckers, the boat captains, and the lovely ladies who promoted the products.

All the pieces of their ingenious scheme gradually shifted into place. The purest caida libre granules were selected for special clients who preferred something inconspicuous with a greater shelf life. For those who preferred a thriftier product, Talley came up with a nifty solution. Under an assumed name and through a dummy corporation with no ties to Nomad, Talley sold a fifty-one percent interest in two of the Nomad properties to a novice group of pharma entrepreneurs betting on the come. The labs underneath the acquired facilities cranked out a pseudo version of caida libre sold by the new owners at a much lower price to an indifferent clientele.

To get to this point, it had taken luck and clever manipulation by Talley and Millie. It all began with a well-designed feint. Out of the blue, the two founders of Sister Nation dissolved their partnership after a huge falling out over a man. They both made it look so believable, the entire community fell for it. Thread by thread, they wove their sinister plan. The attack on the Sister Nation compound was an ingenious setup by Talley, to free her to move her enterprise elsewhere without raising suspicion. All it took was a couple of well-timed anonymous tips to lure foreign mercenaries to Napa, where they obliterated the Sister Nation memory.

WHILE THE NOMAD TEAM set about getting its ducks in order in Middle America, Mr. Xen sat alone at his desk in Hong Kong gloating over the ruination of Sister Nation. Not that he had anything to do with it personally, but from a business perspective, he was delighted they were gone. He finished off the last of an espresso and pulled out his PC to check emails. Most of them were unsolicited junk mail, which made him wonder why he went through this ritual every morning. One email caught his eye as he was about to sign off in disgust. It was from a trusted associate of his in the United States. It read: *"Good morning, sir, I hope all is well. Didn't know if you heard, but there is a rumor circulating here in the States about a new stimulant soon to hit the pharma market. No further details yet but will keep you informed. All the best, J."*

"Damnit all to hell," Xen screeched as he slammed his PC shut. "Is this crap ever going to stop? It's getting where an honest criminal can't get an even break. I wonder who it is this time. Probably a piss-ant splinter group from that Napa Valley bunch."

He leaned back in his chair and stared at the skylight in the ceiling, searching for answers to his own questions as his eyes followed a jet accelerating to altitude. To be on the safe side, Xen ordered his people to keep an ear to the ground and report anything they heard to him immediately. Still full of himself, he was aware of what to do to pesky competitors—just look at what happened in Northern California.

Xen had no idea the scope of the blueprint Nomad had in mind to invade his precious overseas market. The greedy trafficker was too busy peddling his products in Eastern Bloc drug markets that manufactured over-the-counter pain medications. Profits from the non-prescription segment of the drug business ballooned overnight into the largest-grossing entity in his stockpile of nefarious goods. He had little time to ponder trivial matters like a fledgling enterprise in the States.

CHAPTER 11

WITH NEMESIS STUCK in observation mode, Trey felt comfortable enough to relax and spend more time with his family. He and Jefferson spent eleven magical days in the United Kingdom, capped off when his son won the Open Championship at Carnoustie in Scotland, his second major championship victory of the season. In a magnificent show of talent and maturity, Jefferson dazzled the golf world and amazed a doubting press, as he brought home the Claret Jug.

The first order of business, when they got back to the ranch, was to celebrate with friends and family. Whether it was fate or pure luck during the function, Jefferson accidentally bumped into an auburn-haired, wide-eyed beauty named Reanna Eckhart. As a last-minute invitee to chaperone a nervous girlfriend, Reanna came to the celebration, and currently felt like a third wheel.

From a distance, Jefferson observed her obvious discomfort, walked over to her with a smile, and winked. "Never fear, my lady, I've come to your rescue. You are far too beautiful to remain here in the shadows. What say we show you off? Would you care to dance?"

"Why, yes, kind sir, I would love to. Oh, and by the way do you happen to know the bloke we are here to pay tribute to?" Reanna asked as she accepted his hand.

How refreshing, thought the man of the hour, who snickered and said he would do his best to find the *bloke* and introduce her. Spellbound, they danced, laughed, and talked throughout the evening. Instead of the stuffy, stuck-up crowd of fuddy-duddies she expected to encounter at the gathering, Reanna was having the time of her life, with a wonderfully attentive gentleman whose name she had yet to establish. Suddenly, the music stopped, and the emcee called for silence. Curiously, Reanna glanced over the crowd as the man called Jefferson McCall to the podium.

Jefferson began to walk toward the stage, then turned and asked her, "What do you think of Sam Irwin and Duck Soup? Do you like the band?"

Embarrassed. Reanna nodded and mumbled softly, "Yes."

"How about Bob Seger? Do you like his music?"

Again she nodded.

"Good, then stay put, I'll be back shortly."

Before he spoke to the gathering, Jefferson glanced over at Reanna and winked, and all the eyes in the place shifted in her direction. Oddly, she lost her uncomfortable feelings. It was as if she knew she belonged right there at The Circle M, smiling up at the man of the hour. He spoke from his heart with the smooth, easy confidence of a man who had a purpose in life and was well on his way to securing his goals. At that moment, she wanted to be by his side to support him on *their* life journey.

After he concluded his speech, Jefferson rejoined Reanna on the dance floor and Duck Soup cranked up "Like a Rock" by Bob Seger.

Reanna was impressed as they played the first few bars of the song, then overwhelmed to see Bob Seger stroll out on stage. The magic had only begun for Reanna and Jefferson.

TEXAS-BORN AND RAISED, Reanna Eckhart grew up as an only child in a small ranching town in the central part of the state called Bandera, locally known as the Cowboy Capital of the World because it was the staging area for many a cattle drive back in the day. A quiet, slow-paced town with solid country values, where her father settled after the second world war and built a sizable ranch. Her mother worked in the clothing section of a downtown department store and managed the household at the ranch. No stranger to hard work, Reanna grew up doing chores, learned to be self-sufficient, and before long, there was not much that she could not handle, especially if it came to ranching. As a family, they understood hardship, family values, and faith in God, and they voted their conscience and managed difficulties with solutions, not excuses. A stunningly gorgeous young woman, Reanna was never short of suitors—mostly foolhardy boys with one thing in mind. Motivated by her desire to succeed, she had no time for frivolity, or any interest in marrying some rich lamebrain glory-days high school jock who inherited his daddy's fortune and squandered the money on boy toys and extramarital affairs.

Desirous to make a difference, Reanna put herself through college with money she earned at their ranch. Partnered with her father, they bought and sold quality cattle and quarter horses. As a business major at Texas A&M, she focused on entrepreneurial courses that helped build on her and her dad's wealth. After graduating with honors, Reanna went back to Bandera where she incorporated her fresh ideas with her dad's experience to update, improve, and move their brand forward. Before long, the Eckhart Ranch became known for breeding the highest quality livestock in the Texas Hill Country, especially quarter horses.

Early in her twenties, already a successful entrepreneur, Reanna realized there was a significant void in her life—she yearned for a man to share her dreams. Not just any man, but one who was a special, caring man of principle. Done forever with Ken dolls sporting handsome faces and beach body physiques, with no personality or ambition. She'd rather carry on a conversation with a mannequin than listen to them ramble on about themselves and their conquests.

She was almost to the point of giving up when her best friend asked her to go with her to The Circle M for a big shindig. *Like they'd known each other forever,* described Reanna and Jefferson that first night.

Lost in each other after their chance meeting, they'd laughed their way into the early morning. Both were in hysterics over her not knowing he was the man being honored. All too quickly, it was time for her to go; neither one wanted it to end. As Jefferson leaned over to kiss her goodbye, Reanna felt the strangest, most wonderful sensation come over her. She threw her arms around him, drew his face toward hers, and kissed him passionately.

It wasn't long before Reanna moved in at The Circle M. She took a huge interest in Jeff's golf game, amazed at the control and power her man generated with such an effortless golf swing. Eager to learn, Reanna took care not to be a distraction as she observed in silence. Being among the top of American Quarter Horse breeders, she was fully aware of the commitment it took to be one of the best in the world. Mac and Trey occasionally came to the golf facility to join them for a refreshment break. Reanna and Mac went for walks through the gardens getting to know each other better, and to talk ranching, mostly horses. In no time, the McCalls embraced her as one of their own and were delighted when the couple got engaged.

Both families agreed Tara should assume the role of wedding planner, which she eagerly accepted. Tara suggested, until a location for the wedding was determined, no firm date would be set for the nuptial. It had to be somewhere exceptional, far away from The Circle M, in that their ranch seemed to be a magnet for disaster in the past. After considering numerous alternatives, the families agreed to a destination wedding at Sandy Lane in Barbados. Sandy Lane was one of the most exquisite resorts in all the world. Boasting three superb golf courses—The Old Nine, The Country Club, and the world-renowned Green Monkey—should Jefferson or the wedding guests feel the urge to test them out. The guest list was limited to thirty invitees per family to make things manageable.

Next on the agenda was to organize transportation. As her husband's and son's business manager, Tara dealt with many diverse companies through the years. One of her favorites happened to be the most exclusive cruise line in the world—Global Oceanic. A bright, engaging gentleman named Leif Larson, the current CEO of Global Oceanic was her contact back then, who over the years became a close friend. When his secretary notified him that a Tara McCall was on the line, Larson picked up immediately.

"Tara, how are you this fine day? Well, I hope. What can I do for you?" Larson asked cheerfully.

Getting straight to the point she answered, "We are all fine, Leif, thanks for asking and hope you are too. The reason for my call is twofold. Our son Jefferson and his fiancée Reanna are getting married. Trey and I would love to invite you and your lovely wife Lalani to attend the wedding at Shady Lane in Barbados. And we wondered if we could charter one of your smaller all-ocean-view-suite vessels for a two-week cruise, roundtrip from Miami to Barbados?"

"What great news about the wedding. Congratulations. My wife, Lalani, and I are honored to be invited and happy to accept. Of course, we would love to be of assistance in any way we can with transportation. It just so happens Global Oceanic has a brand-new one-hundred-passenger ship that would be perfect for your cruise. Let me know the dates so I can work out the details on our end and send them along to you. It's a magnificent vessel, ideal for you and your guests," Larson preened.

After a slight hesitation, he added, "One other matter if you don't mind. You, Trey, and I have always had a close business relationship. Seeing as your boy Jefferson is taking the golf world by storm, we here at Global Oceanic would like to add him on as one of our family and offer him a multi-year endorsement contract to represent the cruise line. With the blessing of my cruise line board, I'd like to throw in the Barbados cruise as a signing bonus. Let's say the timing of your call could not have been more perfect."

Tara had to catch her breath before she replied, "Leif, I, we are honored by your proposal. I'm sure Jefferson will be delighted as well. "

"My pleasure! We've loved having the McCalls as part of Global Oceanic's family. I'll send you a detailed contract for your review including our wedding gift of the Barbados cruise. Have your legal team peruse the documents, and if they have any questions, please feel free to have them contact me personally. When you decide on the dates for the wedding, let me know and we will take care of all the travel arrangements."

Tara stuttered, searching for the right words to express her gratitude. "This may … you have … What an absolutely marvelous gesture on your part. Thank you so very much for being such a great friend to us over all these many years. I will provide you with all the details. Leif, you have made my day."

With the wedding plans firmed up and the unexpected cruise line endorsement offer on the table, Trey and Jefferson were thrilled and relieved. It meant they could focus their time and effort preparing for the PGA Championship, hosted at the Ocean Course on Kiawah Island, South Carolina.

CHAPTER 12

CHANCES WERE THE WEATHER in South Carolina would mirror what Jeff faced at Carnoustie in Scotland for the Open Championship: gusty ocean winds, possible rain showers, although considerably warmer than overseas. A Pete Dye–designed track, the Ocean Course had tiny greens, tough driving holes, and demanding par threes. Sandy waste areas dotted with wispy sea grasses dominated the rough and came into play more as wind speeds increased. Balance was key to playing well in the wind, which became the primary thing the McCalls worked on in preparation for the championship.

Following their major championship routine, Trey and Jefferson flew to South Carolina a week early to settle into their rental house and get in as many pre-tournament rounds as possible. Trey took their preparation a step further at Kiawah. Even though Dance was on the bag for the championship, they hired a local caddy to accompany the McCall team around the course for the practice rounds. Being a very good player in his own right, the veteran caddie, Sam Knowles, knew the ins and outs of the Ocean Course. Dance welcomed Sam's input and listened attentively to the local knowledge he'd accrued during countless rounds of golf over the challenging seaside links. For the most part, the Atlantic Ocean bordered the layout, which meant that wind was most likely going to be a factor. Jefferson thrived in the wind because of his ability to hit the ball solidly, and his incredible short game gave him confidence to take chances when necessary. Trey knew his son was ready, he could see it in his boy's eyes.

Monday evening Tara and Reanna showed up in time to witness a beautiful sunset as the sun slipped away as if swallowed whole by the marshland in the background. Jefferson lovingly wrapped his arms around his fiancée, blessed to have her in his corner. They had a calm, relaxed air about them, totally on the same page in their drive and aspirations. Reanna was there to give Jefferson all the support she possibly could.

For each of the four days of the championship, the Ocean Course lived up to its reputation as one of the toughest in the major events rotation. Unpredictable winds blew at inconsistent speeds from different directions each day, the temperatures fluctuated from the low nineties down to the low sixties as weather fronts entered and exited the coastal area. Thunderstorms caused a several-hour delay on Saturday. Fortunately, with a field of seventy players making the cut, they were able to finish the third round as the sun was going down. Sunday seemed a combination of all the previous days rolled into one. Contestants were constantly putting on, then taking off rain gear, umbrellas going up then coming down. Winds continued to swirl around the course at various velocities, playing havoc with golf balls in mid-flight and ending the life of numerous umbrellas, turning them inside out with their gusts.

When he entered the final three holes, McCall was two shots out of the lead playing in the second-to-last pairing. All three holes followed the shoreline; a brutal wind gusted off the golfers' left out to sea. After a birdie at the sixteenth, Jefferson waited patiently for the group ahead to finish the 221-yard seventeenth. A roar from the green at sixteen meant the leader made a birdie to retain his two-shot advantage. Finally, the green was clear at seventeen; the wind howled off the left, gusting, swirling, dying down, then returning with a vengeance. An instant before he started the club back, a gust blew the ball off the tee. Unfazed, Jefferson bent over, tossed the tee aside, and placed the ball on the turf. Then he smashed a three iron on a low trajectory, drawing toward the left side of the tiny green guarded by bunkers left and ocean right. As Jefferson watched his shot, he knew he'd hit the proper shot to put the ball on the green.

Sometimes golf was cruel even to the very best players. His shot landed on a slope tilted severely to the right, instead of the bounce he expected toward the hole, the ball dived left and ran through the left bunker into the tall grass beyond. All he could do from there was hack the ball out into the bunker and hope to get up and down for bogey. Sadly, his ball rolled into a seam left by a poor rake job in the group ahead. With the ocean only a few yards from the right side of the green, his best option was to play to the front edge of the green, where he two-putted for a double-bogie five. Barring a catastrophic finish by the leader, Jefferson's chances for a victory were slim. He birdied the last hole to keep his hopes alive but to no avail; he finished second, by two shots. In the scoring tent, he shook his head while he carefully reviewed his scorecard, then signed it.

Jefferson sat back in his chair and flashed back to something his father shared with him years ago. *"Son, if you play this game of golf long enough, anything that can happen to you—will.*" He slowly nodded his head as he thought about that and what Trey added. *"It's the nature of the game, you don't have to like it. But to be successful, you must accept it."*

While Jefferson gathered his wits in the scoring tent, Trey's thoughts drifted to how much golf mirrored life in that it required discipline, stamina, preparation, patience, self-control, and execution under pressure—the very same principles he exhibited on a daily basis at Nemesis. And the reason Trey was able to reinvent his life from the professional golf tour to cybercrime investigation, with the capability to navigate the fine line between both careers.

WHEN THEY GOT BACK TO TEXAS from Kiawah, Jeff and Reanna invited her parents, Marcus and Sheila Eckhart, to The Circle M ranch to help finalize plans for the wedding. In a freak accident days before they were scheduled to leave for Kiawah, Sheila suffered a bad fall and bruised her hip. On the mend now, she was excited to be part of the preparations for the big day at Sandy Lane. Sidney Baker, the McCall's female lead council and longtime confidant, worked behind the scenes for months using Warlock to vet and organize the guest list invitees for the two households. After which she coordinated flights and assigned cabins aboard ship for the lucky attendees approved for the mega-social gathering.

Leif Larson provided them with one of his most exquisite ships in his cruise line, *Serendipity*, manned by his most experienced crew sailing from Miami to Barbados on September 21 and returning on November 4. At an average speed of twenty knots, the ship would be at sea for three-and-a-half days each way, one week total in transit, leaving a glorious week sandwiched in the middle to enjoy the wedding and what Barbados had to offer.

Sidney arranged for Reanna and Jefferson to exchange their vows on a private beach nestled in a lovely, secluded cove, followed by the wedding reception at the resort. During their stay, the newlyweds made a stunning private villa at Sandy Lane their home, while the guests had the option to stay on the ship or in a luxury room at Sandy Lane. Twenty highly trained Nemesis personnel provided security, along with sixty passengers and a crew of twenty; the total on board came to exactly one hundred.

On the evening of September 20, passengers and crew on the luxury voyage to Barbados congregated at a five-star resort hotel near the port of Miami for an open-bar reception and a sit-down surf and turf dinner arranged by Sidney Baker. Each person collected their picture ID for the two-week excursion when they checked in at the welcome desk. Without exception, from now on until they docked back in Miami, everyone had to display their credential on a lanyard worn around their neck.

Serendipity set sail at noon for the first leg of the cruise with its crew and lighthearted passengers safely boarded, a few the worse for wear from the previous night's welcome party. An impressively designed ship, *Serendipity* was one of the sleeker, swifter vessels in Larson's fleet and without a doubt the most lavishly furnished. It was the optimal size to accommodate the one hundred folks aboard without feeling the least bit cramped. It had the speed to outrun storms if necessary or reroute around them. Suites were surprisingly spacious, each with a balcony facing out to the ocean. Although the boarding process took longer than usual since IDs were so closely scrutinized, the rest moved along swiftly, and they left the dock on time bound for Barbados cruising at a speed of twenty-five knots. Seas were calm, a welcomed state for those prone to seasickness or late-night recklessness.

TO HIM IT SEEMED AS THOUGH EVERY media outlet in the world broadcast the McCall wedding as breaking news on a continuous loop. Xen grew tired of the fanfare, fed up hearing about such an ostentatious waste of money—on a "destination wedding." There was more to his disdain than just that. Since Xen had been in the international import-export *business*, Nemesis had been a thorn in his side. No telling how much money they cost him over the years with their meddling. The McCalls were so high and mighty up there on their pedestal, glaring down at the heathens below. It pissed him off that there had been nothing he could do to stop them. Then it hit him. He couldn't believe he hadn't thought of it when he first heard the news. A dual scheme to wreak revenge on the McCall family and at the same time send a stern warning to his other adversaries to leave him alone. Seconds later, he was on the phone to line up a ship and a crew of mercenaries.

Serendipity's course followed commercial sea lanes, and so far, all was well, not a hint of anything suspicious. Blips on the *Serendipity's* radar were attributed to the popularity of the route she was on to Barbados. Unfortunately, one of those blips was not a friendly—the *Incubus* manned with mercenaries hired by Mr. Xen. Their mission was to keep an eye on the cruise ship, report in each evening, and await specific orders as the ships approached their destination.

Although Xen was cognizant of the existence of Warlock, he was not fully aware of its uncanny capabilities. At this moment, he was clueless that not only had the mega-computer uncovered his given name, Kim Tong, and his life history, the program hijacked all communications between him in Hong Kong and his men aboard *Incubus*.

When Miranda Stevens first picked up the communiques, she recorded the conversations and played them back to Trey and Tara McCall aboard *Serendipity*. The timing bothered Trey. Why now? For what reason? A sideshow maybe? A diversionary tactic to draw attention away from a more significant operation in the works? Nothing else made sense.

WHILE TREY AND XEN played mental chess in the Atlantic Ocean, a small army of scientists experimented with deadly contagions on a small island in the South China Sea. Operating under specific orders from Xen, they worked around the clock to develop pathogens communicable by physical contact or through the air. Bacterial proteins that he intended to blend into everyday products like hairspray, air freshener, disinfectant wipes, and the like, designed to induce forgetfulness, fatigue, apathy, and symptoms of severe depression and paranoia.

Once perfected and administered, Xen's pharma colleagues would introduce an antidote to counter the maladies and make the patients feel on top of the world. A miracle cure delivered in vaccines and capsules, made available to the masses, laced with enough narcotics to ensure a steady stream of addicted clientele worldwide.

CHAPTER 13

FOR THE FIRST FEW DAYS of the cruise, the seas were unseasonably calm. Taking advantage of the conditions, the captain of *Serendipity* increased her speed. *Incubus* followed suit but maintained a reasonable distance between the two vessels so as not to raise suspicion. While Nemesis monitored communications between Xen and *Incubus*, the mood among the civilian crowd was kept light and festive. If the situation became threatening, Nemesis was prepared to take appropriate measures. There happened to be a United States Navy aircraft carrier on a port visit anchored off Bridgetown, Barbados, to lend a hand if necessary. In the meantime, daylight activities included much more than the usual shuffleboard and lounging by the pool. Golf clubs and balls were at hand for passengers to hit shots off artificial turf, where Trey offered helpful tips for golfers who wished to hone their golf swings. For those who chose to sharpen their aim, a skeet-shooting stand was set up on the deck above. A casino ran twenty-four-seven for gamblers to test their luck while a full gym with personal trainers gave passengers a chance to melt off a few pounds the exquisite cuisine aboard ship added to their waistlines. Bars and lounges located strategically about the ship offered cocktails and wines of the finest blends and vintages. If anyone was bored, it was through no fault of the cruise line or the McCalls.

An entirely different scenario existed aboard *Incubus*. Hired soldiers trained, cleaned weapons, and surveyed their quarry in an atmosphere that was anything but festive. Every evening at eight p.m. sharp, the commander aboard *Incubus* reported to Mr. Xen. Warlock intercepted their conversations that were meticulously scrutinized by cybercrime agents back in Texas and aboard *Serendipity*. Nemesis watched and listened for anything fishy.

SERENDIPITY WAS MAKING RECORD TIME on the placid seas. So much so the captain called Trey to the bridge. They were well ahead of schedule, and the skipper wondered if the passengers might like to spend half a day on a private island the company owned. It was a short detour from their current course. In addition to an extra special treat for the passengers, it gave the captain an opportunity to stock more supplies. Trey agreed to the spur-of-the-moment junket, a maneuver that was sure to shake up his pursuers.

In the inlet off the shore of the privately owned island, the water was crystal clear; local schools of fish in hues of a rainbow darted about beneath the surface. Colorful umbrellas decorated the beach, lounge chairs rested evenly in rows. Huge palm trees swayed in the gentle breezes, and inside tiki huts, wait staff dispensed food, drink, water sports paraphernalia, and souvenirs. While dinghies full of supplies were transported from the island to the ship, passengers were shuttled close to shore and waded onto the beach. The island jaunt was an unexpected yet delightful afternoon of fun in the sun, embellished with umbrella drinks and delicious pupus. As sunset approached, passengers were shuttled back to the cruise ship; *Serendipity* weighed anchor and resumed on its original course to Barbados.

Trey snickered a little at dinner when he checked out Miranda's memo from Texas. The communique from Xen to *Incubus* was laced with profanity. The unplanned stop *Serendipity* made to the island initiated an unscheduled call from the captain of the *Incubus* to his boss. At first, Xen was furious that the man broke protocol. Xen's orders were specific, unless it was a dire emergency, the eight-p.m. status call was to be the only communication between them. After the captain calmed him down, the two men had a civilized conversation. All the captain meant to do was apprise Xen of the course alteration, which could have been for any number of reasons—engine trouble, emergency on board, or mechanical malfunction. It was agreed the *Incubus* should keep its distance and continue to observe.

WHEN THEY REACHED BARBADOS, *Serendipity* dropped anchor offshore from Shady Lane; the wedding party and guests booked at the resort disembarked first and were ferried to the dock. Guests who preferred to reside on the ship were transported later for the rehearsal dinner and after party in the ballroom. The wedding was scheduled to take place several hundred yards down the beach at a charming, secluded cove at seven the following evening.

Erwin Crichlow, the resort events planner, handled the arrangements for Sandy Lane. Crichlow was a native of Barbados, his wife, Hiroko, was not. Xen contacted Hiroko to do him a small favor. When

Hiroko hesitated, he cautioned her that her father was currently under surveillance in Hong Kong and could be permanently detained with one phone call. Reluctantly, she agreed to provide him with the McCall wedding party agenda for the week, including locations and a detailed housing chart for the participants. In particular, he was interested in the bride and groom's accommodations. Warlock picked up and recorded all of their conversations.

UPON HEARING THE CAPTURED COMMUNIQUE, Trey and Tara assigned the bride and groom their own Nemesis bodyguard for the duration of the wedding cruise. For Reanna, Trey chose Cassiopeia Drakos, born to Greek parents who migrated to the United States several years prior to her birth. Cassiopeia came to Nemesis from the Army after surviving two tours in the Middle East. Fearless and skilled in combat, Cass, as she preferred to be called, was an expert with firearms, a black belt in martial arts, and adept at survival in hostile environments. Yet with all her history and qualifications, she came off as an innocent, breathtakingly beautiful young woman. Every man in the room turned to check her out when she entered, which she laughed off as the curse of inheriting Greek genes.

For Jefferson, Tara chose another combat veteran, Raife Whelan. A medal-of-honor recipient for his unselfish bravery under fire in combat, he was solid as a rock—six-foot-one inches tall, on a 180-pound frame of muscle, built around a thirty-inch waist. Out of habit, Raife wore his hair short and his face clean-shaven. He was ruggedly handsome in an outdoorsy way, sporting a year-round tan, with piercing steel-grey eyes that could stare a hole right through you. A daunting presence who carried himself with an air of purpose and the wherewithal to back it up.

Nemesis's prayers were answered when the beach wedding went off without a hitch. A docile ocean breeze kept the attendees comfortable. Jefferson kissed his bride to seal the deal, and all adjourned a few hundred yards down the beach for the reception.

Cass and Raife acted as ushers seating patrons on the proper family sides for the ceremony. After which, they left quietly to reassess their camouflaged sniper positions with unobstructed views of the beach, the hotel, and private residences. As a further precaution, they concealed motion sensors and cameras around the residence occupied by Jefferson and Reanna.

AS WITH THE WEDDING, nothing happened during the reception, or for the first few days after the festivities. Xen would have to act soon; in two more days, the McCall crowd would pack up to leave Barbados. Aware of the time constraint, security tightened, although the guests didn't notice. Even Jefferson and Reanna were at ease and joined in with the family for golf, boating, swimming, and sightseeing with no signs of suspicious activity anywhere around. Trey perceived it as a ploy by Xen to lull Nemesis personnel into a false sense of security. Chairman Trey McCall summoned Cass and Raife to his cabin to ask their opinions as agents with the most recent combat experience.

Not one for small talk, Trey got right to the point. "So, Cass, what do you think of the situation?"

"Sir, I believe they are going to test us tonight. It's the most feasible time, while all our guests are partying in a location they can circumvent. Tomorrow night everyone will be scattered about, packing for the cruise home."

"And, Raife, how about you?"

"Sir, I think Cass is right. We should deploy our agents in the underbrush up and down the coast around sunset. Their best bet is to come at us from out of the west around the point, giving them the most cover for the longest period of time. From our camouflaged positions, Cass and I will keep an eye on them, while our agents circle in behind and either capture or finish them off."

"Perfect. Plan to be in position at dusk this evening." Trey dismissed the agents and gathered the McCall family together for an update.

LIFE ABOARD *Incubus* went from boredom to pandemonium in a matter of seconds after Xen contacted the captain of the ship, giving him the order to make ready for the invasion at nightfall. While Xen related the details of the mission to his commanders at sea, Nemesis agents listened in, recorded what was said, and instantly passed it on to Trey and his team on the island. As Raife predicted, the invasion force of a dozen men chose to come from the west around the point as darkness approached, then disembark on a secluded part of the beach a quarter of a mile from the guest house where the newlyweds resided.

DISCREETLY, SIDNEY BAKER organized a last-minute *bonus* clambake, to be held on the opposite side of the hotel from the residences. Featuring an open bar, fresh seafood dinner buffet, dancing to a steel drum band, and fireworks to cap off the evening. All the guests signed up for the night of food, drink, and dancing. Now that the innocents were occupied and out of the way, Trey's people finalized and coordinated the welcome committee task force's locations and assignments.

Sidney Baker's idea to have a fireworks display for the improvised gala to mask the sound of distant gunfire was brilliant.

Late afternoon, Trey McCall assembled all his agents to go over their individual assignments and answer any last-minute questions. Nemesis had twenty-one soldiers on the island spaced equidistant from each other in the brush bordering the beach and thick sea grasses encircling the guest house. Each had earbuds tuned to the same secure frequency, AR15s equipped with infrared laser sights with extra thirty-round magazines, a nine-mil Smith & Wesson, and a Gerber serrated combat knife. Dressed in camo outfits and black/green face paint to blend into the foliage. Trey issued one final order before his agents broke to inspect their gear and go over last-minute logistics: Nemesis forces were not to engage unless fired upon.

AS PART OF THE EXPANDED SECURITY afforded to dignitaries who visited Sandy Lane, the guest residence occupied by the newlyweds had an impenetrable saferoom that Jefferson and Reanna would move into just before dark. It was about the size of a small suite at the hotel, with all the accoutrements. Access was hidden behind a large sliding panel in the library of the house beautifully blended into a wall of dark wood. With its own separate oxygen and water supply, it was fireproof with an emergency escape tunnel leading up to a grass-covered hatch exit near the beach. Defensive measures were taken care of; all Nemesis had to do now was wait.

A THIRTY-FIVE-YEAR-OLD Serbian named Damir served as commander for the incursion force. Damir left the military when he grew tired of taking orders from imbecilic army officers and getting little in the way of compensation for risking his life in desolate mountain regions. Soon after he heard about the outfit Xen put together, and the lucrative payday, Damir decided to join.

Given the weather forecast, for the life of him, Damir couldn't figure out why Xen wanted to attack on the first night. To begin with, they would travel downwind to their destination where every little sound would ride on the wind, easily heard ahead on the island. To make things worse, the forecast called for a full moon, which would make them much more visible to possible lookouts on the beach. He felt it was more advantageous to go on the second night amid overcast skies with a wind from the opposite direction. When Damir voiced his concerns to Xen, the arrogant fool dismissed his argument pointing out that they had the element of surprise and the order stood.

Had it not been for the attractive salary and generous bonus this assignment promised, Damir would have resigned and walked away. But then again, perhaps he read too much into it and overreacted. Damir promised himself if they pulled off this raid tonight, he would take his money and buy a small island where he would retire. A peaceful paradise to spend the rest of his life relaxing with a beautiful young babe in a hammock on the beach, drinking Red Stripe beer while tropical sea breezes caressed the palm fronds, providing shade from the sun overhead.

AS THE OCEAN APPEARED to swallow a golden sun, eighteen men disembarked *Incubus* in three reinforced rubber rafts headed for the beach around the point. Small whitecaps formed on the waves as the wind freshened, soaking the men and tarps that covered the equipment. For the moment, clouds filled the sky, and they traveled in almost complete darkness, forced to rely on memorized landmarks on shore to keep them on course. Then the clouds disappeared, and the sky suddenly lit up, with a full moon that shone with a brightness near that of the sun, casting shadows as the two main landing crews gathered on the beach. The third raft remained anchored offshore in case reinforcements were needed. An ominous feeling overtook Damir as he and his men made their way toward the guest house.

Everything was too quiet. Contrary to the norm, the shore area was devoid of any bird or scampering animal sounds associated with a beach setting at night—something or someone had frightened the wildlife away. Seriously disturbed, Damir considered calling off the mission, until the Serbian recalled his conversation with Mr. Xen earlier. Reluctantly, he signaled his men to hasten their pace. Ignoring a cardinal rule of engagement, the mission leader substituted expediency for efficiency, which left the door wide open for mistakes. At this point, Damir didn't care. It was up to him to follow the orders given by his superior. He and his men were winded when they reached the grassy lawn outside the guest house.

While his men knelt to rest, Damir surveyed the front of the impressive residence with infrared binoculars. To his surprise, he saw no one and heard nothing. Maybe Xen was right about the McCalls becoming lax in their duties so close to their departure from Barbados. Experience kicked in, and Damir took his time checking in the trees, the scrub bushes below, and the rooftop of the house searching for Nemesis personnel. Still, he detected nothing; the deafening quiet unnerved him. Warily, he signaled his men to proceed slowly across the lawn to the porch of the house.

Damir felt more than saw what was happening and shouted for his men to scatter for cover a moment before a voice pierced the silence to inform him that he and his men were surrounded. Reflexively, he fired a burst from his automatic rifle in the direction of the voice and watched as a speaker located high in a palm tree exploded like a skyrocket, illuminating the front lawn of the guest house.

In desperation, the mercenaries retreated toward the beach firing at anything that remotely bore resemblance to a human shape. Several statues were demolished in the fray; fortunately, none of Trey's defensive force was hit. From their lofty sniper perches, Cass and Raife picked off four of the escaping hostiles, Nemesis agents seriously wounded another two. Five more surrendered at the beach when they noticed red dots dance about their bodies from a bevy of AR-15s aimed at them.

USING THE NOISE AND CONFUSION as a distraction, Damir took a less direct route to the beach as he belly-crawled around to the rear of the house and then used the foliage as cover to work his way farther down the beach. If only he could get to one of the boats, maybe he could escape back to *Incubus*.

A near miss by Cass that took a chunk out of the stucco on the side of the house alerted Damir that he'd been spotted. Now scampering for his life, Damir was furious with himself. Why didn't he listen to his inner voice? How could he have been so damned stupid? One of the rafts was just ahead tethered to an ancient palm. He glanced around, then broke cover to race the last twenty yards to it. Only a few yards short of the boat, he heard a voice behind him tell him to halt and drop his weapon. Panicked, Damir dived behind the palm to take cover and peek back at his pursuer. Surely his eyes were playing tricks on him;

could it really be a beautiful woman drawing a bead on him? When he did not respond to her second command, she fired a warning shot that kicked up the sand beside his right foot. In his mind, the Serbian had little choice. The moment he twirled around to fire at her, Damir felt something hit him with enough force to knock him down on his back. Blood gushed from a gaping hole in his chest, spilling out onto the warm, sandy beach; his last vision in this world was a lovely woman standing over him as a gentle breeze tickled the fronds on the giant palm. His dream had come true—just the wrong woman, wrong beach, wrong palm.

Reinforcements in the third rubber raft witnessed the scene on the beach and hightailed it back to *Incubus* to report what they'd seen to the captain, who immediately made his way to international waters. After setting his course to full speed ahead, the captain reluctantly contacted Xen to give him the bad news.

WHEN HE RECEIVED THE SHIP-TO-SHORE call from *Incubus*, Xen was in his massive hot tub at his penthouse in Hong Kong, enjoying the pleasures of his harem of gorgeous women who frolicked around him in the frothing, steaming water. His ear-to-ear smile instantly turned into a menacing frown. Xen leaped straight up out of the water; his state of bliss shattered by what he heard. In a fit of rage, he ordered his bevy of beauties to get the hell out of the hot tub and vacate the premises immediately. Familiar with his mood swings, the girls left on the run, in degrees of undress, much to the delight of male guests waiting for the down elevator in the hallway.

ONLY ONE OF THE BEAUTIES STAYED BEHIND, his personal secretary and bodyguard, Akira Ito, a Japanese lovely who had been with Xen as his most trusted ally for decades. Ninja-like, she was intense, gorgeous, yet deadly, having studied and perfected the most aggressive martial arts. Brilliant in mind as well as body, Akira spoke seven languages fluently, nearly accent-free, including English. After she slipped her flawless body into a kimono, Akira joined Xen in the library of his gigantic suite. At a moment like this, he needed advice from a confidant with no scruples.

Visibly distraught, Xen explained what had just taken place in Barbados, the men he had lost, and more importantly the failure of the mission. Baffled as to how Trey McCall and Nemesis anticipated his every move, he was desperate for fresh ideas of how to proceed from here. Listening closely, Akira's eyes lit up.

Observing her reaction, he asked, "Well, do you have something you would like to contribute?"

"Yes, I believe I do. You say this enemy of yours knows your every move, despite the fact you have taken all the proper security precautions, am I correct?"

Xen nodded.

She continued, "Let me contact some friends of mine who are, let's say, way ahead of the curve as far as security matters are concerned. I believe they could be of great assistance in this matter. It would be my pleasure to contact them for you if you would like. And if I'm not mistaken, your little invasion did create a media distraction away from a much more important agenda matter."

"Yes, you are so right. It's just that the security issue with Nemesis troubles me. Check into it and let me know. I should have come to you in the first place."

His confidant nodded, then moistened her lips. "You are a wise man, shall we return to the warmth of the hot tub to complete our unfinished business?"

As he grabbed her hand to lead her, his ear-to-ear grin returned; her kimono slid to the ground when they arrived. An hour later, Xen was sound asleep in his bedroom.

TEN YEARS AGO, Akira, a brilliant, alluring young lady only nineteen years old, caught Xen's eye. Before long, Akira was working as his personal assistant. A position she secretly parlayed into a lucrative corporate espionage business. During her covert dealings, she'd learned about Warlock and how Nemesis spied on its adversaries, but she kept it to herself. She knew better than to trust Xen with anything that important; he was too mercurial and driven solely by greed. With the information she possessed, Akira could make a quick fortune. Or hold on to her cards and play her hand later on in the game. She chose the latter.

WHEN THE SKIRMISH in Barbados hit the world press organizations, it was passed off as a foiled robbery attempt by local crooks seeking to make a big score off wealthy guests at Sandy Lane. Still, it occupied the headlines for weeks with breaking news, which wasn't breaking or real. Fabricated stories were fact-checked, discarded, then reincarnated. Attendees on site had no idea what really happened. They believed the commotion at the residential beach was all part of a huge, dramatic fireworks display.

CHAPTER 14

EMPLOYING THE US HIGHWAY SYSTEM as their office, Nomad techni-
cians mass produced the Mayan-inspired additive in their mobile home
labs on the way to their four Nomad underground warehouses. From
there, the product was transported around the world by land, sea, and
air. Talley patted herself on the back once again for another brilliant idea
to confound nosey investigators. She'd sold fifty-one percent interest in
several underground facilities to local yokels, who continued to produce
the same narcotic-infused substances Sister Nation introduced to the
marketplace in the past. Her forty-nine percent was tucked away inside
an assortment of dummy corporations, managed by an overseas pseudo
conglomerate, under the auspices of Albatross LLC, a Croatian holding
company she set up in anticipation of the Sister Nation's downfall.

The good ol' boys' subterranean labs were operated solely
under their new management. Neither Talley, Millie, nor Nomad
were mentioned in the cash transaction. Cocksure that the Warlock
computer program run by Nemesis was eavesdropping on the Nomad

groups' communication, Millie and Talley resolved to never mention caida libre or Le Serena in any correspondence written or spoken.

All the early warning signs were there; it was inevitable the facilities that produced narcotic additives would fail as had their predecessors. Until then Talley and Millie would make a nice chunk of cash to put toward Nomad, before they vanished. Nemesis would most likely follow the new owners down the rabbit hole, leaving Nomad to sail along above reproach.

THE NEMESIS CYBERCRIME unit realized international organized criminal elements like Xen's were aware of Warlock by now. It would only be a matter of time before they figured out how to neutralize or at least circumvent its current abilities to snoop without detection.

Fearful of losing his edge, Noah Bouchard, the mastermind behind Warlock, worked tirelessly in his lab in Canada to stay ahead of innovations taking place in a lightning-paced cyber industry. Nearly an octogenarian, Noah thought of it as a challenge to keep his mind fresh and his reactions sharp. At some point, Noah would lose a step, something he and Nemesis prepared for with their ace in the hole—Tara McCall. She shared Noah's passion and, thanks to his tutelage, understood the unlimited potential of Warlock.

Routinely, she visited Noah and his wife Greta at their home near Banff, known as the Monastery, where she spent most of her time with Noah in his lab, soaking up knowledge from the cyber-master. Tara had a gift; Noah spotted it and cultivated it. She was intuitive, revolutionary, and fearless. If something were to happen to the elderly computer genius, Tara had the wherewithal to continue executing Warlock protocols without missing a beat.

TREY HAD SOME SERIOUS DECISIONS of his own to make about their cybercrime business for the future. Well on his way to becoming one of the best players ever on the PGA Tour, Jefferson could not be expected to assume the helm of Nemesis when Trey retired. Although Trey continued to fight the good fight, worldwide corruption ran rampant, and it seemed two new criminal enterprises showed up to every one they eliminated.

In their suite at Sandy Lane, after an exhausting day doing her part to smooth over the mess in Barbados, Tara McCall was sound asleep. So lovely, she aged like fine wine. The only giveaways were a few silver hairs peeking out of her jet-black hair, and maybe a wrinkle or two that snuck in when she smiled. Ever since she and Trey reunited decades ago at a high school reunion, she had been his rock—always strong and supportive. Concerned about the current state of flux generated by their adversaries, Trey regretted the constant danger he subjected her to. What would she say, he wondered, if she knew what he was thinking right now? Knowing her, she'd probably give him a piece of her mind, tell him to forget all that silly foolishness, and sternly remind him the world needed men like him to combat all the evil.

Trey burst out laughing when Tara stirred and asked him what he was thinking.

"I would love to share if I could get all my thoughts straight. Right now I'm so confused. We have so much to be thankful for, and I don't want to jeopardize that. Someone could have gotten hurt in that firefight tonight. And Nemesis …"

She interrupted him right there, "Hold on. We all knew what we were signing up for when we joined Nemesis. Don't even go there with me. Nemesis makes the world a better place. Don't forget divine intervention. Relax and let the One who's in control, be in control."

Transfixed on his wife, he took in all of what she'd said. Finally, he responded, "Well, I guess I had that coming. You are absolutely right, of course, and that is one reason I love you so much."

"Well then, why don't you come over here and show me your appreciation," Tara countered with a wicked, seductive glint in her eyes.

Unable to resist such a welcoming suggestion, Trey slid over and kissed her passionately and she responded in like. As gentle sea breezes stirred the sheer drapes on the open window of their suite, they made love to the tropical sounds of the whistling frogs of the Barbados night. Without fail, Tara always made their world better; still, he had lingering concerns over the future of Nemesis. Who would take over the helm when he left, and would that person's passion be enough to motivate the team to stay the course against an increasingly cruel and senseless world?

AS THE *Serendipity* weighed anchor to leave Barbados for the trip back to Miami, Talley and Millie were busy in mid-America, working out details of how to introduce their newly developed Mayan formula into the international marketplace. Talley racked her brain for days before she came up with an idea that just might work. It was widely known that a major player in the Asian drug trade, a Mr. Xen, had a proclivity for beautiful women. Speculation went as far as to say he had his own harem from around the globe that he put on display at his outlandish parties. How about if Talley obtained a pair of invites to one of his wingdings and sent two knockouts the man couldn't miss. If the rumors about Xen were true, Nomad would have two chicks in the hen house. Millie could set up a dummy business, address, phone, fax, and email for the girls, independent of Nomad. No matter if Nemesis picked up communications between the bogus company and Xen, as long as it had nothing to do with human trafficking, the international investigations group would probably give it a pass.

Talley picked the cream of the crop from her stable. Both were not only beautiful, each was a college graduate, thanks to the money they'd earned at Slice of Heaven. Evangelina, Eva Moreno, was a Filipino lovely with flawless skin and alluring eyes, a slim yet curvy figure, with a fiery personality that refused to take no for an answer. And Victoria Novak, a five-foot-ten well-endowed Eurasian knock-out who tantalizingly filled out an evening dress. Her long jet-black hair cascaded to her waist, shapely legs, blue-green eyes, and a smile that melted hearts. Two showstoppers that turned everyone's head when they entered a room.

Mr. Xen fed his narcissism and overzealous ego with expensive art, lavish furnishings, a custom designer wardrobe, along with his troupe of female lovelies. At the end of each quarter, he hosted an exorbitant gathering for friends, business associates, and his most ardent customers. It just so happened that the end of the third quarter was fast approaching, which set up the ideal opportunity for Talley's two girls to get *recognized*.

Talley called in a huge favor from an old friend and secured a couple of invites for her girls to the shindig at Xen's penthouse in Hong Kong. If history held true, the prodigious dwelling would be bursting at the seams with bodies, business tycoons with their significant other or favorite companion, social climbers, loyal customers, suppliers, and of course scores of gorgeous ladies. The invitation said from seven p.m. until …

EVANGELINA (EVA) AND VICTORIA arrived just after 9:00 p.m. and threaded their way through the guests to the outside bar on the spacious patio. Both dressed seductively, leaving little to the imagination. Eva leaned nonchalantly against the bar. Victoria took a seat on a barstool, lit a cigarette, and blew out a plume of smoke as they surveyed the crowd looking for Mr. Xen. Across the way, a nattily dressed gentleman stared at them trying to figure if, when, or where he had seen them before. A few moments later, the man in question stood directly in front of them, introduced himself as their host, and welcomed them to his humble abode.

Victoria stood to greet him; her voluptuous assets met him at eye level as she was a good head taller than Xen. Awkwardly, he turned to Eva, took her hand, and gave it a gentle kiss. She smiled and winked with a devilish glint in her eye. Victoria took a drag on her cigarette and snickered under her breath, elated their host was so totally consumed by lust in their presence.

"I, uh, well, see that you smoke, I, we, don't usually allow smoking at my get-togethers ..."

When Victoria made a move to put her cigarette out, he gently grabbed her hand. "However, in your case, I'm going to make an exception, on one condition. You must honor me with a dance when the band plays the next slow song." His eyes were glued on Victoria's cleavage as she purposely bent over to adjust the hem of her skirt.

Victoria took another long drag on her cigarette, then ever so slowly, threw her head back to exhale the smoke into the night air, then uttered in a low, seductive, guttural tone. "But of course, Mr. Xen—tonight, your wish is our command."

SPURNED BY PURE CARNALITY, Xen frantically guided them away from the claustrophobic affair upstairs to his personal elevator for an express ride to his elegant private lair in the bowels of the building. His building was one of the most coveted addresses in Hong Kong. None of the other apartment owners knew he actually owned the ultra-exclusive high-rise building, and he wanted to keep it that way. It was much easier to converse with his neighbors if they believed he had the same grievances toward the management of the superstructure as they did.

The express elevator whisked them down to a subbasement that concealed a well-hidden staging area for a rapid escape by submersible into the South China Sea. Around a corner from the watertight sub berthing station was an elegant bedroom suite designed with one objective in mind: to lure his prey into his enormous bed that spread out over a quarter of the room. The anticipation of a romp in the hay with the two beautiful women was almost more than Xen could stand.

NO ONE EXCEPT AKIRA had ever had the pleasure of joining him in his underground domain. Members of his harem humored him in the "game room" of his penthouse, never in the grotto, his uniquely special place down below. Ever vigilant, Akira detected the conspicuous attention her boss paid to the two beautiful strangers that came late to the party. Things like that rarely bothered her, knowing he always came back to her bed for the night. She had a feeling these two were different, so she kept an eye on them for a while. For the moment, the three of them were conversing at the bar outside. Nature called, and Akira left her post to go to the ladies' room. When she returned, they were gone, all three of them. Slowly, she moved around the rowdy crowd searching for the tall brunette with the huge bosom, but she was nowhere to be found. By chance, she glanced toward the private elevator in Xen's master bedroom in time to see the doors closing and immediately guessed where they were headed. She was *furious*.

DECADES OF MARTIAL ARTS TRAINING taught her not to act in haste. Akira sat on the bed for a couple of minutes to gather her thoughts, then crossed the hall to her room to change into her sneakers from her high heels. She walked confidently to the emergency stairwell in Xen's bedroom hidden behind what appeared to be a solid wood panel and pushed on the upper right corner. There was a noticeable click as the panel silently slid sideways into the wall. Once inside, Akira picked up a flashlight attached to overhead jam and began her trek down seventy floors from the penthouse to the grotto.

On the long climb down, she cleared her head. Revenge murder was not a rational response. In her case, it would be disastrous as far as her future was concerned. If the diminutive self-proclaimed Don Juan wanted to play games—she was more than up to the challenge. As his private secretary, Akira was savvy to his connections worldwide, the scams he perpetuated, the organizations that were after him, and more than enough skeletons buried in his closet to get him hung many times over. By the time she reached the bottom floor, Akira knew what she was going to do.

Before she made the long ascent back up to the penthouse, she sat on the bottom step to catch her breath, content to remain oblivious of what Mr. Xen and the two strangers did or did not do in the grotto—it no longer mattered. For the longest time, she'd felt twinges of guilt for blindly obeying Xen's orders, justifying her actions out of what she thought was love for the man who loved her. The truth was he was incapable of love. *No more blind obedience*, she thought. Oh, she would make him believe she was still doing his bidding, and he would fall for it—for no other reason than his ego.

The climb back up the stairs should have been brutal, but now that she'd seen the light, it was a breeze. She actually enjoyed it in a cathartic way. Hours later, Xen slid in beside her in bed. Akira snuggled up against him, and he cupped her breast in his hand and fell asleep, just as he had done every night since they'd been together.

IT WAS A GOOD THING SHE ABANDONED her plan to confront Xen and his two new playmates. Akira may not have been able to contain her wrath had she witnessed the theatrics in the grotto. Caught up in the moment, Xen was delirious, oblivious to anything but the attention he was giving and receiving from the two sexual dynamos. When he was spent, Victoria and Eva left him exhausted in bed while they shuffled off to shower. Totally smitten, Xen stared like a teenager at their exquisite figures as they dressed, wishing he could manage one last hurrah. No chance of that since the previous session damn near killed him. Reluctantly, he slipped on a robe and accompanied them back into the elevator.

Weak in the knees from the marathon he'd just endured, Xen spent the elevator ride to the penthouse in a dazed silence. Never had he had a night like this—*never!* When they reached the top, Xen came to his senses long enough to hand them his card and make them promise to call him the following afternoon. Zombie-like, he crept to his bedroom and collapsed into the bed next to Akira. Oblivious to the fact she couldn't help but detect the scent of sex on his body. Like the uncivilized animal he was, Xen had not even had the common courtesy to shower before nestling up against her.

THERE WAS NO WAY OF KNOWING the number of spies Xen had in Hong Kong, and Victoria and Eva were too experienced to blow their cover with a premature celebration in the limo ride back to the hotel. Better to wait until they reached their suite. Even then, they made a diligent sweep of the place to make sure there were no cameras or listening devices to pick up unguarded conversation. Only when they were sure the coast was clear did they let loose, popping the cork on their first bottle of champagne. It was six o'clock in the morning, still time to party for a couple of hours, take a nap, then call their host from last night to thank him for a most memorable time. At noon, Victoria woke to find Eva sitting on the living room sofa, smoking and sipping champagne from a fresh bottle.

"Hope you don't mind. I stole one of your cigarettes. It's the same brand I smoked, until I quit. Last night you came off as so cool, way sexy, and totally in control exhaling that smoke over Xen's head, the horn-dog almost lost it. I forgot how much I enjoyed smoking—you don't mind, do you?" Eva inquired.

Victoria grinned and shook her finger at her girlfriend. "No, smoke all you want. Just don't blame me if you get hooked again. Who knows, it might just work for you too. By the way, when we make this call to Xen, I sense he's going to want us to come over tonight for a redo of last night. What say we string him along for a while to make him squirm, what do you think?"

Her partner in crime giggled. "I think that is a marvelous idea. We'll give it a few days, by then the old fart will be so worked up he'd give anything to have us pay him a visit."

Before she made the call, Victoria poured herself some champagne, lit her own cigarette, then reached for the phone to punch in his number. "Good afternoon, Mr. Tong's residence, his personal secretary

Ms. Ito speaking," Akira said professionally. "He is in the shower right now, please state the nature of your business and a number where you can be reached."

Not expecting a woman to answer, Victoria was ill prepared to respond to the personal secretary's request. Instead of giving her a straightforward reply, Victoria stammered a mouthful of idiotic gibberish about not having a number where she could be reached and would call back at a more convenient time.

ON THE OTHER END, Akira broke the connection and burst out laughing at the reaction of the bimbo from the previous night. Before deleting a record of the call, she jotted down the number displayed on the phone. She found the name of the condo-hotel complex where the call originated in a reverse directory, in case she decided to call or pay the girls a visit at a later date.

TWO DAYS LATER, the girls called Xen again; this time Eva took the reins and put the call on speaker. Xen answered and was not at all happy that the girls hadn't contacted him sooner.

When Eva was allowed to speak, she explained, "There must have been some kind of mix-up. Victoria and I called the other day to thank you for such a memorable time. We expected you to call us back. When you didn't, we thought we must have let you down."

There was a long pause at the other end. "What do you mean mix-up? Let down, how? I don't understand."

Victoria chimed in, "Hey, lover, Victoria here, missing you terribly. Wishing we had connected on my first call. Eva and I were all set for another wild night in the cavern like you promised. Thought maybe you were just another of those one-and-done guys who gave us the brush-off. Eva talked me into letting her try once more; she really digs your action in the rack. I must admit, so do I. We're leaving on a business trip this afternoon. What say we call you when we get back in town? Ciao."

"What phone call? When are you ..." His phone went dead.

Xen was baffled. He checked to see if they called two days before and, if so, had left a message. There was no record of a call. Akira walked in, and he asked her if she'd answered a call for him a couple of afternoons ago and forgot to give him a message.

"No, sir. Were you expecting an important call?"

He snapped at her angrily, "Yes. I mean, no, it is really of no consequence. You are excused."

She closed the door.

AKIRA SNARLED AS SHE TURNED to walk away and silently mouthed, *You are excused.* To be dismissed like one of his house whores made her insides churn.

One of Akira's duties as Xen's personal secretary was to ensure the penthouse and grotto security systems were constantly maintained and updated when necessary. Unbeknownst to Xen, she had new state-of-the-art micro spycams installed in the grotto. One specifically zeroed in on the combination lock of a seven-foot-tall steel-reinforced safe in the bedroom—where Xen kept his top-secret papers. The feed from the cameras was sent directly to a monitor concealed in a cabinet in Akira's bedroom closet. Obsessively paranoid, Xen changed the combination every morning so only he knew what it was at any given time. She was certain if she gained access to that safe, Akira would find more than enough concrete evidence to bury him.

Xen was careful to never go near the safe on the occasions he bedded Akira in the grotto. He only approached the dial to work the combination when he was down there alone. The miniature spycam engaged as soon as anyone rotated the dial, indicated by a tiny blinking light on the side of the receiver in Akira's closet. To make sure the video was clear enough to make out the numbers, she checked each time he went through his daily ritual with the safe. It was spot-on every time he changed the combination.

One afternoon after Xen left for one of his biweekly golf games, Akira turned off the new system monitoring the grotto and rode the elevator down to see if the combination she copied that morning opened the heavy door of the safe. She donned a pair of thin latex surgical gloves to maneuver the dial, and to her delight, it worked on the first try. Carefully she sifted through an assortment of documents to get an idea of what her boss valued so highly. It was a bonanza of classified material with lists of foreign agents, informants, assassins, lobbyists, and corrupt politicians. Digging deeper, she uncovered documentation that made the hair on her arms stand straight up. There was serious dirt on half the planet's most powerful men and women—including heads of governments, captains of industry, military elite, entertainers, athletes, you name it.

My god, she could own the man and many others if she wanted. But would she live to enjoy it? If he didn't kill her first, one of the others most certainly would. Even if she managed to get away from Hong Kong, her days would be numbered. And here she thought she was so clever going toe-to-toe with her boss, even believed she could actually outmaneuver him. What a fool she had been, or had she?

Now that Akira could lay her hands on up-to-date incriminating evidence on people resolute to run the world, there was one organization she knew of that could put this treasure trove of information to good use, and at the same time give her protection from the criminal world. Before she made contact with her potential benefactors, she must first covertly collect as much damning evidence as she could from the safe.

ON TUESDAYS AND THURSDAYS, Xen played a high-stakes golf game on a course an hour away from the penthouse. Departing around ten a.m., he usually got back by 7:30 p.m. for dinner. Judging from the contents she'd observed on her first go-round, it would take several visits to the safe to copy the files. Xen had no inclination of her clandestine plan. On days he was at the golf course, her boss assumed Akira went out shopping or some other useless waste of time.

Fortunately for Akira, the two new harlots from the latest quarterly blowout were toying with their prey—playing Xen like a fiddle. Clearly, the old man's mind was set on making those two the newest additions to his ever-growing harem. Akira saw it as a welcome distraction to keep his mind occupied with sexual conquests and away from business. Between the golf and Xen's preoccupation with maneuvering Eva and Victoria back to the grotto, Akira had enough free time to scan, copy, then place the copies in the safe. She concealed the originals in a floor cavity in her bedroom closet. The one place Xen swore to never visit again, after she'd kept him in her boudoir for hours one day while she tried on outfits. A brilliant plan of subterfuge on her part.

It took nearly a month for Xen to confirm a Friday night date with Victoria and Eva. Akira shook her head in disgust while she observed

Xen acting like a schoolboy, riding up and down in the elevator all day to make sure everything was just right for the evening. When Akira received an expletive-laced summons to come down to the grotto, she was frantic. What could he possibly want? Her mind raced back to the previous day when she completed her mission while her employer was away playing golf. Meticulously she retraced her movements in her mind, step by step to be certain she'd put everything back exactly how she'd found it. What had she missed? How could she have been careless this close to the finish? As soon as the elevator reached the bottom and the doors opened, she exited to the right for the bedroom. When she rounded the corner, she saw him holding something up in his hand.

His face was twisted, his voice rife with anger. "And where, my dear, do you think I found this?" It was a vial of lipstick with a disgusting stripe of purple on its cylinder.

So relieved she almost fainted, Akira managed a reply. "I have no idea, sir, and why should I?"

"It's yours I suspect, and I found it over by the safe. You know that is off limits. What in the hell have you been doing down here, anyway?"

Akira placed her hands on her hips and glared at him in disgust. "Not a damn thing, thank you very much! Might I suggest you find out whose lipstick that is before you start accusing people of things? That's just crude. My good man, I wouldn't wear that slutty shade on a dare. It must have rolled under the bed the other night when you brought those sluts down here. The maid probably dislodged it while she made the bed and it ended up near your precious fucking safe. If that is all, I'm out on my own for dinner tonight, then retiring early," Akira hissed as she twirled around and marched back to the elevators without another word. Sweating bullets on the ride up, her bottom lip quivered; she didn't know whether to laugh or cry.

A few minutes later, she answered the buzzer from the grotto. Seemingly in a fit of anger, Xen had thrown the vial of lipstick as hard as he could against the wall of the safe, shattering the case into pieces on the floor leaving purple lipstick stains on both. His attempts to clean up the mess had only made it worse, and he begged for her assistance. When she arrived, Xen gazed at her and maybe for the first time in his life felt embarrassed—like the little boy who'd just been scolded by his teacher in front of the whole class—scrambling for a hole to crawl into. Dutifully, Akira swept up the fragmented pieces on the floor and wiped down the front of the safe. His head stayed down, his eyes glued to the floor. In a roundabout way, she understood silence was his way of apologizing.

She smiled to herself and went back upstairs. He owed her one, but for now, his preoccupation with Eva and Victoria took precedence. And that gave Akira enough time to organize her escape with the cache of information. Fully aware the libelous material became radioactive as soon as word got out it was missing, she waited until the very last minute to contact the only group she felt could save her, Nemesis. Specifically, the head of the organization, Trey McCall.

COOLING HIS HEELS BACK IN TEXAS, Trey glanced over the report from his agents summarizing the raid they'd thwarted in Barbados. It was his responsibility to evaluate the overall handling of the mission as well as grade individual performances as excellent, acceptable, or poor. Every one of his team had done an outstanding job without sustaining any significant injuries and deserved the highest possible rating. As he scribbled his signature on the report, the inner office secure line buzzed.

Chairman McCall picked up immediately, "Yes, ma'am, what can I do for you this fine day?"

Tara sounded frantic. "Trey, you need to get down here to the lab pronto. If what we just received is any way near what it appears to be, it could be one of the most incredible breaks in international cybercrime fighting ever. Please hurry, I don't want to discuss this over the phone."

Instantly he leaped out of his chair and raced over to the crime lab building. Tara led him over to her desk and showed him a text from a burner phone she believed belonged to Akira Ito, Mr. Xen's most private secretary.

It read: *Sir, this will be the only message I'll be sending from this phone. I have a small window of time to escape Hong Kong before what I have done is discovered. When it is, I will be one of the most hunted persons in the world. I have incriminating evidence on some of the world's most influential figureheads in business, government, entertainment, and more. All of which I am willing to trade for sanctuary from the criminal elements sure to be on my tail. You are the only people I can trust. I beg you to accept my plea for help. A.I.*

When he'd finished reading it, Trey peered quizzically over at his wife. "Wow, what do you think? Is she for real or is this some sort of retaliatory ruse for Barbados?"

"Sounds to me like Xen wronged her in some way, probably for no good reason. I think she's had it with him and wants revenge. Sounds like a legit plea for help from us."

Trey gave her a thumbs-up. "That's the way I see it. Text her back, tell her we'll help any way we can."

In response, Akira sent: *Thank you. I am forever grateful. More soon.*

AKIRA'S SCHEME CALLED for her to leave Hong Kong, with Xen's blessing, by convincing him one of her confidential informants uncovered vital information about a new additive and requested a meeting with Xen in person. A carrot on a stick that normally would have piqued his interest, if it weren't for the amorous exploits he fancied with the two hussies he was pursuing. Early one afternoon, she started her scheme in motion. Xen's mind was a million miles away while he readied his den down below for another visit from his favorite twosome. Akira surprised him with news about a new product he might be interested in promoting. Clearly annoyed, he put her off.

"Okay, okay, whatever, I don't have time for such nonsense right now. You go find out what this is all about, take your time, when you get back, we will discuss it then. Now, get the hell out of here and let me be. I'm busy!"

So far, so good, Akira chuckled to herself on the ride back up top in the elevator—so grateful that Nemesis was onboard. Her detailed escape strategy included the use of multiple disposable phones and aliases on forged documents and credit cards to book a flight to San Francisco that evening and reserve a rental car in San Francisco. When the coast was clear and she was safely on US soil, Akira would contact Trey McCall.

Predictably, Xen wasn't even aware she'd gone. A little over thirteen hours after she left, Akira landed in Northern California. On her way to baggage claim, she visited the women's restroom, removed the sim chip from her phone and flushed it down a toilet, then tossed her burner phone in the trash. In the terminal, she bought another. She collected her bags and took the BART rail to the rental car staging area where Akira selected a luxury Lexus SUV. As planned, she used the navigation system in the Lexus to drive to San Jose where she took a room at one of the airport hotels. From the parking lot of the hotel, Akira texted Trey to call her at this number in five minutes. She answered on the first ring and explained what had transpired since they last communicated.

"Now that you're in the States, what's your next move?" Trey asked curiously.

Akira hesitated, "Well, sir … I thought I would leave that up to you. I'm sure the information I have in my possession will be of great interest to you and your organization. As I said in my first text, all I require in exchange is sanctuary from Xen and his associates."

"Understood, we are anxious to see the material—and prepared to give you asylum. Let me work out a few logistics. We'll have you here within twenty-four hours, if not sooner."

"Thank you, the sooner the better. I've taken every precaution I could think of to get here. Still, Xen is so well connected, it frightens me."

"I promise to expedite everything from our end. When I've worked out the details, I'll call you at this number."

True to his word, Trey had a Nemesis plane en route to San Jose six hours later. As directed, Akira dropped off her rental car at the Executive Jet FBO in San Jose and took a seat in the terminal awaiting the McCall jet from Dallas. Three and a half hours after boarding the Gulfstream G280, a much-relieved Akira Ito touched down at the McCall landing strip at The Circle M.

BONANZA WAS AN UNDERSTATEMENT when it came to the documentation in Akira's possession. As they viewed the material, Tara and her sister, Miranda, were astounded at what the world's elite were capable of. Drugs, sex, pedophilia—it was all there. These were not doctored evidentiary articles, but authentic proof of outrageous behavior by trusted people, respected for their supposed patriotism, thought to be worthy of adoration by their public, admired even honored for their dedication and sacrifice. Nemesis agents were appalled at what they read.

Most disgusted of all was Mac McCall. The very hint that he'd fallen for their subterfuge made him physically ill. Many of those participants had been friends of his over the years, people he had done business with, hunted with, worst of all confided in. All the while, he had no idea they were so pathetically twisted. Mac wondered how he'd misread so many. It all boiled down to one thing: he'd trusted them all. He bemoaned any world that existed without trust and faith.

CHAPTER 15

TREY MCCALL WAS IN HIS OFFICE reading over the notes he took after reviewing Akira's confiscated documents. Mac stepped in to put in his two cents, then suddenly drifted off point, talking about when he and Molly built the ranch from scratch. His recollections were spot on, until he shifted to a totally different subject. Then mid-sentence, Mac stood up and left. As of late, Mac seemed out of sorts, spending a considerable amount of time up on the rise where Molly and Tomas were buried, speaking to them as if they were still alive. Clearly, his focus laid in the past with his late wife, Molly, and her contributions to The Circle M. Tara voiced her mounting concern, wondering if they should get a professional opinion.

Fortunately, a recently retired neurosurgeon turned rancher lived not far from The Circle M. Dr. Ralph Jenkins specialized in dementia and Alzheimer's and was regarded by his peers as one of the most knowledgeable in dealing with either disease. Doc Jenkins agreed to come to the ranch to evaluate Mac's situation. To keep Mac in the dark about the doc's true mission, Trey and Tara introduced him as a novice rancher who wanted to pick Mac's brain about cattle and horses.

Since Mac loved to help tenderfoot ranchers avoid the pitfalls of the inexperienced, he was all for a meet and chat with the newcomer in the neighborhood. It proved the perfect sham to allow Dr. Jenkins to observe the eldest McCall. For the next few months, the doctor came by frequently to check for signs of deterioration in Mac's mental and physical functions. Recently, Doc observed how much his patient dwelled in the past with total recall yet fumbled with present-day things. After several months, Jenkins confirmed what they all suspected, Mac was in gradual mental decline. For now, it was nothing to be overly concerned about; however, as his symptoms progressed, his condition would need to be closely monitored.

It wasn't the worst news in the world. Mac was in great spirits, almost always with a big smile on his face. Anxiously, he would tell them about what Molly was going to do to The Circle M or the size of the bobcat Tomas brought down at dusk from two hundred yards. All things that took place well in the past. None of it in real time, just harmless banter that kept Trey's father happy. As his condition worsened, Mac spent considerably more time outside than he did in his office, often walking for hours surveying his magnificent ranch. It seemed he had a story about every tree, plant, horse, cow, or wildlife creature. When a particular calf was born, in which tall oak the bald eagles hatched their offspring, or under which of the Cypress limbs overhanging the banks of the lake he and Trey caught that mammoth bass. No one cared when the old man took to whistling off-key in a world of his own. Day by day, he pleasantly slipped away; it was sad to see him go, although it seemed he was having such a good time getting there.

The malady Mac suffered from was unpredictable at best. Mac returned to the here and now as soon as he found out Reanna was pregnant with a due date in the spring of next year. All of a sudden, he was full of vim and vigor, excited about the new great-grandchild on the way. Secretly Mac hoped it was a girl. It was time to break the all-boy trend. Besides, if it was a girl, they could name her after her Great-Grandmother Molly McCall.

One afternoon, Mac took Trey aside and suggested, "Son, I've been thinking. What say we build the kids a house on the lake, you know, as a belated wedding present or an early baby gift?"

Trey was astounded. It was as if Mac was back. "I, ah, think that's a great idea, Dad. There's plenty of choice spots for them to pick from. Why don't you give them the good news."

Reanna and Jefferson had no idea what to expect when Mac summoned them to his office. The kids were surprised to see how alert and high-spirited Mac was. When he broke the news, in between tears of joy, Reanna blubbered, "Grandpa Mac, if you aren't just the most special human being God ever put on this earth. You don't know how much this means to the both of us."

Jefferson rushed over to hug his grandfather and quietly whispered in his ear, "We can't begin to thank you for everything you have done for us. And now, this. It's so … I don't know … unexpected. We will accept your offer, but only if you pick the lot for us."

Mac chose their plot wisely, one with a magnificent view of the lake and the golf complex. Across the water was the rise where Molly rested in peace with an unobstructed view, to keep an eye on her first great-grandchild. As a tribute to his grandfather and grandmother, Jefferson and Reanna studied scores of old blueprints Molly created, until they found a design they fell in love with. Their decision warmed

Mac's heart and brought back fond memories of his wife working diligently to perfect her designs, then joining the workers down in the trenches to make her ideas come alive.

AS IF HE'D HAD A SHOT OF YOUTH SERUM, Mac went to the building site every morning at six o'clock to shout over the noise at the foreman and put in his two cents just as Molly would have done. No doubt the project breathed new life into the man who never missed a morning for almost six months. Except for the Sabbath, when he observed the work in progress from up on the ridge. Carefully, he would explain to Molly what had been accomplished that week along with what else he thought they should be done, as if hoping for her feedback. A sparkle returned to Mac's eyes; the feeling he was making a contribution gave the old man something to look forward to each day. For the first time in quite a while, Mac dealt more in the present than the past.

FOR SEVEN AND A HALF MONTHS, construction crews labored on the new lake house. Step by step they measured, cut, hammered, glued, installed, painted, sealed, and stuccoed. Finally, it was done. Workers touched up cosmetic details, cleaned up their messes, and placed excess materials in storage in case repairs were ever needed. Around midday, the foreman noticed Mac had not been at his normal spot shouting instructions to him. Worried, he called Trey to ask if the elder McCall was all right. Now that the project was done, he wanted to show Mac the finished product. Trey called around, but no one had seen Mac since the evening before when one of the agents noticed him walk away from the new house mumbling and shaking his head. Eventually, they found the stubborn old codger sound asleep below deck in their cabin cruiser docked at the marina.

Afraid Mac was regressing, Tara asked Dr. Jenkins to stop by when he had a moment. When Doc Jenkins arrived. Mac was resting comfortably in his bedroom.

With confusion written all over his face, Mac addressed his guest. "How do you do, sir, I don't believe we've been introduced, my name is Mac. And yours?"

Acting as if nothing was wrong, Doc replied, "Nice to meet you, Mac, my name is Ralph Jenkins, I recently bought some property down the road from you and just wanted to stop by to get acquainted."

Mac's eyes lit up. "Did you say Jenkins? That's odd. I seem to remember the name Jenkins from somewhere. Do you have any kin from these parts?"

Dr. Jenkins just smiled and slightly bowed his head. "Why yes I do, a brother of mine, a retired doctor, who lives nearby."

"That's right, Doc Jenkins. Know him well. He comes by from time to time to shoot the breeze and play some chess. Good man, your brother. Well, thanks for stopping by. Don't be a stranger, welcome to our little piece of paradise, Mr. Jenkins." With that, Mac closed his eyes and was sound asleep in seconds.

Leaving the old man to his nap, Tara, Trey, and Ralph Jenkins retired to the library. Once they were seated, Dr. Jenkins explained to the two concerned parties what was going on with Mac. It was not unusual for patients with dementia or early stages of Alzheimer's to become confused or forgetful, then to fabricate events to satisfy their delusions. Deeply concerned, Tara asked him if he thought Mac could stay at the ranch as his condition worsened. To her surprise, the doctor remarked, "Absolutely. Mac should remain in familiar surroundings where he felt comfortable as he slipped in and out of reality." Although Doc thought it would be a good idea to hire a skilled private nurse who specialized in Alzheimer's care. Doc knew of several highly qualified nurses who resided in the Dallas area if they were interested.

After the doctor left, Trey and Tara strolled hand in hand down to the lake to nestle together on a wooden bench that faced the crystal-clear spring-fed lake. For close to an hour, they sat there in silence allowing their thoughts and emotions to settle into the reality of Mac's condition. All was in God's hands now.

TRUTH WAS A MYTH and trust a fabrication in Xen's world. Here at Nemesis, truth, trust, and justice were staples of life. Finding herself now in an unfamiliar environment, Akira didn't know exactly what to expect from Trey, Tara, and Miranda. As a result, she came off as nervous and a bit apprehensive, until she realized how knowledgeable and professional Nemesis personnel were. The Nemesis trio eased her concerns with their relaxed manner. Their questions were on point seeking information without accusation. At the conclusion of the first interview, she was positive she'd made the correct decision. When the inquiry wrapped up, Trey suggested they all go down to the golf complex. It was a popular spot on Taco Wednesday featuring authentic Mexican cuisine that attracted most of The Circle M residents. An ideal venue for Trey to introduce Akira to Jorge Vargas, the ranch supervisor, and his wife, Sidney Baker, legal counsel for the McCalls.

During the evening, Akira met Cassiopeia Drakos and Raife Whelan, the agents who were instrumental in thwarting the ambush in Barbados. Both were part of the McCall extended family, now assigned as her personal bodyguards for the immediate future. Akira marveled at the light and festive atmosphere; everyone let their hair down, and rank flew out the window on fiesta night. Never had she seen the like. There was no posturing here, and all were having a great time drinking, eating, laughing, just letting go.

Not one to shy away from a challenge, Akira dived in like a native. Not having occasion in her former life to sample tequila, she discovered it was actually quite good. Her favorite, Herradura Silver, went down smoothly. Before the night was done, she did shots with the more experienced tequila connoisseurs, probably not the best idea for her rookie experience with the potent Agave drink. Her cohorts bet that she'd pay a wicked price in the morning when she was scheduled for her second interview—first thing after breakfast. Odds were against her making it to either. When the regulars arrived, they were shocked to see Akira already seated, eating breakfast, refreshed, and ready to face the day. The ice was broken. She was one of them, accepted as an equal, a far cry from how she was treated in Hong Kong.

IT HAD BEEN TWO DAYS since Xen had seen or heard from Akira; he'd focused his attention solely on his two potential concubines. Now that the dust had settled and the girls readied themselves to depart, Xen rang upstairs for Akira to have his breakfast prepared—he was famished. When she didn't answer, he winced, then remembered she was on an assignment to chase down a lead. He'd neglected to ask her where. Nothing he could do about that right now; Eva and Victoria were on their way out the door. Frantically, he hung up and raced after them, begging for them to stay one more night.

"No can do, lover," said Eva. "We have some last-minute paperwork to fill out in order to file our taxes before the deadline. I'm sure you can understand."

Xen gave in. "Yes, that I fully understand. The government be damned, I say. When will I see you two again?"

As they scurried out the door, they replied in unison, "Soon, lover … soon."

ACTUALLY HE NEVER DEALT WITH TAXES, Akira was the one who handled that sort of stuff. Where in the hell was she? "Damn it to hell," he shouted to no one there. "All you bitches drive me fucking insane."

Seething, he spent half an hour seated in his massive shower under the force of multiple showerheads pounding hot water down on his body. With his emotions somewhat under control, Xen emerged from his shower wrapped in an oversized Egyptian cotton towel and sat on the corner of the bed to cool off and gather his thoughts. Ravenous, he donned a sweat suit and headed for the kitchen to make himself something to eat.

Mr. Xen fumbled through leftovers in the Sub-Zero refrigerator hoping to find something that piqued his interest and decided on a casserole Akira called chicken cacciatore. Just as he'd seen her do, he preheated the oven to 350 degrees and set the timer for twenty minutes. When the chime went off on the oven, he took it out and spooned a good bit of the contents into a large soup bowl. It was delicious, so he finished the entire casserole. Then he opened a bottle of white wine, poured a glass, and sat in his overstuffed leather chair to browse old television mystery shows. His eyes drooped closed, and he nodded off; an hour later, he woke with a start.

Why hadn't Akira called him with an update? It was not like her to forget. Xen checked for missed calls or messages on his mobile—there were none. Red-faced with anger, he punched in her number. No answer. He dialed again, same thing. Now seriously pissed, he launched his cell phone into the painted brick wall across the room, shattering it into a gazillion pieces. Then stomped into his office in search of his backup mobile, from which he sent her a vile text. No reply. Another text followed telling her to respond immediately or don't bother to come back. Nothing. As soon as he pushed send, he regretted the tone of the message, but it was too late. The damage was done. Again, his temper had gotten the better of him. All he could hope for is that she did not take him literally. Surely, she understood his moods by now and would laugh off his foolish comments.

MR. XEN HAD NO IDEA Akira never received his calls, messages, or emails that now floated around in some vacuous Cloud wasteland. For the rest of the day, Xen downed double martinis and sent her messages begging her to respond. Vodka took its toll. Eventually, he passed out in his favorite leather chair in front of the big screen. At five a.m., the bewildered scammer awoke with a screaming headache and what felt like a mouth full of cotton candy. He staggered to the kitchen for a drink of water, only to drain an entire pitcher in multiple gulps. In an attempt to ease his pounding headache, Xen stuck his bald head under the faucet and turned on the cold water. Droplets cascaded off his head, down his face, and off his chin; the shock of the icy water helped clear his jumbled thoughts. Back to his phone, he made a few more attempts to reach Akira, to no avail. Totally manic, Xen was about to send the mobile phone in his hand to meet the same fate as the one he shattered against the wall yesterday.

At the last second, he caught himself in mid-throw and dropped it to the carpet below his feet. Maybe Akira ignored him because she was having a tantrum of her own. Since he laid eyes on Eva and Victoria, he hadn't exactly made her feel wanted or needed. Could be jealousy and her way of punishing him. If she didn't contact him by the weekend, he would send out the cavalry.

WHILE MR. XEN BEMOANED his predicament, Akira was in conference with the principal agents of Nemesis in Texas. It was day three of her debriefing by Trey McCall and his team. Verifiable proof exposed bent puppet masters who controlled figureheads in big business, organized crime, as well as evil-intentioned countries vying for dominance on the world scene. Even with Warlock, it would have taken Nemesis years to dig out, collect, and verify the material Akira willingly handed over to them on a silver platter.

Best of all, Akira had personal contact with a majority of the persons of interest in the documents. Others, she knew in the cyber world under assumed names. It was Mr. Xen who put their true identities to paper and image for his personal records; bottom line, Xen was an unwitting accomplice to his own collapse. Each uncovered identity added a loop to the knot on the hangman's noose around Xen's neck. Part of the beauty of Akira's defection was, as of yet, no one on the other side had a clue the chronicled damning evidence existed much less who was scrutinizing it. Xen couldn't afford to raise holy hell; the damaging material had his fingerprints all over it. One peep out of him, and he was history.

With the assistance of Warlock, Nemesis prioritized the data Akira furnished into groups ranging from most threatening to least threatening, then focused on half a dozen subjects who fit into the most aggressive category. Detailed files were created on their comings and goings, who they associated with, who financed them, plus the location of their base of operations. Three of the six were the most corrupt, financed by the same outfit based in Eastern Europe, owned and operated by the same man, Dmitri Volkov. Akira recognized the name from past dealings on behalf of Mr. Xen.

AS A YOUNG MAN, Dmitri disowned his heritage in pursuit of fortune and power. Clinically speaking, Volkov displayed narcissistic schizo-phrenic tendencies coupled with sociopathic predisposition. In layman's terms, the man was seriously mentally ill—possessing neither conscience nor compassion—only an unwavering desire to crush anything and everyone in his way. Throughout his life, he bulldozed his way to success, becoming a multibillionaire along the way. Money was his motivator: the more he made, the more powerful he became. He represented pure evil and was nothing more than a coward who would abandon his associates in a heartbeat to save his own skin. Akira shuttered at the thought that Dmitri Volkov and Mr. Xen were so much alike, nothing more than predators lacking any hint of moral compass.

THE WEEKEND CAME AND WENT, and Mr. Xen still had not heard one peep from his personal secretary; his anger turned into full-fledged paranoia. Panic-stricken, Xen called around and put out feelers to all his informants to be on the lookout for Akira Ito. A week passed, still nothing. No longer could he allow his assistant to be MIA; she knew far too much about his business and personal life. If he'd only paid more attention to what she said before she left. Any little hint she might have let slip as to where she was headed would help. Nothing showed up in her bank accounts or her credit card transactions. Mentally exhausted, Xen took a breather in his comfy leather chair to settle his nerves when something hit him like a ton of bricks. *The lipstick.* What if the damn vial of purple lipstick he found by the safe in the grotto was really hers? Could the little bitch have somehow broken into his safe? But how? Clumsily, Xen rushed to his private elevator and impatiently poked at the button until the door finally opened. Once inside, it seemed to take forever to reach the bottom.

Squeezing out before the doors fully opened, Xen raced to the safe and worked today's combination; as the last digit clicked in, he jerked the door open. To his surprise, everything appeared to be in order. Anxiously, Xen thumbed through random files to make sure, and was about to close the safe when he observed something peculiar. Resting in the margin of one of the files were two long jet-black hairs. *How in the hell did the black hairs get there?* Not his, Xen was bald. *I am so frigging SCREWED!* he thought. Akira was on the loose with his kryptonite in her possession. Irregularities to his filing system inside the safe suggested these were copies. Assuming she wore gloves, there would be only one set of fingerprints on the originals—his.

In his zest to gain more power and influence, he'd opened himself up to retaliation from all sides. By now, all the hard work Xen put into developing the incriminating records would be in the hands of others to evaluate. If word got out that he prepared them, his life would not be worth a penny. In anger, he slammed the safe shut and plopped down hard on the bed to think. What could he do to escape this nightmare? Who could he call for assistance? Sadly, he realized Akira was the only person in the world he'd ever trusted. Anyone else he called for help would most certainly turn him down or turn him in.

Without warning, his whole body rebelled against him in a massive panic attack. Rapid heart rate, dizziness, sweats, shakes, shortness of breath, and a sense of impending doom overwhelmed him. If he was to survive this predicament, Xen couldn't stay in Hong Kong. Even though time was of the essence, he forced himself to calm down and focus on an escape plan. Willing himself horizontal, Xen closed his eyes and laid his head on a pillow until his symptoms slowly dissipated. An hour passed, then another, and finally, he opened his eyes. With a grin on his face, he rode the elevator to the penthouse.

DURING HIS DOWNTIME, Xen organized a workable escape scheme. First, he'd take his submersible across the bay to the private airport where he kept a small fleet of planes. Once there, he'd board his Lear for a two-hour flight to a remote airfield he used in the Philippines, where a driver would take him to a hideaway he had not seen in years but kept available for emergencies. Brilliant!

Xen swept up all the cash from his floor safe up top—over two-hundred thousand pounds, as well as documentation under an alias that gave him access to a bank account worth over five million US dollars. More than enough to pay all the obligatory bribes that were a part of life in the Philippines, while he lived comfortably in his villa above Mindoro Strait, for years if necessary.

After a last-minute check around the penthouse, Xen packed a few essentials and took the elevator down to the airlock, where he boarded a Braun submersible. He took one last mental picture of his magnificent building, climbed into the pilot's seat, sealed the cockpit, and remotely opened the outside hatchway to fill the chamber. When the water reached capacity, he flipped a switch on his control panel to start up the engine, then maneuvered the vehicle gently out into the bay and remotely closed the hatchway behind him.

Fifteen minutes later, he surfaced and guided the boat under some dense overhanging branches near the shore, shut everything down, gathered his gear, and leapt to shore. Eight hundred yards from where he'd abandoned his motor craft was the runway. Casually, Xen walked toward the hangar, boarded the Lear Jet and stowed his gear. A certified pilot with sufficient hours to fly a Lear, Xen occupied the copilot seat while the pilot filed a flight plan to Singapore. After takeoff, they circled the bright lights of Hong Kong, and the skipper set the controls on automatic pilot for the four-hour flight. Weather was good all the way.

An hour and a half into the four-hour flight, Xen excused himself to go to the restroom. When he reentered the cockpit, he knocked out the pilot with a blackjack, and jumped into his copilot seat to take the plane off automatic pilot. Xen dived to a lower altitude, slowed the plane, reengaged the autopilot, then drug the pilot out of his seat and muscled the body out the door. Rapidly, he moved into the pilot's seat and answered the frantic call coming in on the radio from air traffic control.

In an anxious voice, Xen explained they'd had engine trouble and experienced a rapid loss of altitude, but the aircraft was under control now and climbing to altitude. However, his copilot sustained an injury and was currently unconscious, and he requested a flight plan change to Manilla. With no challenge, the flight plan change was granted, and Xen set his course for a remote airstrip on one of the smaller Philippine Islands. He touched down lightly on the tarmac and eased the aircraft underneath camouflage netting strung up against the jungle backdrop to avoid detection from above. A jeep pulled up to whisk him to what tripled as the airport terminal car rental-limo service facility. Xen handed five thousand US dollars in cash to the man in charge of the airport. After counting out the money, the airport manager nodded to the driver who put the jeep in gear and sped away. Behind the building, another driver in a dark suit and hat waited next to an open passenger door of a well-preserved Mercedes. As soon as Xen ducked in with his overnight valise, the door shut with a solid thud, and off they went to the villa on the sea. Sadly, this special treatment would last only as long as his money held out, as would his paid array of employees who awaited him at the villa. Forty minutes later, over bumpy, almost nonexistent roads, the Mercedes pulled up to a structure that had not changed much over the years. Although it could definitely use a new coat of paint.

RELIEVED TO HAVE MADE IT to his hideaway, Xen gave his driver a generous tip with instructions to be ready to pick him up at a moment's notice if need be. Once inside, he took the stairs two at a time to the upstairs master bedroom. It was exactly as he remembered, a suitably spacious room with a Brazilian wood floor and shuttered mahogany doors that opened onto a balcony with a magnificent view of the Mindoro Strait. On his way to admire the view, he tossed his duffle on the bed and threw open the balcony doors. After filling his lungs with the smog-free air, Xen hustled downstairs to grab a beer out of the refrigerator in the bar. Ice-cold San Miguel was one of his favorite beers in all the world—and the Philippines his favorite island country. With some of the most exquisitely gorgeous women in the world.

A vision of loveliness interrupted his daydream. Not sure whether she was a hallucination or for real, Xen reached out to touch her. She giggled and scampered away, not a rebuff, more of a tease. Intrigued, he followed her into the massive gathering room at the center of the manor. Fashionable and functional with its pockets of conversation areas brandishing luxuriously upholstered chairs, custom coffee tables, and sectional leather sofas that formed a semicircle facing each side of a gigantic open fireplace often used for cooking during social occasions.

Unexpectedly, the lovely vision plopped down on one of the couches and beckoned him to join her. As soon as he sat down, she introduced herself.

"Master Tong, my name is Hiraya, and my mission is to see to your *every* need."

"Please, refer to me as Xen. Master Tong sounds too formal for our relationship."

To reinforce her intentions, she took his hand and led him back to the master bedroom where the offspring of a handsome Filipino father and a lovely Japanese mother fulfilled her promise and satisfied his every whim. Afterward, Xen closed his eyes as Hiraya massaged his body. Pent-up tensions melted away, and soon he fell sound asleep with a smile on his face. He awoke midmorning to the sounds of the jungle outside the wall surrounding the villa. Hiraya was nowhere to be found so he shaved, showered, dressed in casual attire he had delivered to the manor from a gentlemen's shop prior to his arrival, and traipsed downstairs for breakfast.

When he walked into the kitchen, his house girl was fixing an omelet. "Good morning, Master Tong, sorry, I mean Xen-san," Hiraya cheerfully chimed.

"Morning to you as well. I thought you might join me last night or this morning."

Hiraya giggled. "I would have, only you were so weary after your journey, I didn't want to disturb you."

Grinning to himself, Xen thought, *If running for your life is this rewarding, I should have gone on the lam years ago.*

BACK IN THE MIDWEST, Talley and Millie were having a hell of a time keeping track of the events over in Hong Kong. Until recently, their agents Eva and Victoria kept them up to date. The two Nomad infiltrators were in solid with Mr. Xen; they played him like a fiddle and had him dangling like a puppet from their strings. All of a sudden, everything went dark—dead silence. No one answered the phone, not even the obnoxious bitch who managed his daily affairs. It was like they magically disappeared. Talley directed her girls to stay put in Hong Kong in the event Xen came back unannounced.

Millie wondered if the perverse bastard finally outsmarted himself and had to bug out. Could be the syndicate *eliminated* Xen for past transgressions, a message to others not to mess with the mob. Perhaps it was a blessing that Xen was out of the picture; things might open up more in Nomad's favor. For years, the middleman was a stumbling block for them. Their quasi-*natural* stimulant could save the Eastern cartels millions in production costs by purchasing the Nomad product at reasonable rates.

At the same time in Albania, Dmitri Volkov took a call from one of his best operatives concerning Mr. Xen. Dmitri's agent tried unsuccessfully for a week to contact Xen in reference to drug shipments that were inexplicably overdue. The Russian didn't care at all for Xen, but it was not like the greedy bastard to be late with deliveries—the man loved money too much to let that happen. A pleasant thought entered Dmitri's mind, *What a perfect excuse to remove the middleman!*

HE SMILED, ALMOST SALIVATED, at the visual of Xen squirming as Dmitri delivered the bad news in person. Oh, how he relished those moments. The first order of business was to put out a worldwide bolo for Mr. Xen, with a substantial reward of one million pounds going to the person whose information led to his location. Word spread quickly through the underworld network. It wasn't long until the militia man recognized the picture of Xen as the man he picked up in his jeep after Xen landed in the Philippines. Although the militia man was paid well for his silence, it certainly wasn't anywhere near a million pounds. In less than the week, Dmitri knew the location of his least-favorite associate.

The question became, should Dmitri pounce right away or let the creep assume he was free and clear? Compared to Dmitri's massive wealth, there was no way Xen had enough money to buy the loyalty he needed. The Russian added a couple of his best Filipino men to the landscape crew to surveil his prey inside the walls of the villa. Both newbies glimpsed Hiraya at the same time and rolled their eyes, as their target opened the front door to let her in. There was no mistaking the diminutive bald man was Mr. Xen. Dmitri's men worked their way around the house until the pseudo gardeners were in position to film Hiraya through an enormous plate-glass window while she serviced the man on a spacious couch. When the show was over, Dmitri's men sent the X-rated movie to Dmitri Volkov, who wasn't as impressed with the action as he was with the awe-inspiring beauty of the young woman straining to keep the expression of boredom and disinterest off her face. Observing her disdain, Dmitri sent a text back to his boys to find out if Hiraya was interested in changing teams for double the money she was being paid.

CHATTER COMING OUT OF THE PHILIPPINES about a Mr. Xen and a Russian by the name of Dmitri Volkov in Albania caught Tara McCall's attention. For years, Tara suspected Volkov and Xen were involved in nefarious practices in the pharmaceutical markets in the Eastern Bloc. Nemesis now had confirmation Xen and Volkov were associates. Moreover, they learned as soon as Xen discovered his secretary absconded with his incriminating files, he'd fled from Hong Kong to a place of safe refuge on a small island in Mindoro.

In Trey McCall's office, Akira carefully read over the transcripts of the captured conversations and smiled. She could not have wished a worse revenge on Xen than what he faced from the Russian. Dmitri Volkov was the last person on Earth anyone would want chasing them. Not only was he an animal and a ruthless enemy, he took great pleasure in personally inflicting pain on his adversaries. If only she could be present when Dmitri tortured Xen. Breaking into her thoughts, Trey asked Akira if she had ever been to this island villa.

"No, I have not; however, on occasion when Xen was drunk, he spoke of a place where he would go to retire—a refuge where he could hide from the world."

Trey nodded and grinned. "What an unexpected piece of good fortune. It will be interesting to find out where this new information leads us."

AT LUNCH WITH TREY AND TARA, Miranda mentioned an interesting exchange regarding Volkov and Xen from a party wanting to know if the Russian was still doing business with the insolent middleman. If not, they had a product Volkov may be interested in.

"Out of curiosity, where did the communique originate?" Tara asked, suddenly very interested in what her sister had to say.

Her answer was dubious. "I don't exactly know. Our calculations say about halfway between Sioux Falls, South Dakota, and Topeka, Kansas. According to the coordinates, that is in the middle of nowhere—nothing for miles in any direction. When I say nothing, I mean absolutely nothing at all."

Scratching her head, Tara said, "Did you recheck the coordinates with Warlock?"

"Only three frigging times. Same every time."

Trey interjected, "Could it be from a mobile device, iPhone or iPad, maybe?"

Miranda shook her head. "That's what I thought at first, but those types of devices have definite signatures recognized by Warlock. These particular messages had varying signatures. Honestly, sir, I'm out of my league with this one," answered a bewildered Miranda.

Never had Tara heard her sister utter those words before. Which left them with only one recourse: to call Noah Bouchard in Canada. After Noah listened to Miranda's explanation, he asked her to send him the original messages she received from the server. Later that day, the computer genius called back, admitting the person who sent the messages was very clever. By introducing their own set of protocols into the system, they figured out a way to disguise the signatures of the sending device.

MILLIE CURRENTLY SAT IN A CAPTAIN'S CHAIR at the front of an enormous motor home moving down a deserted Midwestern interstate. If she could have been a fly on the wall for the McCall's conversation with Noah, she would've appreciated Noah's reference to her as clever. Being innovative and motivated, Millie Snowden figured out that mobile devices were identified by signature, and she designed an app to alter that signature/number/IP address of that device after each use. On her iPhone for instance, the app chose any active phone number at random as a proxy. Its signature reflected the name and address of the cloned owner. As soon as any transmission ended, the app automatically shut itself off. Each time Millie opened her phone, all she had to do was click on the app and a new signature/proxy number appeared.

The first message Millie sent to the Russian was totally ignored, not a surprise, in that Dmitri Volkov was probably preoccupied in his search for Mr. Xen. On her second attempt, she was much more aggressive with her language, stating she was a longtime supplier, with product that she was ready to ship to Xen, except he was nowhere to be found. If Dmitri did not respond, she was going elsewhere to do business.

Seconds later, she received a response from Dmitri. *Listen here, asshole, whoever you are. I've got underlings that handle this kind of shit. How dare you pressure me. Go through channels or fuck off.*

Millie had his attention. *Fine with me. Just wonder why you'd want underlings to handle a revolutionary new product that is going to set Big Pharma on its ear. An undetectable natural non-narcotic addictive formula that could make you billions. But hey, your choice. No problem, I'll put it up for the highest bidder. Bye!*

Dmitri's return message arrived full of excuses and an apology. Of course he was interested and asked to schedule a meeting, then requested her contact information. Millie ignored the missive. Instead, she sent back she would be in touch soon to find out if he was still interested. Time was money, and this discovery was far too novel to sit on the shelf collecting dust. Click, she disconnected.

GLARING DOWN AT HIS PHONE, Dmitri couldn't believe the asshole cut him off. No one in their right mind ever had. Livid, Dmitri leaped up from behind his desk. In an effort to figure out who might have come up with such a revolutionary stimulant, he paced around his office racking his brain—he came up empty.

CHAPTER 16

SMOLDERING MAD, Dmitri Volkov was not used to waiting on anybody for anything. It had been three days since he got that text concerning some newfangled magic elixir. The sender said they would be back in touch soon. In his world, seventy-two hours was not his definition of soon. About to give up on the whole thing, his phone dinged.

Hope you have had time to consider my previous offer. It still stands until end of business today at five p.m. Eastern time. After the deadline, my product goes up for bid.

Before he responded, Dmitri reread the text, then sent, *Yes, I am very interested but must have more details of new product unique properties. Can we arrange a meeting?*

Yes, only it must be at a place and time of my choosing.

Agreed. When and where?

Soon.

Again, Dmitri attempted to reconnect to the sender, and again, no luck. *Damn, they were good.* In frustration, Dmitri let out every curse word he knew in English and Russian. Who was this person who obviously had a death wish? Imagine a man of his stature, manipulated like a dangling puppet, he did not like it one bit. With Mr. Xen still very much an issue, this mystery texter had gotten under his skin. In a way, he admired the person's tenacity and courage. Surely, they were aware of his reputation, yet stood their ground daring to try his patience.

CONVINCED SHE HAD PIQUED Dmitri's curiosity, Millie was aware he was a man she should fear—but didn't. In reality, the Russian was no different from most of the crooks she'd dealt with in her criminal career, including the late Lucky Richards. Her first priority was to decide on a meeting place, one with a relaxed atmosphere to give them the opportunity to freely negotiate without distraction.

WHEN MILLIE RELAYED THE NEWS to her partner, Talley Marsh was impressed, glad she'd left the promotion of caida libre to Millie while Talley dealt with some unresolved real estate matters in California. Talley was happy to report she'd convinced an up-and-coming group of drug dealers to purchase a fifty-one percent interest in an addictive supplement business in the Golden State, formerly Sister Nation. Similar to the deal she'd done for the two underground labs in the Midwest—shielded under the umbrella of Albatross, LLC. Blinded by dollar signs, the dealers jumped at the pot of gold but ignored the small print. By agreeing to the terms set forth by the sellers, the new managing partners became the responsible party in any and all legal disputes, absolving Millie and Talley from any reclamations individually or attached to Sister Nation past, present, and future. It was a brilliant maneuver whereby Talley and Millie still collected forty-nine percent of the profits the renamed company generated in the old brick-and-mortar stores along the Left Coast—without having to deal with any of the headaches. In addition to a plausible plan to move the caida libre stimulant directly to clients, which saved millions in middleman fees. Finally, after a long dry spell, tied down with construction and production expenses, things were moving forward. When all came to fruition, Nomad could recoup their overhead in no time.

WHILE NOMAD RATCHETED UP PRODUCTION for international distribution of caida libre, an interested third party took it all in. Desiree Richards sat in the catbird seat in Montreal watching and listening via spycam. The common denominator among the principal actors in the big picture was Millie, in that she interacted with them all. An enviable position for Desiree, enabling her to bide her time until she could create serious chaos among her adversaries. None of them knew where she was or what she was up to—most thought she was dead.

One night after listening to Millie go on about her wonder stimulant caida libre for the umpteenth time, Desiree called Boris to find out if he could get her a sample. Specifically, the product called Spice of Life that came in packets like sweeteners in fast-food joints. Advertised to give hot or cold beverages more zip, not to mention the wonderful added benefits it lent to other aspects of life. If what she heard was true, it might just be what she needed to put pep back into her aging body.

To her delight, Boris had a good friend in New Orleans who dealt with Nomad and agreed to send Desiree a couple of cases of Slice of Life to test. It wasn't as though she wanted to stir up anything romantically with Boris; their relationship was plutonic, more like a mother with her favorite son. What Desiree sought was strictly business related, clarity of mind, increased energy, attention to detail. Qualities she would need further down the road to outmaneuver Nomad, Bogus Pharma, the likes of Dmitri Volkov, not to mention Nemesis.

DMITRI VOLKOV WAS CONFLICTED. Would it be better to expose Xen as the thieving, conniving slime he was, or should he pursue this supposed fabulous undetectable additive he could purchase and receive directly from the manufacturer? After considerable deliberation, Dmitri let Xen believe he was secure. As of now, the little shit felt safe in his current environment with no apparent reason to leave anytime soon. After Dmitri's men persuaded Hiraya to join his team, the Russian was at liberty to concentrate on the mystery texter.

MILLIE TEXTED DMITRI with her decision to meet in Bermuda. Even though he'd left it up to her, Dmitri turned it into a hassle, in what was meant to be a show of power and control. Millie didn't budge and threatened to call it all off. He backed off, and she determined the date and time. Nemesis intercepted the communications between Millie and the Russian, copied the messages, and placed them in a secure file for Tara and Miranda to evaluate, along with Dmitri's emails and texts to and from Mindoro.

MR. XEN WAS TOTALLY unaware that his adversaries knew of his whereabouts in the villa—Hiraya made sure of it. She kept him occupied. Now his eyes and ears, Hiraya fed him only information she was ordered to by her handlers. Reports she sent to Albania were intercepted by Warlock. Always a tease, Hiraya took delight in describing everything in vivid detail. Over time, the Filipino girl gained Xen's full trust and became his personal assistant.

No longer did he trust the news on TV or what he read in print, convinced by his lovely assistant that it was all government propaganda. At her insistence, Xen had little contact with the outside world. Bimonthly, he checked in with his personal banker on the library phone she'd tapped. Hiraya listened to the recordings for anything suspicious.

Selfishly, Hiraya neglected to report *all* the financial transactions she performed on Xen's behalf to her handlers. At times she would accompany him into the bank, where she overheard him give the banker the passwords to his accounts. Mr. Xen, of course, had no idea she had defected and believed her to be a loyal companion. On occasion when they were in town, he would allow her to shop while he enjoyed San Miguel beers in the shade at a cantina near the docks. Out of sight from her handlers and her boss, Hiraya would go to the bank and use the passwords she memorized to withdraw money from Xen's account, which she slipped into the zippered side of her large tote. Since the bank manager recognized her, there were no issues. On the way back to the cantina, she'd purchase inexpensive items to show her master.

On one occasion after placing her packages in the car, Hiraya walked into the dark cantina, hesitated briefly to give her eyes a chance to adjust from the bright sunlight outside, and spotted Xen at the end of the bar chatting up a young prostitute. Cool, calm, and collected, she walked up to the hooker and slapped her so hard the bitch flew off her barstool and slid across the grungy germ-infested floor. On her one and only attempt to get up, the whore was met by a swift kick to the face that rendered her unconscious. Shoving the body aside, Hiraya took her employer's arm and escorted him outside to the applause of the patrons and the bartender.

In his warped ego-fed perspective, the reaction by Hiraya proved her undying devotion to Xen by destroying a rival in a jealous rage. From that point on, Hiraya noticed a change in the man, a softer attitude toward her, and a gentler touch when he held her. Which gave her a slight twinge of guilt, but not enough to change her true alliance. Fear of Dmitri's wrath outweighed her loyalty to Xen. Not to mention, the generous wage Dmitri sent her way was preferable to the brutal punishments he promised to those who crossed him.

MEANWHILE, AT THE CIRCLE M IN TEXAS, Mac McCall slid deeper into dementia—lingering mostly in the past. For hours, Mac stared up at the ridge where his dear wife, Molly, was buried. Funny thing was, Mac never complained; he wore a smile a great deal of the time and gave the impression he was happy to live in the world of his memories.

When asked for his prognosis, Doc Jenkins took on a pained expression. It saddened him to tell the McCalls what was inevitable. Mac was going to get worse at an increasingly rapid rate and would progress into acute Alzheimer's, from which the man would perish. If there was an upside to the disease, Mac McCall would be in his own world with no clue what was happening. It was not unusual for patients to pass peacefully in their sleep.

As her due date approached, Reanna McCall began to feel the discomforts of pregnancy. Months ago, they'd found out that she was going to have a baby girl, who they'd all agreed would be named Molly

Elizabeth. The chances of Reanna sleeping through the night were nil once Molly Elizabeth started kicking like a mule in her belly. As a distraction, she began to count down the days and talk to Molly in her womb. When Jefferson said he thought it was cute, Reanna scolded him saying that's what a parent was supposed to do, so the child knows their voice. It was a reprimand done in jest. Nevertheless and not to be outdone, Jefferson spoke to Rea's belly, so Molly would learn his voice as well.

WHILE PREPARATIONS WERE UNDERWAY for the baby, Trey and Jefferson snuck away when they could to keep Jefferson's game sharp. There was an important tournament looming on the horizon in April— the Masters. They sorted out a few minor issues in his swing before Jefferson returned to the road. Although things didn't pan out the way they thought they would. Jefferson's game was sporadic and unimpressive. Trey joined his son in California to find out what was going on and quickly figured it out. Jefferson's focus was off, his mind far away dwelling on Mac's dementia and Reanna's delicate condition back home.

Following an ugly second round at Torrey Pines, where Jefferson birdied the final hole to make the cut on the number, he and his father sat down and had a long talk—more of a father's gentle counsel than a pep talk.

In a soft voice, Trey referred to the cycle of life. "Death is an element of life as is birth. Mac has lived a full and prosperous life, one in which he has given far more than he has received. We must think of his illness as a gift from above, a docile way to pass, with his mind full of pleasant memories that put a smile on his face every day. Your grandfather has a good friend taking care of him who understands the stages of his affliction. The last thing Mac would want you to do is dwell on his condition. He'd want you to continue to make him proud. Nothing would please him more than for you to fulfill your dreams. Along with the inevitability of his death is the promise of a new life coming into our family to bring joy and happiness to us all. That, my son, is simply the cycle of life."

Sitting on the edge of his bed, listening with his head down, staring at the floor, with tears in his eyes, Jefferson stood to give his father a hug and held on, until Trey gently pushed him away. Wiping away the boy's tears, Trey pulled him close again.

Jefferson knew his father was right, and with newfound inspiration and drive, Jefferson's game shifted. His final two rounds at Torrey Pines moved him all the way up the leaderboard to finish solo second. And in his remaining two events prior to the Masters, Jefferson collected two top-five finishes.

APRIL AND THE MASTERS were on them before they knew it. Trey, Jefferson, and Moondance flew out the week before for early preparation. Staying in the same rental house as the year before made it feel like an old home week in comfortable surroundings. As was his custom, Moondance turned down an invitation to stay with them in lieu of staying with a *friend* for the week. Wednesday of tournament week, Tara and Reanna flew over on the private jet. It was less than a two-hour flight from The Circle M airstrip to Augusta, an easy trip for Reanna in her current stage of pregnancy, with a clean bill of health from her pediatrician. Trey and Jefferson met them at the airport, gathered their luggage off the baggage cart, and placed the bags in the trunk of the Masters' courtesy car. After unloading and unpacking at the house, the four of them settled down for a pre-Masters' tournament dinner of steaks cooked outside on the grill, with fresh vegetables, a garden salad, and peach cobbler a la mode for dessert. Reanna pouted, sad that she couldn't watch Jefferson in person at Augusta National, quickly reminded why, by a subtle kick in the gut from Molly.

For the first two days of the Masters, the weather was ideal, temperatures in the high seventies to low eighties with light winds. Nine under led the way into the final two days; Jefferson was four back at one-thirty-nine, a sixty-nine followed by a two under seventy. Multitudes of patrons got their money's worth with the course yielding lots of birdies and eagles. Overnight, the beautiful weather changed, temps dropped accompanied by thunderstorms and gusty winds forecasted for Saturday to continue through Sunday.

The third day was one of those where storms moved in and out and circled back. With lightning in the area, players were removed from the course multiple times only to have to resume their position on the course thirty minutes later. Luckily, the final group finished as the sun was going down. Only one shot separated Jefferson from the lead after he fashioned a round of sixty-eight. In the final twosome on Sunday, he would be paired with Hugh Corbyn, an international golf star with multiple tournament wins worldwide and contender in numerous major championships—both players seeking their first Masters victory.

Saturday was difficult, Sunday was brutal. Temperatures were in the fifties with winds gusting up to forty miles per hour swirling down and around the draws, whistling through the massive Georgia pines lining the fairways. After the first nine, McCall was still one behind Hugh Corbyn both carding one under thirty-fives, each relying on gutsy shots and nifty short-game skills. Through the par five fifteenth, they matched scores for the second nine. On the par three sixteenth Corbyn had the honor with a one-shot lead over McCall for the championship. Swirling winds around Augusta National were famous for delivering drama to the closing holes of every Masters. As they waited for the green to clear, the wind picked up, mostly against, then left to right.

Using a six iron, Hugh drew his shot into the wind. In mid-flight, a gust caught it, killing its momentum, dropping the ball straight down into the water in front and left of the green. Patrons surrounding the sixteenth groaned when it splashed. Digging deep into his arsenal of shots, Jefferson played a seven iron back in his stance and hit a low screaming draw at the right center of the green, and the ball caught the center slope and finished eight feet underneath the hole. His opponent's troubles continued as Corbyn missed a twelve-foot bogie putt, while Jefferson made birdie to take a two-stroke lead with two holes to play. Both parred seventeen and hit their tee shots in the fairway at eighteen.

Corbyn's second finished twenty-five feet past the hole, while Jefferson hit his to fifteen feet right of the hole. The walk uphill to the green was awash in emotions for Jefferson. Two putts to win his first Masters. His mind couldn't wrap around how awesome yet terrifying it was. He slowed down to take it all in. The patrons were ten deep around the green, giving him and Corbyn a standing ovation. His eyes teared up, and his heart raced. As if by magic, when his foot touched the putting surface, a calmness overcame him, and he knew he was going to make his putt. His opponent putted first and made his for birdie. The patrons cheered their appreciation. One shot separated the last pairing. A respectful hush enveloped the eighteenth green as Jefferson addressed his putt. He envisioned the ball dripping over the front lip of the cup before he stroked the putt. One more look and it was on its way. The ball never wavered off the line and dropped ever so gently over the front edge on its last rotation. He went to his knees on the green and wept tears of joy for what he and his father had accomplished.

On his way to the scoring box, Jefferson spotted his dad and made a beeline for Trey, threw his arms around him, and buried his head in his father's neck, tears streamed down their faces. Back at their Augusta rental house, Reanna and Tara were hugging each other, screaming at the top of their lungs, and Molly Elizabeth kicked like hell to join in the celebration.

IN TEXAS, DOC JENKINS and Mac watched the tournament glued to the TV. When Jefferson's final putt dropped, as clear as a bell, Mac said, "Well, what do you know. How 'bout that, Doc, isn't he something else. Won the frigging Masters. Tough as nails, it's in his blood."

Delighted as well, Jenkins chuckled, wondering if the old bastard had been putting on an act all along. He knew he wasn't, but wished he was. Everybody around The Circle M could not wait to welcome the new Masters champion back home. When the plane set down at the Ranch's landing strip, there was already a huge crowd of employees to greet them. By the time he reached the main house, the party was in full swing.

The first thing Jefferson did when he got to the house was to find his grandfather, who was sitting on the wraparound porch outside, scoping out the landscape that he and his family had transformed into a legacy that would live on forever. When Mac heard the screen door creak open, he smiled ear to ear and stood to embrace his grandson. For a brief period, it was as if the senior McCall was clearheaded and rational, listening and asking questions, trying desperately to stay in the moment. Then as if Jefferson weren't there, the old man resumed staring out into the distance at the ridge where Molly was buried. It was just before dusk, shadows fell across the landscape and over Mac's mind, invoking a symptom of Alzheimer's called *sundowning* that produced a variety of behaviors such as confusion and mood swings. They sat in silence for a while until Doc Jenkins showed up to keep Mac company.

HONORING HIS COMMITMENT, Jefferson played the following week at Harbour Town, and squeezed out a top ten on the tight Harbour Town Links. Then hurried home as Reanna was close to her due date. Lingering Masters fanfare paled in light of the excitement brimming over when Molly Elizabeth McCall would make her appearance. According to her pediatrician, the baby could come at any time. Which was great news to Reanna who was getting more than uncomfortable waddling around, praying for her water to break. Two weeks later, early in the morning of May 1, Jefferson and family loaded Reanna into the GMC Yukon and drove her to the hospital only a short distance from the ranch, her contractions at four minutes apart. At 2:34 p.m., Molly Elizabeth McCall came screaming into the world, ready to rule the roost. Everyone fussed when mom and baby came home from the hospital, wanting to hold and play with the new arrival. Letting them know she wasn't a human football they could just hand off to whomever, Molly Elizabeth bellowed her disapproval until cradled in Mac's arms.

Immediately, she became silent and stared up into the old man's eyes, her frown turned to a smile, and laughter replaced the screams. Holding her tight, Mac whispered something in her ear that generated a giggle as his great-grandchild nestled herself to his chest. There were tears of joy in Mac's eyes. You could see the pride in his expression, knowing a part of Molly was back where she belonged taking charge at The Circle M. For the rest of the evening, the two were inseparable until they both ran out of steam. Mac shuffled off to his room, Reanna and Molly Elizabeth headed for the nursery.

When the family congregated for breakfast, they talked about how Mac and Molly Elizabeth stole the show the previous night. With all the hoopla, no one noticed Mac had yet to make an appearance. Certain his father slept in, Trey suggested everyone remain seated while he went to fetch his dad. When he knocked gently on his father's bedroom door, there was no answer, so he knocked louder. Still nothing. Concerned, Trey turned the knob and walked in to find Mac sitting upright in his bed with a smile on his face, a photograph of his Molly from back in the day clutched close to his chest. Oddly, Mac did not acknowledge his son in any fashion. Fearing the worst, Trey rushed to his bedside and peered into two sightless eyes, his father's skin cold to the touch. As he grasped the reality that his dad was gone, the smile on his father's face provided all he needed to know. Mac waited until his great-granddaughter Molly Elizabeth was born so he could welcome her to the family before he passed on to his maker.

A celebration of life took place on the front lawn, where Mac and Molly had the first big shindig celebrating the monumental reconstruction and expansion of The Circle M. Duck Soup, the versatile cover band from Austin, came to pay tribute to the life work of an unselfish rancher who'd made everyone's life around him better. Nemesis provided the tightest security ever at The Circle M. Snipers were in place in hides. Armed agents on high alert walked the perimeter and among the crowd. Pretty much all of East Texas showed up to mingle with folks from all over the world and walks of life, salt of the earth human beings who came to celebrate a special life. Flags flew at half-staff for a quiet American hero few people knew existed—by his own choice. As further proof of the cycle of life, Sidney Baker Vargas went into labor the next day and gave birth to twins—Levon and Novél—new additions to the McCall extended family, who would one day positively affect the McCall legacy.

FAR AWAY IN HONG KONG, Eva and Victoria, Mr. Xen's fantasy duo carried out Talley's orders to remain in East Asia and gather what info they could on Xen and his associates. It was highly unlikely the man would sneak back to his penthouse; it had been months since he'd left, with no indications or rumors of his return. Former ladies of the evening, the two party girls took a shine to the clientele Xen entertained and opened up a small, exclusive escort service catering to the rich and famous. It turned out to be a lucrative endeavor in a most unusual way.

Many of the invitees to Xen's parties could have bought and sold him twenty times over. One of those gentlemen, Ari Moon, took to the American girls and their uninhibited freedoms of expression. Rumor had it the man was a multibillionaire who owned a number of businesses in this part of the world, including a pharmaceutical manufacturing plant in Taiwan to which Xen brokered elemental ingredients. Although Xen had never knowingly met the man, an invitation was sent to Ari for every function held at his penthouse.

ON EACH OCCASION a representative of the company showed up for the parties, a smallish quiet man in his late forties, early fifties, stayed to himself studying the crowd of wealthy and eccentric guests. Inconspicuously disguised, Ari Moon observed humankind as he'd done since his youth, when he discovered he learned a lot more about people by watching and listening, than by engaging in useless chit-chat with self-promoting braggarts. Throughout the evenings, he'd work his way around the crowd, hoping to eavesdrop on a worthwhile conversation, or to pick up on the latest in-crowd gossip that flowed like champagne. Always an admirer of beautiful things, Ari attended Xen's functions to scrutinize the celebrated array of gorgeous women. There were always plenty of them roaming around the premises. On their first visit, it was Ari Moon who first noticed Eva and Victoria. Infatuated, Ari promised himself one day soon, he'd have them at his beck and call.

That day came sooner than later, after Xen took flight and Akira Ito vanished. With those two out of the picture, Ari found out where Eva and Victoria called home in Hong Kong and paid them a visit. When the girls greeted him at the door, they didn't recognize the well-dressed, distinguished gentleman with the engaging smile, an appearance far different from that of the meek little man he portrayed at Xen's parties. Politely, Ari introduced himself and asked in a calm, mesmerizing voice if they had time to discuss a business opportunity. Believing him to be a potential client, Victoria ushered him out to the veranda to enjoy the cool evening air while Eva went to grab the champagne.

When all were comfortable, Eva poured the bubbly. For a while, they made small talk until Victoria asked Ari how he found out about them.

"Actually, I've known of you two for quite a while. I first saw you at one of Mr. Xen's penthouse parties. Then many times thereafter at similar functions. To any red-blooded man, you two would be hard to ignore," Ari said smiling. "Then all of a sudden, poof no parties."

"Yeah, we wondered what happened. Any idea where Xen and Akira might have gone?" Victoria probed.

Staring into her sensual eyes, Ari replied, "I'm glad you asked me about those two. In my various businesses, I hear all sorts of rumors and innuendos, most of which I disregard as gossip. However, I heard from some very reliable sources that the two are not together. Supposedly, Mr. Xen is somewhere in the Philippines, while the whereabouts of Akira Ito is unknown. I heard she made off with some incriminating documents that have a rather large number of individuals on the world scene very concerned. To that point, do either of you have access to Xen's penthouse by chance?"

It was Eva's turn to smile as she went to her purse and pulled out an all-access keycard to the penthouse. "Will this do?"

"Oh my, yes, I believe that will do quite nicely. By the way, do you know if anyone is in residence now?"

Victoria wondered where he was headed. "No, we check from time to time. Haven't seen any evidence to suggest anyone has been there."

"Great, then how would you two like to accompany me there to do a little undercover detective work?"

JUST AFTER ONE IN THE MORNING, the trio slipped into the luxury condo and split up to search the entire top-floor dwelling top to bottom for any defamatory documents Ari had referred to. None were found. Then Victoria suddenly remembered a tall, free-standing safe in the grotto mancave. Using the keycard to gain access back into the express elevator, they rode it down to the bottom floor. When the elevator doors opened, Eva saw that the Braun submersible was absent from the launching area. As they approached the expansive bedroom, they found the space a mess, with papers strewn all over, and the door of the safe opened a crack. Curious if any documents were still inside, Ari opened the door fully. To his amazement, there were quite a few. Each document would require careful scrutiny to determine whether they were of any value to him.

Ari was not after material that pertained to him; there wouldn't be any. Thankfully, the worst illegal thing he'd personally done in his life wouldn't qualify as a misdemeanor. No, he was digging for dirt on his colleagues, politicians, and business competitors. In his business circles, it always paid to have a bit of unsavory insurance, an ace in the hole, to spring on the opposition to convince them to see things your way. He instructed the girls to leave nothing behind. They scoured the grotto, gathering all the papers they could find and placed them in abandoned boxes to carry back to the girls' condo. After double-checking, they tidied up the place as best they could and left. On the elevator ride back to the top, the carriage stopped halfway, and the doors slid open. In stepped the building manager who gave them the once-over.

Bluntly, the man addressed them. "I'm Jeffries, the property manager here. While making my usual rounds, I noticed the express elevator coming up and inserted my keycard to stop it on this floor. Mr. Xen has two keycards to this elevator, one in his possession and the other he occasionally loans to Ms. Ito. I thought either he or Ms. Ito had returned, but instead, I find you three in his private elevator. So, who in the hell are you and what is going on?"

Victoria sighed deeply and replied in her most sultry voice. "Sir, my name is Victoria. I'm sure you remember me and Eva from some of the outlandish galas Mr. Xen threw in his pad."

He nodded. "Oh yes, of course I do. Still, that does not explain your being in his private elevator at this time of the morning."

Eva responded, "Let me clear this up. We all work together in a firm that Mr. Xen supplies with products he represents. Victoria and I run the public relations firm for Mr. Luna here, and we have been courting Mr. Xen to encourage his participation in a venture with a subsidiary of our company for quite some time. Mr. Luna left some very confidential papers with Ms. Ito for Mr. Xen to examine and sign. When we could not reach either of them, we had to resort to using the keycard Xen gave to me and Victoria on our last visit. Those papers are extremely important documents, and we cannot allow them to fall into the wrong hands. We brought the boss along to identify the documents. That's it."

"But at this hour of day?" Jeffries questioned.

"Mr. Luna just arrived from overseas and has another flight scheduled for later this morning. Because of the sensitivity of the issue, it was the only time he could fit into his busy calendar," Eva informed him.

The manager shrugged his shoulders and stepped out of the carriage with his apologies. Their captivating beauty came in handy when dealing with the opposite sex. All the way back to the girl's condo they joked about the encounter; Ari Moon was impressed at how quickly Eva fabricated such a believable tale, especially the Mr. Luna part, absolutely majestic.

ONCE INSIDE THEIR CONDO, Ari made a spur-of-the-moment offer to Eva and Victoria. "Ladies, now that I have seen you in action, I would like to hire you on a permanent basis. You two fit in perfectly with a promising venture I am entertaining. I have no doubt we can work out the details, including a few fringe benefits."

Eva responded, "Wow, Mr. Moon, we can't think of anyone we would love to work for more than you. But this is so sudden, and we have a lucrative business of our own. We'll need time to think it over. How about we let you have our answer by week's end?"

He thought that only fair and agreed to pay them a tidy sum to help him organize the contents of the boxes they confiscated while they made up their minds. Seated around the kitchen table in the condo, the threesome made a cursory run through the material they salvaged from Xen's penthouse. They sorted the data into three categories: business associates and competitors, politicians and world leaders, and entertainers including musicians, actors, and athletes. By four in the morning, adrenaline highs wore off and fatigue took over. They called it a night. The girls retired to their bedrooms, Ari took the couch.

ARI AWOKE MIDMORNING to find Victoria and Eva in bathrobes outside on the veranda having their morning coffee and a cigarette. As Moon approached, he caught the end of their discussion about what a difference a day made. It became obvious to him that they thoroughly checked him out while he slept and were going to take him up on his offer. They marveled at their good fortune. In the last twenty-four hours, they had gone from running an escort service to being hired by one of the wealthiest men they had ever encountered. An accolade Ari gladly accepted with a smile.

Admiring his new hires, Ari stepped out on the veranda. "Sorry, ladies, but I couldn't help but overhear that you've decided to come to work for me. I do so hope I heard correctly. You know success in life can sometimes be as simple as being in the right place at the right time. And it doesn't hurt to be lovely creatures with brains like you two."

They giggled and blushed, then sandwiched him between them in a group hug.

He took that as confirmation. "To business, then. I want you to sell your escort business and join me as my personal assistants to head up my public relations department. As an incentive or signing bonus, if you will, I will cut a check for each of you in the amount of five hundred thousand pounds."

Victoria was the first to find her voice. "Are you … you can't be … serious? I mean, get real, half a million pounds each. That's *insane*."

"You ladies don't know me that well yet, but as you will quickly find out, I don't joke about money. You two are exactly what I, we, need to bring attention to our new enterprise, and I intend to pay you handsomely for your services."

AT FIRST, THEY HAD RESERVATIONS about abandoning their business to join forces with a man they hardly knew. But after last night at Xen's place and now with his incredible offer, they had no qualms about their new undertaking with the cute little man with the twinkle in his eye. Eva and Victoria agreed to keep their affiliation with Nomad a secret, in case things didn't work out.

When they gazed down at the middle-aged man, they detected that special air of confidence successful people seemed to possess. Far from the doltish wallflower he portrayed at Xen's parties, they found the older man to be sharp as a tack, one who didn't miss a trick. They discovered, in his own adorable way, Ari was fun to be around; but a stickler for tying up loose ends. Evidenced by a sharp rap at the front door by a courier service with a simple contract Ari had sent over for the ladies to sign to make it all official.

SATISFIED THAT BUSINESS had been taken care of, Ari Moon left with sorted documents from Xen in hand, along with the signed contract. Back home, he deposited the papers in a vault room hidden behind a paneled wall in his expansive library. The area of a medium-sized apartment doubled as a fireproof safe room with its own regulated environment, filtered water supply, and a natural gas generator for electricity. Divided into three sections with an emergency escape exit in the rear, the living space included a front sitting room with two sleeper couches, coffee table, and two leather lounge chairs facing a big-screen TV, and a swinging door opened into the kitchen. Along the side wall was a built-in wet bar and a full bath. A doorway in the rear led to the second room, a combination office/library/storage space. The third contained a bank-sized walk-in vault that held his most prized possessions; jewels, stock certificates, artwork, and now the documents procured from Mr. Xen's grotto. He sat at the metal table in the center of the room, where he carefully examined his most valuable acquisitions making use of overhead lighting the length and width of the table. From his brief, random survey of the documents, Moon knew they were copies, left by whoever took the originals—most likely Akira Ito.

Nevertheless, they would be useful in compiling dossiers on individuals he hoped to expose with facts they would not be able to refute. It was in his nature to be thorough, and he vowed to make certain of their accuracy. During the process, he would take pleasure in watching the guilty parties turn on themselves like rabid animals. One name he was particularly interested in was Dmitri Volkov—a man he hated with a passion, the traitor who was directly responsible for the deaths of his parents and brothers and sister.

BACK IN THE GIRLS' CONDO, Victoria and Eva were on speaker phone with Talley and Millie giving them the lowdown on Ari Moon, careful to stress that they did not tell Ari about their Nomad relationship and wouldn't without permission. Talley was delighted with the initiative of her two agents and proud of herself for leaving them in Hong Kong.

INTERESTED PARTIES IN TEXAS and Quebec eavesdropped on the lengthy call.

In Montreal, Desiree listened with a wide grin on her face, pleased to pick up so much vital up-to-date info. Still, she was content to remain in the shadows, watching and waiting to pounce.

In Texas, with Xen being one of the flagged names on Warlock's list, the recorded call went straight to Tara. Most of what she heard on the recording, Nemesis already knew or had guessed. It was nice to learn Akira's whereabouts was still a mystery and that they knew about the cache of files she made off with. The call that originated in Hong Kong was picked up in Kansas. The Hong Kong number belonged to a Filipino woman by the name of Evangelina Moreno; the number in Kansas was another dead end, which was becoming a bothersome happenstance.

At least Nemesis could add the name Ari Moon to the flagged list and put a tap on Eva's phone. One thing the conversation confirmed: Mr. Xen was no longer in the big picture. Research revealed that Ari Moon was a very wealthy entrepreneur who owned and operated a variety of manufacturing facilities around East Asia. He had no criminal record, and his reputation on the street was that of a tough but honest negotiator.

IN THE VAULT AREA OF HIS SAFE ROOM, Ari Moon filed away the dossiers—save for one—which he placed on the large metal table. Ari examined the dossier of Dmitri Volkov in depth, every last detail of the worthless bastard's life. To his credit, Xen did a remarkable job compiling all the data from the man's birth to the present. It was amazing that Volkov wasn't executed for his actions or at least put in prison for life. Which spoke to the power of money, so persuasive it could make people turn a blind eye to the most perverse human atrocities. Documentation bore out that Volkov committed more than one premeditated murder by his own hand, and affidavits confirmed Dmitri ordered the deaths of hundreds more. Meticulously kept records showed bribes paid to world leaders, members of Congress, and lobbyists for everything under the sun, with names, addresses, phone numbers—the works. It took Ari most of the day and half the night to put all this information in chronological order by crimes committed. Satisfied that he'd organized things to his liking, he turned off the light, closed the door behind him, spun the dial on the vault to lock it, and walked out into the library.

At the bar, he poured himself two fingers of Pappy Van Winkle Special Reserve, a fine single malt to sip while he sat to think. Just as he settled back into his comfortable leather chair, his phone rang. Normally at that hour, he would ignore it, but this time he checked to see who it was. When Eva's name showed up on caller ID, he answered the phone. In an excited voice, she asked if he could make time for her and Victoria to visit, they had something they wanted to share with him.

He downed his whiskey and returned to his vault. By the time they got there, he'd have something for them as well. In the hour it took for them to get there, Ari fashioned the beginnings of a grand scheme. Without a major diversion, he would not be able to draw

Dmitri Volkov out of his shell of protectors—Ari bet his girls could. When they arrived, Ari met them at the door and escorted them to the library. A trio of chairs sat around a good-sized coffee table on which he'd laid out three folders. While Eva and Victoria were in transit, he'd made each of them a copy of Dmitri Volkov's file. While they got comfortable, he poured champagne all around. The girls glanced curiously at the folders, but he waved them off and asked them instead about the news they were so anxious to share with him.

Victoria couldn't hold back her excitement. "Mr. Moon, Eva and I weren't completely forthcoming with you yesterday."

Ari cocked his head and glared at her with a perplexed expression.

"Oh, nothing that would merit that scowl on your face. Believe me. You see, Eva and I are independent contractors in Hong Kong, on assignment for an organization we often provide services for in North America. A company that manufactures and ships ingredients to pharmaceutical concerns in the Eastern Bloc using Mr. Xen as an intermediary. Our assignment was to gain Xen's confidence in order to assess whether his services were actually needed any longer, since the company we represent expanded their logistical capabilities and can now ship directly to East Asia. From what we'd already discovered, the man was obsolete, and our recommendation was going to be that he be removed from the payroll."

Eva chimed in, "It just so happens one of Xen's best customers is a Russian named Dmitri Volkov. While we were occupied with Xen, our employers negotiated a deal with Volkov to ship additives directly to him without any middleman involvement. We have been given permission by the company to make you the same offer with the caveat that your orders will take precedence over his. Our management found Volkov to be belligerent, vulgar, and untrustworthy. They currently supply him with basic product at an inflated price, whereas for you, they are willing to provide the refined product at a reduced rate."

Eva smiled at Victoria and winked at Ari. "So, after all that, I guess our question to you is, are you interested?"

THE REACTION ON ARI'S FACE showed both shock and delight. "I must say, you two are amazing and unpredictable. I commend you both for again exceeding my expectations. To answer your question, yes, I am interested. My question back to you is one of loyalty. Do you foresee any conflict of interest here?"

Victoria spoke up, "None at all, the organization in the States is all for it. They believe we can build and expand upon this relationship."

Ari leaped out of his chair and danced Eva around the room. Then Victoria, who turned out to be a bit awkward with their height difference, much to his delight; his eyes lit up in pure ecstasy. Now that they were all on the same team, the girls opened up about Nomad, the outfit's managers Talley and Millie, and their new product caida libre. Astounded how things melded together, Ari asked where Nomad was based. At that, the girls laughed and said that was the beauty of the whole deal; they were mobile, hence the name Nomad, and their labs were on wheels in massive, reconfigured motor coaches. After a few more questions, Ari was satisfied he'd chosen wisely.

Before he moved on, Ari poured them each another glass of bubbly. "Ladies, you have made my day. Ironically, the folders you have in front of you are copies of what Xen compiled on Dmitri Volkov. I've included a smidgeon of my personal history, specifically merciless atrocities I suffered at the hands of Dmitri Volkov. I want you to sabotage every aspect of this man's life."

The cold, angry stare in Ari's eyes was reason enough for them not to question his dictate.

AMID MULTIPLE SCENARIOS coming to light, the Nemesis cyber lab at The Circle M was bogged down with information overload and overlapping investigations. Miranda brought in her man Ty Dossier to concentrate solely on the complex riddle of the puzzling cell phone signatures. In all his thirty-plus years on the Dallas police force, Ty had never encountered the like. Nor had any of his colleagues on the Dallas PD. Baffled, Ty called Tina Tremblay and Rose Conner in Canada, who referred him to Noah Bouchard at the Monastery in Canada.

Already aware of the issue, Noah advised him he was working on the mystery. Whoever it was built an app to reset to a new signature the instant communication was closed down. Ordinarily not that difficult to configure. However, in this case, the sequence followed an unusual protocol, a complex random code, that even Warlock may never crack. Discouraged though never defeated, Noah promised to keep after it and would update Ty on his progress.

IN THE MIDDLE OF THE NIGHT, Ty woke with a start and sat straight up in bed. Perhaps there was an easier way to find the illusive communicator—a more conventional way. Every phone call bounced off a cell tower or satellite. Warlock had ample time to track the signal and determine the coordinates of the party in motion. A majority of the mystery calls originated from the Midwest, along desolate strips of interstate highways. What if Ty and Miranda took a working RV vacation to tour the heartland of America? Miranda was going stir-crazy in the lab; it would do her a world of good to get out and do some work in the field. Why not attempt something different? What could it hurt?

Trey thought it was worth a try and had them fly to Wichita, Kansas. A rented motor coach was waiting for them when they arrived.

Posing as novice tourists, Ty and Miranda roamed up and down I-35 and I-29 in the motor home, stopping from time to time to check out landmarks and interesting vistas along the way. Nights they stayed at the most populated motor home camping grounds they could find, asking questions about the area as novice campers tended to do. By and large, the motor home crowd were a friendly and helpful bunch, and their tips came in handy. As a result, the couple saw some incredible countryside most tourists never see. After a week of relaxed driving in little to no traffic, the two agents almost forgot they were working.

On a cool evening at a campsite alongside a beautiful lake outside of Coon Rapids, Minnesota, Ty reeled in his third good-size walleye to fry up for dinner over an open fire. As they finished their meal, Miranda put her head on Ty's shoulder and thanked him for picking up that she needed a break. After Miranda cleaned up and Ty extinguished the fire, they laid silently in bed listening to the creatures of the night serenade them.

Miranda broke the silence. "Ty, do you really think we can find this phantom caller we're chasing? What if Warlock can't identify them, and we're just spinning our wheels here?"

Ty ran his hand over her silky hair as he gazed out the window at the wide-open spaces. "I think we are going to have to take things as they come and not rush them. Our caller is eventually going to lead us right to them. We are exactly where we need to be."

Comforted by his words, Miranda fell asleep and awoke in his arms in the morning.

AFTER THEY MADE SURE the fire from the night before was completely out, she and Ty packed up their gear and headed north on I-35, then took a state road west to intersect with I-29 South. As they drove down the interstate toward Sioux Falls, South Dakota, Tara McCall contacted them to report a suspicious call was just placed to Dmitri Volkov from a location some twenty miles from their location. According to Warlock, the caller was headed south on I-29 before the signal disappeared when the contact terminated.

Even though Ty didn't know exactly which vehicle the caller was in, there was an outside chance a second call would be made. As he accelerated through sparsely populated farmland to merge onto I-29 South, traffic was light, which bettered their chances of making up time on their suspects. Most of the vehicles he and Miranda passed were agricultural in nature—tractors, loaded produce trucks, jeeps, and the like. Ty was driving far too fast to suit the locals, and they let him know it, by honking their horns, shaking their fists in the air, or flipping him off. Unfortunately for Ty and Miranda, they were unable to find the mystery callers, and there wasn't another call that day. Exhausted, they called it quits for the day.

Although he was somewhat disappointed, Ty took solace in the fact that the use of cell towers and satellites worked. After a long day on the road, it was time to find a nice place to park the coach for the night. Tomorrow was another day, and their spirits were high. Tired and hungry, they spotted a sign that advertised a massive travelers' resort and RV park, where they could get a nice meal and a good night's sleep. Nationwide Overnight Motel and Diner, he'd heard that name before or seen it in print somewhere. After they checked in, Ty pulled into their designated spot in the back of the property close to a snazzy new mega-RV.

TY AND MIRANDA SYSTEMATICALLY made the essential hookups and adjusted the expansions of their home on wheels. Part of the ritual in motor camps was to set out lawn chairs under the broad awning, an open invitation for their neighbors to come over to introduce themselves and share a beverage or two. Just as they sat down and popped the top on their first beer, a couple strolled over to welcome them. Soon a small crowd milled around drinking and snacking on sandwiches and simple hors d'oeuvres that magically appeared from their new neighbors. To cut the chilly evening, Ty built a fire in the pit near the RV. Mostly the conversation centered around open road small talk, highway conditions, gasoline prices, rising tolls. To change the subject, Ty asked who owned the ship on wheels parked nearest them.

One of the regulars at the camp said, "Oh that, it belongs to the owners of this park who have done quite well with their franchises. That's just one of a small fleet of those monsters they have roaming about the interstates."

Out of curiosity, Ty asked the man if he knew the owners' names. Ty was thinking of upgrading and wondered if the expense was worth it, what with the price of gas and maintenance. It was a legitimate question, so the know-it-all said he'd only heard them called by their first names, Talley and Millie. Coincidentally, they just happened to be on site. Rumor had it, they had individual suites on all their properties to use during their visits. The trailer park genius now had Ty's and Miranda's full attention.

Matter of fact, the road warrior remarked, "It was probably Talley who checked y'all in."

Aware they lucked into something far greater than they had anticipated, as soon as their guests left, Ty and Miranda hurried inside to contact Trey at Nemesis HQ.

TY'S CALL FOUND TREY AND TARA snuggled together on the bench by the lake enjoying a pleasant breeze off the water under clear skies and a full moon.

"Good evening, Ty," said Chairman McCall. "What's up? Good news, I hope."

"Good evening," Ty responded. "Best news so far, hang onto your Stetson. Miranda and I hit the jackpot tonight with the motor park crowd during an impromptu get-together. Seems the owners of a number of parks called Nationwide Overnight Motel and Diner are none other than Talley and Millie, our old friends from Sister Nation, who I suspect now run Nomad. Yep, looks like they are back together and my guess is one of them is our mystery texter dealing with Dmitri Volkov. Thinking out of the box, I'm not sure how or if Xen fits in with this scenario. Hard to figure."

"Wow! Are you kidding me?" Trey was now up on his feet pacing. "That's awesome. As far as Xen goes, for now, why don't we let karma take care of him."

Ty cackled and added, "Yeah, if need be, we can always use Akira's treasure trove of evidence to nail his ass."

"Precisely."

Before they hung up, Trey filled Ty in on Ari Moon, a recent person of interest Nemesis was investigating. "Our query into Mr. Moon's business life showed no significant illegal activity. Apparently, he's an intelligent entrepreneur who has amassed a fortune making 'prudent acquisitions in East Asia through his conglomerate—Moon Enterprises—its logo a crescent moon.

"I don't get it. Then how does this Moon fella fit into the picture?" Ty inquired.

"When we dug into Ari's personal life, Warlock uncovered an interesting bit of information—Ari's fierce hatred for Dmitri Volkov. Get this. Dmitri was directly responsible for the murders of Ari's parents, brothers, and sister; crimes for which he was never held accountable. We'll keep you posted on him. For now, you and Miranda stay where you are and continue to play RV neophytes." Ty agreed and signed off.

CHAPTER 17

LIVING THE GOOD LIFE in his manor above Mindoro Straits, Philippines, Xen was not the least bit bothered with what was happening in the world outside of his little paradise. Except that his money might run out—monthly salaries and bribes took a huge toll on his assets. On a premonition, he phoned his bank, only to be informed his personal banker had been replaced and his account transferred to another department. He asked to be transferred and was put on hold until he finally gave up. Later in the afternoon, he tried again with the same result. Frantic about the status of his finances, Xen asked Hiraya to drive him to the bank when it opened in the morning.

BELIEVING SHE WOULD RECEIVE a generous gratuity as per usual, she complied. He was inside the bank for an extraordinarily long period of time. Judging from Xen's body language when he walked out of the bank, she knew there would be no gratuity. When Hiraya asked him if everything was all right, all the color drained out of his face.

AT FIRST, HE IGNORED the question, then mumbled for her to take him home. On the way, he said nothing, just stared blankly out the window. Xen raced to his safe to check his funds when he got to the villa, only to discover there was barely enough to pay this month's expenses. Panicked, the former pharmaceutical middleman began to sweat profusely and summoned Hiraya.

As soon as she arrived, he pointed at the safe and screamed at her. "Where in the hell is all my money? I know you stole it, no one else has been in the house besides you and me."

SHE SHOOK HER HEAD VEHEMENTLY as she spoke. "Me? How could I? You are the only one with the combination. After all I've done for you, how could you even think that?"

Hiraya turned and ran out of the room in tears. Truth was she'd taken money from the safe ever since she'd memorized the numbers one night months ago when he was drunk and dialed the combination.

NIGHTFALL FAST APPROACHED. Xen suddenly felt a pang of remorse for his altercation with Hiraya. He called out for her. When he got no answer, he searched the house. She was nowhere to be found, and her clothes were gone from her bedroom. He moped about, in hopes she would pop in so he could apologize. Xen had no way of knowing Dmitri Volkov purchased the bank and froze his account pending investigation. Thanks to the island grapevine, everyone except him was aware he was insolvent and could no longer afford to pay protection money.

Bitterly, he summoned his chief of security, and there was no reply. When he picked up the phone to make a call, the line was dead. Then the lights went out. He could feel the massive compound close in on him. Fumbling around, he finally found a flashlight and hurried to the kitchen. Thirsty, Xen turned the lever on the faucet, a sputter of water came out, then nothing. Alone with no utilities, his world was falling apart. He never developed survival skills living in the lap of luxury. Petrified, he lowered his head into his hands and wept.

At the crack of dawn, bright sunshine shattered the darkness and woke him from his slumber, curled up in a ball on the kitchen floor. During the night, he came up with the idea to make a getaway. He scrambled upstairs to change into loose-fitting clothes and comfortable sneakers. His best bet was to find the landing strip where he hid his plane. He found the keys to unlock the door to his aircraft and put them in his pocket. Much to his dismay, the keys to the manor car were missing. He ran to the garage. It was empty; he'd have to go on foot. What next?

In the pantry, he found bottled water along with packaged food and canned soup. All of which he put in a knapsack. Xen rummaged around the kitchen for a couple of plastic plates. In one of the drawers, he found a retro can/bottle opener and some silverware. By the door, he spotted a Swiss Army knife and a cigarette lighter in a collection bowl. In the laundry closet, he found a blanket he slipped into the knapsack and picked a lightweight rainsuit off a hook along with a ball cap he plopped on his head. Frantically, the terrified city dweller arranged his gear in the compartmental canvas knapsack and hoisted it on his shoulders by the straps. It was a little heavier than he thought it would be, but not so much that he couldn't manage.

Xen ran across a canteen in the maintenance shed and took it back to the kitchen to wash it out, forgetting the water had been turned off. Oh well, if he was going to rough it for a while, might as well get used to it. He unscrewed the cap of the canteen and filled it to the brim with the last two bottles of water in the pantry, took a sip, and swished it around in his mouth to see if it was okay. Satisfied it was, he screwed the cap down. Back in the shed, he snatched up a small hatchet to use as a weapon or to chop wood in case he needed to build a fire. Off he went on his journey to find the airport. Attached to the end of the Swiss army knife was a small compass, which would have come in handy if Xen had any clue in which direction the airport was from his location.

"Damn it, why didn't I pay attention to the route the driver took through the jungle to the manor?" He shrugged and chuckled to himself, "Seriously, get a grip. After all, how many options could there be on an island this small?"

If memory served him, the driver turned left off a dirt road onto the pavement leading to the villa, or was it a right, no, it was a left. When he reached the end of the drive, there were four dirt roads in sight, all turned onto the paved surface in front of him—might just as well have been a million. It was blazing hot and brutally humid. He dropped his backpack on the ground, sat on it, and played eeny-meeny-miny-moe in his mind while he took a sip of water to moisten his dry mouth. What a screwed-up dumbass he was, so proud of his ingenious escape from Hong Kong, then to let down his guard too soon, and now this kerfuffle.

If he had one piece of luck left in his life, he prayed that he would pick the correct dirt road. Which of the four should he choose? Xen picked the third. There was a fifth artery further up around a curve that he didn't see—the one he should have taken.

DUE TO THE POOR ROAD CONDITIONS, he figured it took forty-five minutes to an hour to get from the airport to his villa stronghold. Considering his questionable physical condition, Xen guessed with frequent rest stops he had roughly an eight-to-ten-hour hike ahead of him. Doable if he paced himself. He reset his knapsack on his back and trudged along the dusty road he chose. An hour in, the heat and humidity forced him to take a break. Even though there was plenty of shade from a canopy of behemoth trees in the ancient forest, it felt like a sauna. His shirt clung to his body as Xen settled into a concave spot in the trunk of a huge balete (bal-eat) tree, known as the "Millennium Tree" in the Philippines. Fatigue set in; rife with worry the night before, he'd slept fitfully. Intending to rest his eyes for only a few minutes, he fell sound asleep. An hour later, he heard an unearthly growl that woke him.

A menacing, low-pitched snarl followed from a mongrel dog with bared teeth staring at him, sizing him up. The mangy animal was frothing at the mouth, and its yowls became more intense as it inched closer. The instant it sensed his prey's fear, it charged, inflicting multiple wounds on Xen's arms and legs as man attempted to fight off the vicious animal. Xen got his right hand around the handle of the hatchet, jerked it out of his bag, and took a halfhearted swipe at the attacking dog. The razor-sharp blade grazed the side of the animal, raising a loud yelp and frightening the dog enough for it to limp away, deep into the thick underbrush to lick its wounds.

Most of Xen's injuries were superficial; however, the damage was done. No doubt the dog was rabid. In this environment of heat and humidity, considering the number of times he was bitten, the incubation period was sure to escalate. Was there any worse way to die than from rabies? Paralysis, delirium, coma, then death was what lay ahead for him. Panic set in. He launched the canvas pack onto his back and started to run down the path, hoping to get help when he reached the strip. Soon his run became a pitiful shuffle, then an apathetic creeping death march, that ended when the infamous Mr. Xen fell to the ground and passed out.

It was dark when he next opened his eyes. In excruciating pain, salivating, he attempted to take a drink from the canteen. He spilled more than he drank. Surveying his surroundings, he tried to figure out how he got here and where he was headed. Unusual shapes inhabited the trees; his imagination ran amuck. Even though he sensed he must be on his way, his body would not respond. His wounds oozed blood. He knew he should tend to them. Somehow, he had to muster the strength; hard as he tried, he couldn't and didn't. Then his illusions with glowing yellow eyes came to life; massive shapes with pointed snouts slithered toward him then surrounded him, drawn by the scent of blood. The last thing Xen saw before he passed out again were the wide-open jaws of a crocodile about to clamp down on his right leg.

THERE WERE NO REMAINS AT THE SITE to indicate what happened to him. Rumors circulated about that for some inexplicable reason Xen left the safety of his manor to explore the island. The jungle was a dangerous place for an amateur. Unaccustomed to the searing heat and humidity, the man must have become disoriented and wandered into a bask of crocodiles that populated the area near the creek. Most likely, they drug him into the water to drown him, then stored the body in an underwater den for later.

In a nearby village, a young man named Bayani stood guard outside a grass hut. He admired the fancy knife in his hand that had a gizmo attached to its handle with a spinning arrow inside. A week earlier, Bayani and his father, Rodrigo, the leader of the village were hunting in the jungle when they heard a raucous over by a huge balete tree. A number of crocodiles were about to make a wounded man their dinner. Rodrigo fired a rifle shot into the dirt by the maneater nearest the bleeding man to get its attention and frighten the carnivores away. It was a gamble that worked. The crocs scampered off into a nearby creek, leaving the coast clear for the two Filipinos to carry the bleeding man to their village to treat his injuries. For ten days, Mr. Xen faded in and out of consciousness. Instructed by Rodrigo, shamans administered ointments to Xen's wounds, potions for his fever, and liquids to flush out the poisons in his system.

The chieftain recognized the man as the owner of the villa where he and his villagers worked as gardeners and caretakers for decades prior to his return. If it had not been for the money Xen provided them over the years, their village would not have survived. When outsiders came in and tried to replace Rodrigo and his crew, it was Xen who insisted that they remain out of gratitude for their years of service. They saw this as their opportunity to pay him back.

Xen found a home with the villagers who referred to him as Pastol (*shepherd* in Filipino). Without the natives, he would have died a horrific death, so he proudly adopted the name. Pastol patiently learned their customs, and he schooled them in his. Life here offered him the opportunity to slow down and take things as they came. He discovered how good it felt to give more than he received. He was safe, protected by the villagers who were his allies. They taught him how to survive in and live off the jungle. His physical wounds soon healed, but the deepest mental scars lingered—begging revenge. Someday the opportunity would avail itself, and he would rise out of obscurity to seize the moment. For now, he was content to live a simple life.

WHILE THINGS SORTED THEMSELVES in the Philippines, Talley and Millie sought to tie up loose ends for Nomad in mid-America. If things went as planned, they stood to make a fortune distributing their wares to two very wealthy and influential billionaires. Preeminent to the arrangement, Millie had to finalize the deal with Dmitri Volkov while keeping him in the dark about Nomad's pact with Ari Moon.

The first face-to-face meeting between Millie and Dmitri took place at Cambridge Beaches Resort in Bermuda on the third week in March. A classic five-star resort nestled on a finger of land against the water of the North Atlantic Ocean on three sides, it was peaceful, private, and met the demands laid out by Millie and Dmitri.

Saturday morning at ten sharp, they began their two-hour session. Both sides consented to allow one adviser each for their showdown. It took the entire two hours to reach an agreement. In the end, Nomad agreed to supply Dmitri Volkov with caida libre directly. No longer would either party be in need of a broker. Dmitri, although still peeved at how he was treated by Millie in her mystery texts, was pacified by the potential riches that lay ahead. Millie held the upper hand going in and played it coyly. She was pleased with the final agreement, especially since Dmitri would unknowingly receive an inferior product.

WIPED OUT AFTER HIS MENTAL SPARRING MATCH in Bermuda with Millie Snowden, Dmitri wanted nothing to do with Zoya Volkov, his nagging wife in Moscow, and flew directly to his Albanian villa. Zoya and the kids only came to the villa for a week or two in the summers. For the rest of the year, he was free to use the place for whatever—in his case, that meant unbridled frivolity. No one complained or bothered to contact his wife. Since Zoya was a snobbish know-it-all, who never engaged with neighbors, they figured why not let the bitch find out for herself.

Ari found from one of his jet-set allies that Dmitri was hosting one of his famed blowouts in two weeks' time and arranged for his girls to be invited. Eva and Victoria flew from Hong Kong to Albania the weekend before the event, to acclimate themselves and recover from jet lag after the eighteen-hour flight. They booked a condo at a lovely resort in Vuno not far from Volkov's villa. Once they were settled, it was Ari's idea for them to venture out and experience the local nightlife. He wanted them to attract attention by flaunting their stuff all over town to attract attention and get the locals talking about the two American wildcats who just arrived. That way the girls would not be thought of as total strangers when they walked into Dmitri's bash at his villa extraordinaire.

At Ari Moon's request, the girls dressed suggestively with just enough tease to tempt. For the better part of a week, the two beauties reveled in the intense nightlife in the Coastal Albania community. Their local notoriety preceded them to the party; even the host glanced anxiously at the front door in anticipation of their arrival. If reports about Dmitri Volkov were accurate, it would not take long for him to approach them, much like Mr. Xen had at his penthouse in Hong Kong.

DMITRI, AWARE THAT THE NEW ARRIVALS had become the center of attention at his get-together, fought off a fit of ego-fueled jealousy. Captivated by the beauty of the two vixens, he shouldered his way through the crowd to join the circle currently chatting them up. Eva was mid-discussion with an Arab prince when Dmitri sauntered up. Victoria glanced at him as he eyed her impressive figure. He blushed, but she just gave him a knowing smile and a wink that put him at ease. Regaining his usual haughty demeanor, Dmitri rudely interrupted Eva's ongoing conversation to introduce himself to the girls.

Undaunted, Eva kept talking until she finished her thought, then glared over at him in disgust, calling attention to his rudeness. For an instant, Dmitri resembled the little boy scolded in school and sent to sit in the corner. Eva continued to address the man with whom she was having a discussion, completely ignoring their obnoxious host. Dmitri's face turned red with anger, and he was about to say something to Eva, when Victoria caught his attention. The tall, dark-haired beauty was shaking her head no and wiggling her finger, signaling him to follow her. How could he resist? Dmitri turned on his heels and trailed Victoria out the back to the pool bar. Each got a drink and found a chair away from the crowd.

Before she spoke, Victoria lit a cigarette and took a sip of a perfect dry martini. "Dmitri, may I call you Dmitri? I hope so, anyway, Eva is high strung and a stickler for proper etiquette since she was raised by nuns in the Philippines. Old habits are hard for her to break. Actually, she is a ball of fire when she gets wound up, full of endless energy. I hope we have not offended you in any way—honored as we are to have been invited here tonight. What a magnificent place you have, I would love to see it all sometime."

"Think nothing of it, my dear, I was out of line and will apologize to your friend at the earliest convenience. I would love to show you both around, but I'm afraid now may not be the right time. The villa and grounds are rather large by Albanian standards, and I would prefer to take our time to examine all it has to offer. How long do you two plan on staying in Vuno?"

Holding his stare, Victoria explained they were on a bucket-list holiday, for which they'd set no time restraints or strict agenda.

"Wonderful, wonderful." Dmitri nodded slowly. "That's just what I was hoping to hear. In that case, I may have a special treat for you two if you are interested. I have to check with a very close friend of mine to see if there is still room for two more guests to visit his privately owned castle nestled high up in the mountains not far from here. He is having one of his outings there on the weekend. Lots of worldly people show up for his outrageous bashes. Something to think about, you know, if you're interested in things like that."

With a wicked smile on her face, Victoria leaned over to whisper in his ear. "Sounds delicious. Of course, I will have to run it by Eva. Judging from what you've hinted—it's right up her alley."

"Great, that's great. Why don't you two drop by here tomorrow afternoon? We can take a tour of the place and discuss our plans. I should know by then if there is an opening for The Castle shindig. Okay then, you two have a good time and behave yourselves, if possible. I best get back to my other guests and clients. They're not as interesting as you, but they do help me pay the bills around here. Please tell your friend I am sorry for the way I acted." Then he was off in a flash to join the hustle and bustle inside.

Before she went inside, Victoria finished her smoke and the last of her martini. Taking their host's advice, the girls stayed until two in the morning when the cover band called it quits. As soon as they were safely home in their suite, they gave each other a high five. After the girls got comfortable, Eva poured the bubbly, while Victoria called Ari Moon in Hong Kong with a progress report.

IT WAS NINE IN THE MORNING when his phone rang. Ari was in his kitchen whipping up his breakfast of scrambled eggs and crisp bacon. Priding himself on his ability to judge character, he knew the girls were good; however, their news again exceeded his expectation. In full agreement with them to remain passive, Ari instructed them to stay in Albania as long as they felt necessary and gather as much dirt as possible on Dmitri, his friends, and associates. After Victoria hung up, Eva called Talley and Millie to fill them in on the evening's events. Both conversations from the girls in Vuno were intercepted, cataloged, and transcribed by Warlock.

BACK AT HIS RETREAT IN ALBANIA, Dmitri Volkov admired the majestic contrast of mountains and ocean from the bay window in his guest chalet. The custom-built abode was his version of the ultimate bachelor pad with the latest in ridiculously expensive furnishings crafted out of gold, silk, and marble meant to dazzle his guests. All courtesy of a world-renowned European designer. Not to mention the latest in remote-controlled electronics including TVs, stereos, and security gizmos. To ensure privacy, colossal arborvitae trees blocked the view of the chalet from the villa to foil peeping toms. Like everything Dmitri did for himself, it was overdone to make a statement. The largest expenditure was the tunnel he had built, leading from his art studio off the library in the villa to the guest chalet, used primarily to smuggle mistresses to his den of iniquity. When the villa was finished, the project violated nearly every building code in Albania. Money was power; therefore, bribed officials looked the other way. As justification for his extravagance to his wife, he pointed out, in a pinch, the roomie chalet could house unwanted houseguests, like his sister. Soon after it was completed, Mrs. Volkov visited the structure, thought it hideous, and never returned. He was seated near a warm fire in the chalet when Eva and Victoria rang to say they were on their way for a tour. Rubbing his hands together, he licked his chops in anticipation, then hurried through the tunnel to the villa to shave and shower.

Antsy for the arrival of the two hotties, Dmitri paced the floor in his library. When the buzzer from the front gate bleeped, he passed them through and guided his guests to the last parking stall. Dmitri swiftly whisked them through the art studio door and into the tunnel leading to the gazebo. Not quite sure about all the cloak and dagger, Eva and Victoria eyed him curiously. He reassured them it was merely a short-cut to the expansive grounds behind the villa. When they exited the tunnel into the chalet, his female guests gave him a sideways grimace.

DMITRI SEARCHED FOR AN EXPLANATION. "It's not what you think, really. Well, it is, but it isn't … Allow me to show you the lake, the pool, and the spa."

Still skeptical, the girls followed him out the back to a most glorious setting, overlooking a private lake fed by an inland mountain stream rerouted to empty into the Adriatic Sea. Ingenious landscapers created an aquatic fantasyland including palm trees, a white sand beach, and an infinity swimming/diving pool. A huge deck with ample seating for a generously sized crowd, which included a clubhouse with changing rooms, a snack bar with steps down to grass tennis courts, a croquet lawn, a bocce court, even a putting green and driving range with real hybrid Emerald Zoysia grass.

Their host suggested they begin the afternoon with drinks and a swim, then if the spirit moved them, onto whatever else suited their fancy. Impressed with the amenities, the ladies agreed a swim sounded good, but they hadn't brought swimsuits. Playing the role of a gentleman, he let that pass and informed them swimsuits were available in the women's changing area first door on the left in the clubhouse.

Retiring into the men's locker room, Dmitri changed into a speedo. Neither Eva nor Victoria were surprised that the entire collection of bikini-style swimsuits from which to choose were the scantiest they had ever seen. To make a statement, Victoria searched until she found a top that barely covered her bust, and she and Eva squeezed into thong bottoms. When they came out, Dmitri was seated on the edge of a chaise waiting for them with drinks already on a small table close by. Slowly, from bottom to top, he checked out his guests for the afternoon, unable to disguise his appreciation.

WHILE THEY MADE SMALL TALK and sipped their drinks, it surprised the girls that their host seemed awkward and a bit shy around them. Truth was Dmitri desired them so much he was afraid to say or do anything to upset them. After a couple more drinks, he loosened up and suggested they take a dip in the pool to cool off from the midday sun. Leading the way, he dived in, and the girls followed. As soon as Victoria hit the water, her top flew off, and when she surfaced laughing hysterically, the mood immediately changed from uncomfortable to folly. Before Dmitri got too frisky, Victoria asked if he'd gotten the okay for her and Eva to attend the shindig with him on the weekend.

Dmitri grinned and nodded. What he neglected to mention was that the host of the party ran a thorough background check on the both of them—the man didn't like last-minute surprises. When he discovered the duo had been arrested numerous times for prostitution during their college years, they were added to the guest list. For the rest of the afternoon, Dmitri chased but never caught his prey, which drove poor Dmitri out of his mind with frustration.

DINNER AND BEDROOM CALISTHENICS PLANS were dashed when Eva announced that she and Victoria had a previously scheduled appointment in an hour, and they could just make it if they hurried. Crushed, Dmitri said he understood; his sour expression indicated he didn't. Back in their civies, the trio returned through the tunnel to the girls' car. They both gave him a big kiss goodbye and sped off. Defeated and bewildered, Dmitri called after them saying he would be in touch about the upcoming weekend at The Castle. Victoria held her hand out of the window to acknowledge they'd heard him and waved.

LITTLE WAS KNOWN ABOUT THE OWNER of the renovated castle, other than he was once an average-at-best computer programmer who quit college after he made a fortune from a computer program he stole from his roommate. With his billions, it was no problem for him to secretly purchase the Albanian castle at the asking price—less hassle, less publicity. The magnificent fortress and adult playground turned into a sanctuary from morality where the elite came to enjoy the fruits of their labors. It became a safe haven to indulge in bizarre and decadent practices, out of sight of the witless media and bumbling constituents they sought to control.

Access to the structure as a non-member was limited to a narrow road that wound its way around dangerous curves with severe drop-offs or by helicopter, which guaranteed the passengers a hair-raising adventure battling fluctuating drafts and swirling crosswinds.

If you were a member, you could take a comfortable ride straight up the side of the mountain in a luxurious twelve-passenger cable car, sheltered from sight, wind, and weather, in a camouflaged bullet-proof plexiglass sheath. A small squadron of jet choppers was on ready in a cave hanger for emergency evacuations, accessible by an elevator in the foyer of the main house.

For most of the shindigs, the guest list was limited to fifty guests. There was only one ironclad rule at The Castle: absolutely no cameras, phones, or recorders were allowed. No exceptions, no second chances; anyone who violated that rule was banned for life. Other than that, everything was fair game; nothing was out of bounds or off limits. Influential guests conducted sordid discussions, everything from planned assassinations to hostile corporate takeovers, to coups d'état, initiatives designed to replace entire governments or reduce the earth's population.

Clientele varied in age, lifestyle, and profession. Everything was hush-hush, shielded from the public who would be shocked at the names of those on the guest lists over the years. Idolized individuals who were loved and respected around the world reveled in corporeal debauchery, giving into their wildest dreams and fantasies. There was no other place on earth that held more perverse secrets inside its walls than did The Castle in Albania.

A HANDSOME MAN IN HIS THIRTIES by the name of Miles Stewart was The Castle overseer and facilitator. Since the day he signed on, Miles received his instructions via coded directives from an anonymous individual. He had no desire to find out who was behind it all, unsure he wanted to face such depravity. Miles Stewart was hired to provide a service which he did—no questions asked.

BACK IN TEXAS, THE NEMESIS CREW scanned the latest intercepted calls following the girls' visit to Dmitri's backyard playground. Trey and Tara listened as Eva and Victoria reported to Ari Moon, then to Talley Marsh and Millie Snowden. Victoria confirmed that they were formally invited to an Albanian castle for a weekend blowout called the shindig. The conversations were interesting and informative to the cybercrime investigation team. Trey was curious what Eva and Victoria would turn up and report back to their handlers after their weekend at The Castle.

UP IN MONTREAL, another interested party reviewed the latest recording from Millie. Desiree Richards's ears perked up when she learned that Eva and Victoria were invited to The Castle shindig in Albania. Desiree had heard about it in the past and wished she could have attended one, since it was her kind of thing back then. What excited her most now were the contacts the girls could make and evidence they could procure for Desiree to use against the aristocracy. The timing of it all could not have been better.

That very morning a case of Spice of Life packets, containing the additive caida libre, arrived at her condo as Boris had promised. She was anxious to see if the product worked as advertised. With so much going on, it would be nice to have an extra boost of energy and focus to keep abreast of it all.

She began the regimen right away—one packet three times a day at breakfast, lunch, and dinner. Within a few days, she felt rejuvenated. Her energy level was through the roof, and she maintained her focus without straining. Even her cockiness returned. Now all she had to do was stick to her regimen and wait for the right time to pounce.

VICTORIA WOKE WITH A START from an afternoon nap to answer her phone vibrating on the coffee table. It was Dmitri with the itinerary for the weekend shindig in the Albanian mountains. Being a man of few words, his instructions were simple. Pack lightly, make sure to include a warm coat for the evenings, and be ready at 6:30 a.m. sharp on Friday. The female duo had no false illusions about what the weekend ahead had in store for them. Eva and Victoria were prepared to witness the worst of humankind cloaked in self-adoration, aware the people they were about to encounter cared only to satisfy their lustful appetites and selfish desires. As despicable as that may be, it was an opportunity for the girls to gather vital information for their employers.

Certain there'd be monitoring and detecting devices hidden in The Castle, Victoria and Eva would have to trust their memories to burn images of the participants permanently in their minds. They would have to regulate their alcohol consumption while other guests would be out of it on booze and drugs most of the weekend. Once the girls climbed into Dmitri's car, Eva and Victoria were committed for the duration.

Punctual to a fault, Dmitri arrived at 6:30. Although, he was not in as jovial a mood as one might expect. Instead, he was despondent as if he'd lost his best friend or in this case that he was leading his lambs to slaughter. On the drive to the cable car, the girls did their best to cheer him up, which seemed to work for a while until they boarded the lift for the ride up the mountain.

When the doors opened up at the top, Miles Stewart was there to greet them, understandably taken with the two alluring ladies Dmitri brought to The Castle. Right off the bat, Victoria sensed something was askew. She noticed Dmitri's body wilt, his painted-on smile evaporate, and a heavy sigh of defeat escape his lips. She'd encountered similar scenarios before; Miles had muscled in on the Russian. Dmitri's weekend of frivolity with her and Eva was not going to happen. As special invited guests, neither Victoria nor Eva had a say in the matter. Nor did Dmitri if he expected to keep the elite guests at the party as clients, acquaintances, or business associates. Not desirous to be banned for life, the Russian excused himself and headed to the nearest bar. The master of entertainment for the shindig took the girls, one on each arm, for a tour of The Castle. Victoria blew Dmitri a conciliatory kiss as they passed the bar.

WHAT BEGAN AS A DISASTROUS WEEKEND for Dmitri turned into a blessing for Eva and Victoria. Being escorted by the host gave the two women instant credibility with honored guests and inroads to people they never would have met accompanied by the despised Russian. In their profession, Victoria and Eva had witnessed plenty of bizarre sexual fetishes. But nothing more twisted than what they encountered on their guided tour.

Miles sensed their discomfort, ended the tour, and ushered them outside for some fresh air. The two female spies fought the urge to throw the asshole over the railing to a certain death for hosting such a demonic spectacle. Instead, they lit up a smoke to stem their anger and calm their nerves. Mindful of their mission, Eva and Victoria were more determined than ever to see it through.

For the rest of the weekend, Eva and Victoria stayed within arm's length of Miles. Even though the host to the elite provided his invitees a menu of the most perverse of sexual options, the man's own tastes were more conventional, nothing kinky. As payment for services rendered, Miles became their protector. With him as chaperone, the girls had the run of The Castle twenty-four-seven. They wished they could forget things they witnessed and utterances they'd heard from the chosen ones that remained forever logged in the recesses of their memories.

At the end of the day, it was a welcomed reprieve for the three of them to retire to his bedroom. Miles was handsome, well-endowed, and experienced. A man who gave as much as he received, something his guests at the shindig would never comprehend. After a particularly satisfying love-making session, Eva and Victoria mentioned in passing how grateful they were that he rescued them from Dmitri. Miles cracked up and said he thought as much and couldn't imagine the madman Russian in bed with the two of them—what an utterly disgusting visual. They all rolled their eyes and nodded.

FOR MOST OF THE DAY of his arrival at The Castle, Dmitri sulked. The fact that his prized spitfires were literally stolen right out from under him at the outset put an immediate damper on his prospects for the weekend. Resolved to drown his sorrows at the bar, his spirits rose when a cute young thing approached him and introduced herself as

Passion, a gift from Mr. Stewart to make sure his time here at The Castle was pleasurable. If Dmitri wished, she was his for the duration. All at once, his frown turned into a smile as he escorted her to his suite to get better acquainted. Although Dmitri could not completely forgive or forget about Eva and Victoria, this nasty little fox did her best to occupy his thoughts. Delightfully, Passion lived up to her billing, attending to his every need and desire, so much so the Russian was rarely seen outside his room.

AFTER THEIR BRIEF REFERENCE TO HIM one night, the girls did not speak of Dmitri Volkov until late Sunday night as they prepared to leave the following day. Going against policy, Miles asked the ladies to stay on for a few more days to enjoy The Castle in peace and quiet after the degenerates vacated. Tempting as it was, Eva and Victoria explained they had pressing business elsewhere that needed their immediate attention.

Miles hung his head in a mock pout, then grinned. "Well then, maybe another time when you two are free and preferably without Dmitri Volkov."

On their ride down the mountain and on the drive back to their place, Dmitri was surprisingly cheerful. No one mentioned a thing about the weekend, which put the girls at ease. While his driver took the girls' luggage to their door, Dmitri gave each a kiss on the cheek before bidding them adieu.

As his car pulled away, he lowered the rear window and said, "Ladies, if you can find the time, I would love to continue where we left off at my villa. Think about it and give me a jingle if you are interested."

Whatever Miles did at The Castle to appease the man, it worked like a charm. Victoria responded, "That would be delicious, we'll call soon." Eva and Victoria admired the tenacity of the man, if nothing else.

AFTER THE GIRLS UNPACKED and settled into the familiar surroundings of their condo, they put their heads together to make notes on the vile people they'd encountered at The Castle. They meticulously checked off names on a copy of the guest list Eva procured from Miles's study while he was showering one morning. It took hours to finish the list. There were a number of guests whom they had neither met nor seen the whole weekend. For guests both had interaction with, they collaborated on their observations and documented their conclusions. By sunset, they'd put together a fairly detailed synopsis of the weekend.

First, they reported to Ari, then to Talley and Millie. Both conversations were monitored by Nemesis and Desiree Richards.

ARI MOON LEAPED UP OUT OF HIS CHAIR and did a little jig around the room as soon as he heard one particular piece of information Eva and Victoria gathered for him. A Russian guest let slip that he was present when Dmitri Volkov assassinated Ari Moon's family in cold blood. Ari couldn't believe it; he finally had proof beyond a doubt that it was Dmitri who *carried out* the final order to murder his family.

HUNKERED DOWN IN THEIR COTTAGE in South Dakota, Talley and Millie perused the names of the rich and infamous Eva and Victoria rubbed shoulders with over the weekend. Thrilled at the prospect of adding the narcissistic proletariat to their preferred client list, Millie did a deep search on the dark web as soon as she'd compiled a target list of names. Quite a few of them belonged to an ultra-exclusive elitist group called the Nobilis Familia, Latin for "noble family."

If Nomad introduced caida libre products into the ranks of Nobilis Familia, Millie was positive the word would spread quickly, eventually finding its way to the mysterious head of the noble society for final approval—unless it already had.

CHAPTER 18

WHILE WARLOCK TRACKED Nomad's every move, Trey, Tara, and what seemed to be half of Texas followed their favorite golfer for the next two weeks. First at the Colonial Invitational in Ft. Worth, then at the Byron Nelson in Dallas. Jefferson McCall didn't let his fans down, after a runner-up finish at Colonial, Jefferson birdied the final hole to win the Byron Nelson. That made five wins on Tour for Jefferson.

An off-the-wall thought entered Trey McCall's mind as he watched his son sign autographs after winning the Byron Nelson event. He wondered how the Tour commissioner was dealing with a McCall becoming the PGA Tour's poster boy. Blowing it off as not his problem, Trey shrugged his shoulders, chuckled, and went on to celebrate with his son.

ACTUALLY, THE RISING POPULARITY of Jefferson McCall was giving the commissioner considerable headaches. Recently an unrelenting media rode him hard about the severity of the punishment dealt out to Trey McCall years ago. Hinting the Tour had some sort of personal vendetta against the man, the media pointed out that others on the Tour during that same time frame with similar infractions walked away with little or no punishment; none were permanently suspended.

Over the years, the commissioner thought about it, knowing at the time what he'd done was wrong. The fact was he didn't like Trey, and he wanted to make an example out of him. Things got completely out of hand, and before he knew it, he'd done something he would regret for the rest of his life.

At the time, Trey was overwhelmed and misguided, as young people sometimes get when they are suddenly thrust into the lime-light. With Trey's record and potential, he should never have banned the rising star and taken away his playing privileges, but it was far too late to make amends.

Now the annoying press was breathing down his neck, asking stupid questions about the past. Making rude statements and asking when he was going to suspend Jefferson for being too good a player and not toeing the party line. All because a nitwit reporter got wind of a conversation one of the players had with Jefferson asking him if he would be interested in becoming a player director on the Tour Policy Board. Respectfully, Jefferson said he was not interested—end of story.

Smelling a scandal, the reporter went off on a rampage alleging Jefferson demeaned the role of the board and the office of the commis-sioner. Witnesses at the scene denounced the allegations as untrue, but it started an avalanche. Forced to get involved, the commissioner summoned Jefferson to his office in Ponte Vedra.

The number one player on Tour arrived with Trey, the McCall family leading counsel Sidney Baker, and several antitrust lawyers.

Before the commissioner had a chance to speak, Sidney Baker made it clear this meeting was based on pure hearsay and fabrication. Furthermore, she demanded the commissioner cease and desist or she and her lawyer colleagues were going to feed the frenzy in the shark-infested media pool. Sitting quietly by, Trey stared coldly at the man who'd called the meeting.

Seeing his whole world crumble before his eyes, the commissioner was speechless, his people were at a loss for words. Finally, one of the Tour personnel went into their patented four-corner stall offense of saying a lot about nothing. One snarling jeer from the McCall's attorney Sidney Baker stopped the man in mid-sentence, who meekly sat down and focused on the floor.

SOMEHOW, THE COMMISSIONER FOUND his voice. "Okay, okay, everyone let's all calm down. As I see it, we are all here for the same purpose for the common good of the Tour and the game of golf. I'm sure we can hash this out like civilized people and come to a workable solution."

Trey stood up and faced the man who robbed him of his dream. "I'm not sure that particular remedy is possible in this room. You claim to want what's best for the folks on your Tour, personal experience tells me otherwise. Do you honestly expect me to believe a single word you utter after what you did to me and my family? I don't think you are that much of a fool, are you? Granted, our history is water under the bridge; however, if you persist in harassing my son, let me refresh your memory about a friendly piece of advice I gave you before my boy joined the Tour.

"My family is in the business of uncovering secrets people don't want uncovered. We are the best in the world at it. At this moment, we have no intention of delving into your past. Although, that can change in a split second. Take what I've said whichever way you wish, as a threat or a promise, but keep in mind, my son has done nothing to you or your Tour but help promote your brand in an honest and positive light. If you want things to continue along that path, I suggest you listen to Sidney and cease and desist with this bullshit. I believe I've made our position perfectly clear to everybody."

DURING TREY'S DIALOGUE, the commissioner's face went ashen; he could ill afford for Trey to rummage around in his past, not to mention the public relations fiasco it would create for *his* Tour.

One of the wiseass Tour lawyers stood and blurted out, "That, sir, is tantamount to extortion. Are you willing to face those kinds of charges in a court of law, with all these witnesses in this room?"

Trey sighed and calmly replied. "I call it negotiating. Nevertheless, to answer your question, son, you bet I am. You guys haven't won a fucking court case since Noah floated the Ark."

With that, the silence in the office was deafening. Trey signaled his troops it was time to go and did not bother to close the door on the way out. Visibly shaken, the commissioner was aware he could no longer deflect blame for his actions. All this was because his ego got in the way, there was no question about it. He'd messed with the wrong family. By his own design, there was no one he could consult in his entourage; they were merely yes men there to boost his ego. What had he done? How in the world could he fix it?

None of his options did him any good. What could he do? Swallow his pride, admit he'd made a huge mistake, reinstate Trey McCall's playing privileges, ask the board to grant him the ability to award one life membership a year to a deserving recipient—maybe approve some sort of compensation for McCall. Grasping at straws, his mind raced. Perhaps it was time to retire. His long-term aim was to go out on a high note, now he just wanted out. No doubt the press would barbeque him, whichever way he chose to proceed.

DURING THE ENTIRE PROCEEDING, Jefferson never said a word. Aware his father waited a very long time for this exact moment, he did not want to deprive him of the pleasure. He was proud that Trey stood up for him just like Mac had stood up for Trey when he was young. Serious allegations spawned somber expressions on concerned faces. As weighty as the dialogue became, when his dad popped off about Noah floating the Ark, it was all Jefferson could do to hold back a chuckle.

THANKS TO AN OVERZEALOUS TOUR MINION, the media was alerted about the meeting, and anxious reporters were waiting outside, pressing for answers they were going to manipulate to fit their agenda anyway. Only to be disappointed when the single response they received from participants as they left the building was a curt *no comment.* Trey's stern expression put the fear of God into each and every one of them.

To fan the flames, the *Fourth Estate* ran a few more stories to see if anyone would bite and come forward for their fifteen minutes of fame. No one ever did, and yesterday's big scoop to bring down the Tour faded into oblivion. To smooth over the altercation, the Tour rebuffed the story about Jefferson McCall demeaning the policy board. In retribution, the commissioner banned the reporter who printed the false allegation from ever getting press credentials for PGA Tour–sanctioned events for life. Even though the guy cried foul, pouted, and threatened legal action, the ban remained in place. In addition, his employer canned him for not having a bona fide source for the bogus article.

Rumors from Ponte Vedra about the commissioner stepping down at the end of his current term were confirmed. His successor-to-be was a retired, well-respected, astute businessman with great presence and impeccable credentials—absent the off-putting manner of his predecessor.

THE WAITING GAME to see where cybercrime investigations led lingered on. To busy himself, Trey worked with Jefferson on the golf range and tended to things around the ranch with Jorge Vargas, the ranch foreman and manager. Routinely, the two of them rode the pastures to check on livestock and fence conditions. It brought back fond memories of the old days when they were kids and Jorge's dad sent them out to patrol the pastures, on what the old man called ultra-secret missions. As they rode along, the two men marveled at the massive transformation The Circle M underwent through the years. It was hard to fathom that half a century ago, it consisted of nothing more than a few dilapidated buildings, overgrown pastureland, and unruly scrub brush, surrounded by broken-down fences.

On occasion, Jefferson joined them; each time he drank in more of the history of the ranch and his incredible family. Nowadays, like before, the family was back to picnics by the lake, fish fries, and lazy boat rides. They took to the water in their Sea Ray Sundancer cruiser for sunset dinners, or puttered along in a refurbished houseboat while they sunned on the deck and trolled for fish on lazy summer days. On the golf tour, Jeff rolled along nicely with two more wins—one in Memphis, the other in San Antonio—to make it four for the year. With seven Tour titles in two years, Jefferson equaled the victories Trey managed in his career, creating a point of banter between father and son. All the while, it appeared the McCalls settled into a laid-back, relaxed lifestyle at the ranch, Warlock was on the prowl in search for the supreme leader of Nobilis Familia.

WITH SO MANY MOVING PARTS affected by unforeseen twists and turns, the ongoing investigation continued to be a tedious undertaking. Given all their resources, who would have thought after two and a half decades, Nemesis would still be fighting the same demonic blueprint—inching closer to its purveyors yet not able to squelch its viral message. Emerging contingencies, topped by the unexpected murder of Dmitri Volkov at his villa in Albania, constantly modified the landscape of the case.

NEMESIS UNCOVERED from an intercepted report from Eva and Victoria to Ari Moon that the Russian was found by the landscape maintenance crew floating face down in the bloodied water of his infinity pool on Monday afternoon. Someone had crudely dismembered Dmitri and drowned him. Evidence around the pool suggested the man had company over the weekend: empty champagne bottles and half-filled glasses, wet towels strewn on chairs and lounges, cigarette butts with lipstick on the filters and cigar stubs ground out in ashtrays. The police lab confirmed the fingerprints on the glasses along with

DNA found on cigarette butts belonged to a young lady with the stage name Pleasure, a stripper with a long record for solicitation. Which tied everything together in a tidy little bow. Too tidy for Trey's liking or for the Albanian police.

Trey read on. Further investigation uncovered that Dmitri's wife Zoya Volkov suspected her husband of being unfaithful and had recently hired a private detective. After hours of questioning by police, Zoya broke down and admitted she drove to the villa on Monday morning to confront her husband. She found him passed out on a chaise by the pool, along with all the evidence she needed to confirm her suspicions. From the report, Trey gathered Dmitri was still in the throes of the previous two nights, and was grateful when Zoya took pity on him and made him a drink, a Bloody Mary, hair of the dog, to clear out the cobwebs.

In hopes of instant relief, he downed it in record time. A few minutes later, he was out cold from the heavy dose of sleeping powder she'd slipped into his drink. Zoya pushed his unconscious body off the chaise lounge onto his back. At the edge of his prized pool, she pulled down his speedo and performed a rather sloppy operation to remove his manhood. Blood gushed out of the vacated area into the pool as she rolled his body over into the water. Dmitri flipped facedown and bobbed around like a cork on top of the rippling salt water. With no regrets, she washed the after-operation refuse off the deck into the pool with a hose and left. Asked by the police as to her motive for such a grisly reaction to her husband's infidelity, her reply was simple—to make damn sure her asshole husband was ill-equipped in case there were any virgins waiting for him in the afterlife. Trey grinned and thought, *Got to love karma. It never forgets.*

EVA AND VICTORIA REMAINED in Albania to pick up local scuttlebutt surrounding Dmitri Volkov's demise. A week after the homicide, it was old news. In search of a change of scenery, they called Miles Stewart on speakerphone to take him up on the invitation he extended to them at the shindig.

Miles was absentmindedly doing crossword puzzles in his office at The Castle when Eva's name came up on his caller ID. "Hey, girl, what's up? Great to hear from you, it's been a while. Too bad about old Dmitri although I doubt he'll be missed. FYI, I've missed you and Victoria."

"Hey, Miles, we miss you too. We wanted to take you up on your invitation to keep you company in your lonely castle."

Instantly, he sat up in his chair and checked his calendar. "Perfect. How about this weekend? There's a small group of guests already scheduled most of whom you met last time. We could make it a sort of biz/rec (work/play) kind of weekend. Hey, that reminds me. Remember we were talking one night and you guys mentioned this new product a company called Nomad came up with. You know, with that funny-named stuff that sounded like cat litter. Think you two could arrange for a shipment of whatever-it's-called to be delivered to The Castle. If it's as good as you say, the hoity-toity crowd will flip over it."

Victoria was laughing so hard she could hardly reply. "You mean caida libre? How did you get cat litter out of caida libre? BTW, we market it as Spice of Life, a name we feel befits the product. Yeah, no problem. Just let us know how much Spice of Life you want, and we'll get it shipped to you. Oh, and we miss you so much, can't wait to show you."

WARLOCK PROGRAMS PICKED UP on the references to caida libre and Spice of Life. Miranda ran across both on social media scans as well, referred to as an ancient Mayan mind drug. When Miranda dug deeper, she discovered the feds had been testing caida libre for years without finding any reason to ban it. At first, they were concerned about the euphoric state of well-being it produced. Since there was no proof of short- or long-term side effects and it did not seem to impair judgment or motor skills, it settled in the grey area between approved and rejected. Some test substances stayed in test limbo indefinitely.

Miranda ran her own mini survey about caida libre in her head. Tasteless, odorless, dissolvable granules that increased stamina and extended performance levels without any known adverse side effects. Who in their right mind wouldn't want to try that? Those two Nomad chicks hit a pharma jackpot. If they were clever enough to file for a patent on their product, Talley and Millie would be golden for at least four years or up to twenty if approved. When Miranda checked, she found out Millie filed a patent for caida libre under the brand name Spice of Life for Nomad Pharmaceuticals.

With Dmitri Volkov and Mr. Xen out of the picture, Nemesis devoted more time and resources to Eva and Victoria in Albania in addition to Talley and Millie in Middle America. Trey brought Ty and Miranda back home to Texas to make room for Tina Tremblay and Rose Conner. The Canadian Nomad investors who were purposely left out of the caida libre loop by Talley and Millie—an issue Trey wanted the girls to exploit. To stir the pot, he wanted Tina to contact Talley and insist on coming to the lower forty-eight for an in-person update. A request Talley could hardly refuse since the two Canadian gals were the company's largest investors.

EVA AND VICTORIA STEPPED OUT of the cable car at the Albanian castle to the uproar of a party in full swing. Deliveries of Spice of Life preceded their arrival, and the guests were already experiencing its effects. The girls recognized a great many of the guests from their previous visit. Heads of State and policymakers, Hollywood stars past and present, business and internet tycoons, athletic greats, and musicians assembled once again at The Castle. Thirty in number ready to let their hair down, while they mischievously charted plans to remake the world. Eva and Victoria heard rumblings as they passed among the attendees in reference to something called the Nobilis Familia. Very hush-hush—need-to-know, top-secret. The girls raised their eyebrows in a brief glance at each other.

As promised, Miles made Eva and Victoria feel right at home, and soon they mixed it up with the elite of the world. Before things got completely out of hand, Eva made an announcement to the group cautioning the party-hardy crowd to please adhere to the dosage instructions that came with the Spice of Life product. It was easy to get carried away under its influence. To her knowledge, no one had ever overdosed on the stimulant; however, ongoing studies of over-indulgence and long-term effects on the body were not yet available. Everyone pretended to listen and understand, then went about their business. With fewer guests, things were less chaotic than during the shindig—more open and casually intimate. Regular guests formed their own cliques with individuals they felt comfortable with for the weekend. Meetings scheduled at intervals throughout their stay were not mandatory, although everyone attended. As per usual, Miles was the moderator, who on occasion had to quell some very fiery debates. Alphas detested being challenged and needed a take-charge guy, who accepted no flak from anyone, to calm the waters.

SATURDAY AFTERNOON'S THREE-P.M. MEETING was a critique of Spice of Life. Miles and the girls sought everyone's opinion of the stimulant. Overwhelmingly, the survey of responses was positive, citing no hangovers, dry mouth, or ill effects. The selfish elites were more interested in Spice of Life as a personal-use product than an incentive to build up a dependent clientele.

After the meeting broke up, the guests retreated to their various cliques. Eva, Victoria, and their chaperone remained in the boardroom. Miles poured drinks all around then relaxed in his chair to sort his thoughts. The girls were giddy and anxious to hear his take on things so far.

Miles validated his confidence in them. "Ladies, I can't recall any other time at The Castle when this mercurial group united behind anything as quickly as they did for your ancient Mayan elixir. You two have been the hit of the weekend. More importantly, you've been accepted by the chosen. In their eyes, you are by no means their equal, but you have been granted the privilege to associate with them."

The girls rubbed their hands together naughtily to signify their delight, then gave each other and Miles a high five. As they got up to leave, Victoria posed a question to Miles, "I hope this isn't out of line for me to ask. I mean, if all electronic devices are forbidden, how do you conduct business up here?"

Miles looked down at the floor then smirked as he raised his head. "That, my dear, was something the owner put in place to ensure privacy and secrecy, and why my staff and I collect everyone's electronic devices before they enter The Castle. He has granted me the authority to allow a select few to make use of our communication network. Actually, the services up here are excellent even in inclement weather. And why am I not surprised you two figured that out? Now shall we retire and toast our success with champagne in the master suite?"

For the remainder of the weekend at The Castle, things were less mind-bending and more eye-opening for the girls. The final two meetings were disturbing. Subjects ranged from methods to desecrate the world's population, engineer government takeovers, or manipulate world currencies, all supposedly done for the greater good. Yet Eva and Victoria couldn't see how the noble family had anything in common with people they were supposed to be saving. These elites lived in a bubble of their own making, oblivious to actual problems in the real world. It was all the girls could do to keep their expressions neutral and against their own feelings nod in agreement from time to time. Miles paid very close attention to them during the discussions, as if assessing their reactions. Judging from his positive post-meetings vibes, they must have passed muster.

While at The Castle, thanks to Miles, Victoria made a brief call on her room phone to Millie Snowden to give her their good news. In detail, she described how well Spice of Life had been accepted—substantiated by the number of new customers she read off the list she and Eva drew up. Then wished Millie well and closed the call.

Lots of interested folks eavesdropped on the call. Nemesis, Desiree, and Miles heard every word. As a precaution, all phone calls into or out of The Castle were recorded. It was only natural that Victoria would want to inform the heads of Nomad that their product made a huge splash. Miles would have been suspicious if she had not made the call, which is exactly why Victoria made it.

At the next quarterly board meeting of the Nobilis Familia, Miles planned to gloat, given that many of the staunchest members were totally against him bringing the girls to The Castle a second time. It was Miles who vouched for them and took complete responsibility. Oh, how he loved to rub it in when he was right. Noting how cocksure he was of himself around such a haughty collection of powerful ego-phobes, Victoria paused to wonder just how far up he was on the consortium's ladder.

Unfortunately, their host never hinted about his status. He did, however, appoint Victoria and Eva as his official promotional advocates for Spice of Life. Two devilish angels were brought on board to hype the wonder additive that brought peace, tranquility, and well-being to life. He sent them to make presentations to companies and organizations owned or operated by Nobilis Familia's top echelon. As demand surpassed supply, the international popularity of Spice of Life products exploded. To increase production, Talley bought back all the underground facilities she'd sold to the locals. Absolved from the illegal drug trade, she and Millie retooled the cellars to produce only caida libre. In less than a month, they'd recouped the expense of buying back labs. While the stimulant was still in testing limbo with the feds, for all intents and purposes, it was legal. Like any popular medication or vitamin, there were a few reported problems associated with Spice of Life—dismissed by *experts* as allergic reactions.

WITH SUCH A HOT COMMODITY taking foreign markets by storm, the most prominent cartel collective came to Nomad with an offer to buy them out, waving millions of dollars at them and a deadline for a decision. After the deadline passed, cartel reps came back to ask for a number Nomad would consider. After Talley ran the figures of current and predicted profits, she and Millie determined they would not settle for less than three hundred million dollars. The drug reps laughed and said Nomad was crazy to expect that kind of money. Three months later, the cartel's agents were back with an offer of five hundred million dollars. An amount Millie and Talley accepted.

There were stipulations. For as long as the patent remained in force, the drug consortium would have to provide Nomad, Millie, and Talley, a percentage of the gross profits Spice of Life generated. At the time of purchase, the drug conglomerate would assume all liability concerning Spice of Life—past, present, and future. Nomad had the drug combine over a barrel; Spice of Life was kicking their ass, putting their companies out of business. Pharmaceutical concerns had no choice but to agree. News of the mega-million-dollar buyout traveled fast. Minutes after the contracts were signed, word was all over the net. It was a great deal for Nomad.

It was a better deal for interested parties following the Spice of Life money trail as it blazed through the noble family companies and illustrious membership all the way to the top of the totem pole. Now that Talley and Millie made their huge score, they were anxious to play in the big leagues, desirous to know who the biggest players were; more than that, they wanted to deal face to face with the person in charge. The co-founders of Nomad wondered if Miles was cognizant of the supreme leader's identity. Was he the main player?

MILLIE INSTRUCTED VICTORIA to see if she could use her talents to find out. One night after too much drink and a marvelous fling in bed with the buxom beauty, Miles let slip an interesting tidbit about a subject she touched on over dinner.

In the darkness, Miles stroked the stubble on his face and then he broke the silence. "Been thinking about what you said earlier at the dinner table. Funny thing about all this noble family bullshit mumbo-jumbo that goes on around here. I wish I had a clue about who was behind it all. Everybody thinks I have, but to be honest, I haven't a clue.

As far as I can tell, no one has any idea who this supreme leader might be. All communications are handled by personal messenger, never electronic devices. Even the recordings after each gathering at The Castle are picked up and delivered by messenger. Only the courier has the delivery address for the correspondence—not to say that's actually its final destination."

His scripted slip of the tongue was a brilliant deceptive maneuver on his part to create even more mystery surrounding the noble family and its supreme leader. As Miles expected her to do, Victoria reported her findings to Millie back at Nomad. Millie just smiled.

OVERNIGHT, A DEVASTATING NIGHTMARE sprang out of nowhere for Nomad, an alarming number of Spice of Life customers experienced fatal side effects from continued use of the product. Each quarter, there were more and more unexplained deaths attributed to its use which product manufacturers, CDC, and FDA passed off as statistically insignificant, due to the volume of customers utilizing the product and the vast amount of money that flowed into their coffers.

In a majority of cases, the patients were in excellent condition prior to dropping dead of what appeared to be a sudden heart attack, which baffled the medical profession. Autopsies showed no damage to any vital organs, especially the heart. Although medical examiners did find small amounts of viscous material in the area of the medulla oblongata attached to the brainstems of the deceased. The medulla oblongata was responsible for regulating several basic functions of the autonomic nervous system including respiration and cardiac function.

Concerned over the statistics, Millie Snowden contacted her college girlfriend Esmeralda (Izzy) Barbarossa for more information on the person who introduced Izzy to the Mayan concoction caida libre in the first place. To the best of Barbarossa's recollection, it was a Mayan guide named Kisin. When Millie searched for his name in Mayan, a cold shiver ran down her spine when she discovered Kisin was the Mayan God of Death.

Millie shared what she'd learned with Talley Marsh, who was fully engaged in dissolving their ties with caida libre pending a massive panic.

"Hey, Sissy." Talley frowned, and her eyebrows furrowed. "Any idea where Ari Moon went? We haven't heard one word from him since Dmitri Volkov met his well-deserved fate. For that matter, neither have Eva or Victoria. He's a clever man. I hear he built his enormous wealth by directing others to do his bidding, which ensured his hands were always clean. Where do you think he is now?"

"Sissy, is it now?" Millie glanced up quizzically at her partner. "Then this must be serious. I have no idea where the man is. He's been an integral part of every move up to the point when Dmitri Volkov met his end, then nothing. Why? Was revenge for his family enough? I don't think so. It seems out of character for the man to leave such a large investment in caida libre on the table. Ari's not the type to just walk away without an explanation, although it appears he's done just that."

UNBEKNOWNST ASIDE FROM ONE OTHER, Ari Moon was currently in Puerto Vallarta, Mexico, on his veranda admiring the view of the Banderas Bay from his villa. Absolutely no one knew who owned this beautiful property purchased through a dummy corporation. When he heard the front door close and footsteps on the tile floor moving his way, he turned to greet his partner who joined him on the veranda.

Reaching down, Ari offered the new arrival a cold cerveza from the ice chest at his feet. Eagerly, the younger man accepted the beer and smiled at his confederate.

Ari returned the smile. "So, how is it going?"

Miles Stewart replied, "Never better. Our plan is progressing as predicted. We've received some unexpected aid from the calamity caused by Spice of Life, which is now acting as an impetus to wreak even more discord on the noble family membership. Your ladies Eva and Victoria have no idea who the supreme leader is, after I accidentally on purpose let slip that no one knew who ran the whole operation."

Impressed, Ari slapped his young companion on the back and congratulated him on another job well done. At this moment, Miles was the only living person who knew it was Ari who covertly ordered Dmitri Volkov to murder Moon's own family. It had to be done; they were too vocal, too influential, and stood firmly in the way of his glorious vision for the future. Because Dmitri Volkov knew too much, it was imperative he too had to disappear. Dmitri's jealous wife had done Ari a tremendous favor. Miles and Ari planned to wait out the purge of the world's most exclusive Nobilis Familia reprobates—sipping cervezas right here in Mexico.

AMAZINGLY, ONE BY ONE, the Nobilis Familia fell victim to the chaos. What began as a trickle developed into a flood, as its least valuable members gladly gave up their peers at every opportunity. In their world, it was everyone for themselves. There were no comrades, only predators who devoured their own. As members were singled out and scrutinized by the authorities, they were ostracized by the remaining membership.

NEMESIS STOOD BY and watched the international fireworks. Formerly privileged elites sheltered by wealth and family were arrested, charged with real crimes, and incarcerated. Most of them believed they were socially immune, due to the self-perception of their importance to the welfare of mankind. Trey rocked back and forth in his desk chair with a satisfied wry smile on his face. He was proud of what his Nemesis agents did in the field to make it all possible. Few knew of the contributions made behind the scenes by Warlock and the cybercrime experts. But he did. And they did. Their just reward was to witness the downfall of a criminal element forced to face their felonious atrocities, alone and unprotected.

TO VIEW SOME OF THE MOST POMPOUS asses of the noble family publicly humiliated and stripped of their wealth pleased their adversaries on both sides of the law. It had been the *true* supreme leader's intention all along to eradicate the weak ones, leaving an efficient, streamlined operation void of hangers-on who contributed nothing.

With great delight, Miles and Ari watched as each weakling encountered the destiny they so richly deserved and wondered if he and Ari were destined for the same fate.

IN QUEBEC WITH ONE OF HER DISCIPLES by her side, the supreme leader observed the fall of the high and mighty worldwide with a deep satisfaction growing inside. If only they would have listened to *her* all along, things would have been so different. By her reckoning, the noble family would have already achieved its true purpose. Under her guidance, the world would have a brand-new outlook. It was still a possibility, except for one unanticipated complication.

In her quest to regain her youth, Desiree was now addicted to caida libre. What started out as one packet of Spice of Life three times a day, turned into as many as six packets a day, more depending on her mood. Such large doses would kill a normal person in a short period of time. Her as well, if her drug tolerances hadn't been elevated due to her past addictions. No longer did she view Boris as a favorite son, she saw him as fresh meat for her voracious sexual appetite.

For his own safety and sanity, Boris hightailed it back to Biloxi. In all the years he developed and distributed narcotic-laced products, he'd never sampled any of them for fear he would end up like Desiree. Now that Boris was gone, with no one to monitor her consumption, caida libre continued to take its toll on the strung-out supreme leader.

Consequently, Desiree ended up in a condition worse than years ago when she was committed to a mental institution with an alleged psychotic illness. Neighbors discovered Desiree in her Montreal condominium, barely conscious, mumbling over and over about her daughter—*Millicent*. Opened packets of Spice of Life littered the floor in every room. Greenish powder clung to every available surface in the condo, including her listless body. It was presumed by Nobilis Familia loyalists that she was too far gone mentally to name her successor—or had she and no one paid attention. Beyond medical help, the supreme leader was doomed to spend the rest of her days out of her mind in a padded room, most of the time restrained to protect herself—from herself.

EPILOGUE

WITH MIXED EMOTIONS, Nemesis closed the books on two lost souls. Desiree Richards, who fell victim to karma after dodging its justice for decades, and Robert McCall, who met a bazaar fate in the dark water of the Gulf of Mexico. Both chose the wrong path in life and paid the price.

Although Trey and Tara McCall were still motivated to contribute their skills to Nemesis, they felt it was time to slow down and take things easier in the hill country.

Now in his forties, Jefferson McCall had won fifty-four professional tournaments and added his name to the list of players who'd captured the career grand slam—all four majors.

Years ago, Trey realized Jefferson was not going to be the one to take over the reins at Nemesis. Rightfully so. A generation later than Trey, his son had lived his father's dream of being in the World Golf Hall of Fame. That's not to say that someone else in the family couldn't or wouldn't take over as chairperson.

To no one's surprise, Trey's granddaughter Molly Elizabeth grew up to be a fine, bright young lady, in spite of being a fearless tomboy, as tough as nails with a stubborn streak a mile wide who could outfight and out-cuss all the boys her age. Liz was pretty, but never gave it much thought. Things like that didn't matter to her at that time. What did matter was her love of life and family.

From the day she was born, the McCall family knew Liz was exceptional. Something they first noticed when her great-grandfather Mac held her on his lap and whispered in the newborn's ear. As if she somehow understood, her eyes opened wide and an ear-to-ear smile appeared on her face. As soon as she learned to speak, Liz talked a blue streak and was beyond inquisitive, into everyone's business, and wanted to know how everything worked. Grandpa Trey and her dad Jefferson taught her how to ride, shoot, and fish. Golf was of little interest to her. That's what her father did for a living. Instead, she talked for hours with Trey about Nemesis, fascinated by the mysterious nature of his work and wanted to know all about it.

All the agents fell in love with her and were more than willing to share some of their most interesting experiences in the field with her. As a teenager, Liz trained alongside potential agents and earned a black belt in several martial arts, including Krav Maga. In the cyber lab, Tara was more than happy to show Liz the ropes and explain the basics of how the Warlock computer program revolutionized the way they did surveillance. Miranda gave Liz a tutorial of the systems operation board and let her practice while she stood over her shoulder. Before long, the teen was computer savvy, well on her way to being able to navigate the system on her own.

Canadian agents Tina and Rose met Liz while visiting the ranch and established an instant rapport, amazed that she was still in high school and already had all the makings of a full-fledged Nemesis agent.

Bright beyond her years, Liz graduated from high school a year earlier than the other kids her age, went to college, majored in criminal law, and graduated with honors three years later. Just shy of twenty, she was crystal clear on her path in life. She wanted to run Nemesis and announced so to Trey.

Neither shocked nor surprised, Trey held in his excitement. Of course, he could not show that emotion to her until he knew for sure she was really sincere. Instead, he played devil's advocate with her for an hour, giving her all sorts of reasons why she might want to reconsider: hours were irregular, it was hard to maintain a serious relationship, you could not even tell the people closest to you what you did for a living, you had to deal with the worst of humanity, and any other negatives he could think of. Liz was unshakable.

Trey remembered back in the day when Mac put him through the rigorous boot camp training as a Nemesis recruit, something Trey did to appease his father and as a thank-you for saving him from his sorry life. Trey evolved into loving Nemesis, but it was a struggle. Liz was different; she grew up with a passion for Nemesis already in her blood.

Before she rose to leave, Trey repeated the heartwarming tale of how her great-granddad Mac clung to life in his final days waiting to welcome her into the world before he passed. "I distinctly remember one special night my father held you in his arms and whispered something in your ear as you nuzzled up against him and you giggled."

Trey gave her an inquisitive look when she responded, "I don't remember that night, of course, but I dreamed it a million times. In the dream, he held me tight and softly whispered, *You are the one we have all been waiting for.* Now I know what he meant."

Speechless, Trey gave her a hug and gently escorted her out the door as a tear formed in the corner of his eye. Trey sat back in his chair, and his mind flooded with all the miracles in his life, of the mistakes he'd made when he was young, of his father being there for him when he needed him most, then how rewarding his life became saving others from demons rife with greed and hatred. For so long, he'd anguished over the ideal candidate to replace him as chairperson of Nemesis—assured at last, he'd found *the one*.

THE END

ABOUT THE AUTHOR

JOHN MAHAFFEY WAS BORN in Kerrville, Texas, and attended the University of Houston, where he was a two-time All-American. John was a member of two NCAA national championship teams and the individual NCAA champion in 1970, a feat he accomplished one week after he tied for low amateur in the US Open at Hazeltine National Golf Club in Chaska, Minnesota. He graduated from U of H with a psychology degree in 1970 and turned pro in 1971.

Mahaffey is a ten-time winner on the PGA Tour, including the PGA Championship and the Players. In 1978, John won the individual title in the World Cup and partnered with Andy North to win the team competition at Princeville on the island of Kauai in Hawaii. The following year he partnered with Hale Irwin to win the World Cup for the US in Athens, Greece, and was a member of the victorious 1979 Ryder Cup team.

After playing the Tour for over three decades, John enjoyed the role of announcer/analyst on Golf Channel; broadcasting live golf for the Champions Tour. During his tenure as a commentator, Mahaffey wrote his first book, *Hogan's Boy—A Journey in Golf*; an autobiography of stories and recollections of a career that spanned from the end of the Ben Hogan, Byron Nelson, and Sam Snead era to beginning of the Tiger Woods and Phil Mickelson era—a time in which Mahaffey was fortunate enough to have Ben Hogan as a mentor.

Inspired to write more, Mahaffey embarked on a mission to author a collection of fictional works—the Nemesis series. *Shafted* is the first of the cybercrime thrillers. Golf takes a holiday when the McCall family is plagued by a corrupt narcissist who seeks to bring the golf star Trey McCall's world down around him. The ingenious family of survivors stands up to fight for what is right.

Unfinished Business, second in the Nemesis Series, chronicles the exploits of a disjointed group of unscrupulous disciples, steadfast in their belief that a reengineered master plan of their deceased mentor will bring them wealth and power. Their ultimate goal—to destroy Nemesis and the McCall dynasty.